Anne moved slowly to the glass and surveyed the scene. Jack lay on the white-sheeted hospital bed, nearly covering the length of it. With one wayward lock of dark hair falling over his forehead, his mouth slack, he seemed so vulnerable, so unlike the esteemed surgeon who was openly worshipped and silently feared. In that moment she caught a glimpse of the young man she had married—a brilliant doctor, a good friend, an expert lover. Before the drive to be the best overtook the tenderness. Before he decided his life's work was more important than his daughter and his wife…

She touched her fingertips to the clear pane of glass as if she could somehow connect with him. As if she could bring him back to the way he was all those years ago, when they'd been everything to each other. She grieved not only for the Jack whose future was so tenuous, but also for the Jack she'd lost to stubborn ambition. The man who had been so easy to love, yet so difficult to understand.

She shook off the memories, although she couldn't shake the regret, or the sudden tears, or the groundswell of feelings she'd tried to disregard over the past two years. She had to keep the painful emotions buried, never to resurrect them again, for the sake of her sanity and her soul.

"He's going to need you, Anne. More than he ever needed anything in his life," Hank said. He was Jack's internist and good friend—*her* one-time good friend, before her divorce from Jack. "He's got no one, Anne…. No one but you."

No. She didn't want to hear this. "Hank, don't do this to me…."

Dear Reader,

Many times I've been asked how I come upon inspiration for my stories. With this particular book, the answer is simple—I relied on my experience working in the medical field and my longtime marriage to a doctor. I've become personally acquainted with the physician's psyche, although I've been blessed to have chosen a life partner who has always put family first whenever possible. However, a surgeon's schedule requires some sacrifice, as does a writer's career. But then, give and take is an integral part of sustaining any long-term relationship.

I hope you enjoy *Fall from Grace*, a couple's journey through the past and present as they rely on their memories—and each other—to reclaim what's been lost. Most important, they learn that in the presence of love, there comes a time to grant grace.

All the best,

Kristi

Fall from Grace

Kristi Gold

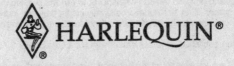

HARLEQUIN®

TORONTO • NEW YORK • LONDON
AMSTERDAM • PARIS • SYDNEY • HAMBURG
STOCKHOLM • ATHENS • TOKYO • MILAN • MADRID
PRAGUE • WARSAW • BUDAPEST • AUCKLAND

ISBN-13: 978-0-373-65404-8
ISBN-10:   0-373-65404-9

FALL FROM GRACE

This edition published by arrangement with Harlequin Books S.A.

® and TM are trademarks of the publisher. Trademarks indicated with
® are registered in the United States Patent and Trademark Office, the
Canadian Trade Marks Office and in other countries.

www.eHarlequin.com

Printed in U.S.A.

ABOUT THE AUTHOR

Kristi Gold has always believed that love has remarkable healing powers, and feels very fortunate to be able to weave stories of hope and commitment. As a best-selling author, a National Readers' Choice winner and a Romance Writers of America RITA® Award finalist, Kristi has learned that although accolades are wonderful, the most cherished rewards come from personal stories shared by readers and networking with other authors, both published and aspiring.

You may contact Kristi through her Web site at kristigold.com or through snail mail at 6902 Wood-way Dr., #166, Waco, Texas 76712.

To my mother, Jean,
for surviving all the storms with such grace.

Acknowledgments

Many thanks to Dr. Don Lewis and Linda Carol Trotter,
R.N., for lending their labor and delivery expertise.
And as always, to my husband, Steve, for guiding
me through the ins and outs of neurology.
Any errors in accuracy are my own.

CHAPTER 1

Beat, dammit. Beat…

As if empowered by the surgeon's silent command, the lifeless heart resumed a steady rhythm, again taking its place among the living, cheating death. Only then did Dr. Jack Morgan allow himself to relax.

At this point during surgery, adrenaline normally coursed through Jack's veins, creating a high that kept him running on all cylinders despite a career that might kill a lesser man. Tonight, he was to-the-bone weary. Too tired for someone still not quite fifty. His limbs felt oddly heavy, weighted with fatigue. But organ donors were few and far between, and failing hearts didn't give a rat's ass about his schedule, holidays or his exhaustion.

After stepping back from the table, he addressed the third-year resident at his side. "You can close, Murray."

"Yes, sir." Her expression reflected gratitude and the same thrill Jack had experienced during his tenure as a student years earlier. That thrill that had been waning for some time now.

While Murray completed the procedure, Jack surveyed the O.R., absorbing the atmosphere he'd so often taken for granted. This was his domain, among friends and colleagues and those patients who needed his skill. The culmination of all his sacrifice, all his blood, sweat and tears.

His efforts, though, had not come without a price. No one waited for him at home. No one had for a while. And for some unknown reason, that bothered him more tonight than at any time in his recent past.

Not one to question moods, Jack gave Murray his verbal approval, along with the standard orders for the recovery process. Then he thanked the team members for a job well done, wished them a happy and prosperous 2007, tossed his gloves and gown into the refuse bin and headed out the double doors to tell the family the father of four now had a new heart and a sound future, barring complications and a lapse into an unhealthy lifestyle. For a brief moment he thought about the motorcycle-accident victim, a twenty-year-old kid who hadn't lived to see the arrival of the new year. But he didn't dwell on that. His sanity demanded he remain detached.

After rounding the corner, Jack stopped at the nurses' station, where Peg Jennings sat with her half-glasses perched on the end of her nose as she scanned a chart. He sought refuge at the counter and leaned his full frame against the cold Formica ledge, flexing the tingling fingers of his right hand in and out of a fist. "Where're the Graysons?"

"On the roof. Where else?"

Peg was a Dallas Regional Medical Center fixture, with twenty years' tenure and a wit as dry as West Texas. Jack liked her a lot. She wasn't inclined to cower and she sure as hell wasn't impressed with his status. She did have a propensity for sarcasm, though. He didn't need that right now, considering the bongo drum pounding in his head.

His annoyance came out in a rough sigh. "What conference room, Peg?"

"The main one." She set the chart aside and steepled her fingers beneath her chin, studying him with concern. "Dr. Morgan, you look like hell. Are you okay?"

"Sure." Since he'd had less than six hours' sleep the past two nights, not to mention he hadn't finished lunch or breakfast, he was as okay as could be expected. He needed a solid surface to sleep on, a couple of analgesics, a quick shower—*after* he met with the family.

As he turned from the station, a searing pain struck the left side of his skull. He clamped his hands over the sides of his head and fought the shadowy abyss that stretched out before him. Fought like a drowning man not to go under.

His knees buckled. A feeling of total helplessness screamed through his brain at breakneck speed. Numbness overtook the right side of his body like frostbite in subzero temperatures. He grabbed for the counter, but couldn't hold on.

God, no!

Annie appeared in his hazy mind, an ethereal presence from a dark place this side of hell. Her hands reached out to him, but he couldn't move. He called to her, a desperate keening cry, yet no sound left his lips. Then she walked away, as she had before.

Too late, Jack…it's too late.

As the blackness closed in, reality settled over him like a thick suffocating fog. For the first time in his life, Dr. Jack Morgan, fearless surgeon, was truly afraid.

And completely alone.

Stroke.

The word echoed like a canyon shout in Anne Cooper Morgan's addled brain, blocking out the flurry of activity in the Intensive Care corridor, where she had been summoned only moments earlier.

Anne stared blankly at the messenger, Hank Steinberg, Jack's internist and good friend. *Her* one-time good friend, before her and Jack's divorce. "There has to be some mistake, Hank."

He scrubbed a hand over his bearded jaw. "No mistake, Anne."

Not Jack. No way could this have happened to Jack. As far back as Anne could remember, her ex-husband had never caught a cold, even when their daughter, Katie, had brought several viruses home from day care. Jack was obscenely healthy. An avid runner. In all the years Anne had known him, he'd never missed a day of work over health-related problems. He was immortal in everyone's eyes, including his own.

Anne's shock yielded to harsh reality. "How? Why?"

"Aneurysm," Hank said. "He bled out night before last, on New Year's Eve."

"Why didn't someone tell me before now?" She knew the answer to that—because she no longer had a right to know.

"I was out of town, so I didn't learn about it until this morning. I called you as soon as I had the details."

Anne needed more details, although true comprehension still escaped her. "What next?"

"Nan Travers is treating him, which is good, since she's the best neurosurgeon in town. In a couple of hours, she'll determine if he's stable enough for surgery."

"If he survives." Anne posed it as a very real possibility, not a question.

Hank attempted a reassuring smile. "Look, Anne, I have no reason to believe he won't pull through this. He's relatively young. Healthy. And because he was here when it happened, he received early intervention." Hank paused briefly before adding, "He's going to make it."

That slight hesitation told Anne more was yet to come. "What are you not telling me, Hank?"

"What he'll be like afterward is my only concern."

Bile rose into Anne's throat, bringing with it the acrid taste of fear. "Paralysis?" The word came out in a croak.

Hank streaked a hand over his nape and studied the blue-and-gray patchwork tiles beneath his feet. "He's exhibiting some on his right side."

"His hand?" She asked the question for Jack as much as she asked for herself. Surgery was Jack's passion. Jack's life. How well she knew that. Their marriage had paid the price for his obsession, and so had their child. But he didn't deserve this. No one deserved this. Even the man who had shattered her heart.

Hank sighed. "The hand's pretty dead right now. The numbness is extensive, especially in his leg. We'll know for sure how bad it might be in the next couple of days, after he's leveled off. If the paralysis doesn't resolve on its own, there's no reason to think he can't recover with extensive rehab. At least, enough to be productive."

"Productive?" Anne released a humorless laugh. "Doing what, Hank? If he can't operate, he'll waste away."

"No, he won't. He'll get better. For Katie. For you."

Anne shook her head. Jack wouldn't get better for her. Maybe for their daughter, but not for her. "He has to do this for himself."

"True. And we have to keep him fighting. We can't lose him over this."

All the well-honed detachment from her former husband couldn't save her from the sudden nausea. Jack was sick. Katie's father. Her one-time husband of seventeen years. Years of abounding happiness and devastating heartache.

She didn't want to feel anything, but she did, and she hated that. "Where is he?"

Hank gestured over his shoulder toward the cubicle. "In eight."

Despite all the latent anger, she had to know he was okay, at least for now. "Can I see him?"

"Sure. He's had some mild arrhythmia, but his pressure's

stabilized. Nan's hydrating him with maintenance fluids to prevent cerebral swelling. He's on pain meds, so he's pretty comfortable, but he's still out of it." Hank sent her a comforting smile. "Guess you probably know most of the routine, huh?"

Yes, as a medical professional with years of training, she understood the treatment and the procedures. Right now, though, all that knowledge was useless. She wasn't the R.N. She was the wife—or ex-wife, as was the case. She couldn't exercise solid judgment at a time like this. Not when thinking with her heart, not her head.

"Don't leave anything out, Hank. Assume I know nothing."

"Okay. I'll remember that." He patted her arm. "Right this way."

Anne followed Hank on leaden feet down the hall. Rationally, she knew Jack would simply look like Jack, only asleep. But still she was afraid.

Once they reached the window, Hank stepped to one side and motioned for her to join him. "I'll be back in a few minutes."

Anne moved slowly to the glass and studied the scene. Jack lay on the white-sheeted hospital bed, his six-foot-two frame nearly covering the length of it. With one wayward lock of dark hair falling over his forehead, his mouth slack, he seemed so vulnerable, so unlike the esteemed surgeon who was openly worshiped and silently feared. In that moment she caught a glimpse of the young man she had married—a brilliant doctor, a good friend, an expert lover. Before the drive to be the best had overtaken the tenderness. Before he'd decided that his life's work was more important than his daughter and wife.

Right now Anne wished he would get up and protest, but he remained motionless. The metal bars on the bed had been raised to prevent him from falling. Jack would hate being confined. But it was for his own good, although he would never see it that way.

Anne touched her fingertips to the clear glass, as if she could somehow connect with him. As if she could bring him back to the way he'd been all those years ago, when they were everything to each other. She grieved not only for the Jack whose future was so tenuous, but also for the Jack she had lost to stubborn ambition. The man who had been so easy to love, yet so difficult to understand.

She shook off the memories, though she couldn't shake off the regret, or the groundswell of feelings that she'd tried so hard to disregard over the past two years. She had to keep the painful emotions buried, never to resurrect them again, for the sake of her sanity and her soul.

"He's going to need you, Anne. More than he's ever needed anything in his life."

No. She didn't want to hear this. "Don't do this to me, Hank."

Clasping her shoulders, Hank turned her around to face him. "He's got no one. Just you and Katie. If he's going to survive, he has to have support. He has to have both of you."

Like someone about to tumble over a cliff, she grasped for anything to save her from this fate. "He has a brother."

"Bert's out of the country, Anne. Jack needs friends and

family right here to help him recover, and that includes you and Katie."

Anne admitted Hank was right, but her survival instincts were much stronger than logic. This summer she'd planned to cut her hours at the hospital and begin work on her master's degree, bringing her one step closer to realizing her dream—a dream she'd put on hold for the sake of Jack's career. Once she had the degree she could sell the house, with its memories, and start over. She could give Katie a mother who was whole, alive and sure of herself. Jack's need might take all that away. She would suffocate in Jack's need.

Anne tried to stay strong, although she was crumbling inside like week-old pastry. She swiped furiously at the tears that slipped past her attempts to stop them. "Katie's only seven. She wouldn't understand seeing her daddy this way. It would scare her to death."

Hank pinned her with a glare. "Are you intending to keep Katie from him? Are you going to just say, 'To hell with you, Jack. Make it on your own'?" He shrugged. "Of course, you could hire someone to take care of him while he's recovering. Is that what you want, Anne? Strangers tending to him? Do you hate him that much?"

No, she had loved him too much.

Her tears fell in earnest now. She didn't know what to do, what to feel. She only knew she couldn't breathe in this stifling atmosphere. She needed air. She needed to get back to work. She needed to think.

Anne walked away and headed past windows revealing the deluge outside that was no match for the storm of emotions within her. She reached the elevator where she would travel to the labor and delivery floor to resume her shift, a place to forget the prospect of death while welcoming new life. And if that didn't work, she would go home and prepare for her daughter to return from school.

Hank let her go without protest, but she could sense his accusing glare while she waited for the next car to arrive. The doors sighed opened and several people streamed out, family members of loved ones clinging to life. She didn't want to count herself among them, so she brushed past the group, seeking an escape, only to run into another man from her past, hospital administrator Maxwell Crabtree, as always looking polished in his tailor-made blue suit, his thinning sandy hair held in place by a light coat of gel.

Before Anne could hand out a polite greeting and be done with it, Max took her by the arm and led her away from the elevator. He stopped outside the ICU waiting room, his expression grim. "I've heard about Jack, Anne. Tough break for him."

His tone was less than compassionate—something that didn't surprise Anne in the least. He'd despised her ex-husband for many years. "He'll recover from this, Max," she said, with only minimal conviction.

"I'm sure he will," Max replied. "And I'm sure he'll have plenty of people helping him with that recovery. I only hope you don't get it in your head that you should be one of them."

The exact opposite of what Hank had told Anne a few moments ago. She felt as though she was engaged in a mental tug-of-war of opposite opinions. "This isn't any of your business, Max."

He narrowed his eyes. "You *are* considering it, aren't you?"

Anne could barely think at the moment, much less make any solid plans. "Jack is Katie's father, and Katie needs him. If that means putting aside the past for her sake, then I have no choice."

"Maybe you don't have a choice as far as your daughter's concerned, but you do have a choice when it comes to how involved you're going to be in his life."

Anne tugged her arm from his grasp and backed away. "Again, this isn't your problem. It's mine." A problem that seemed almost insurmountable.

Max slid his hands inside his pockets and leaned against the wall. "I'll still be here for you, Anne, the way I've always been whenever you've needed someone to pick up the pieces after Jack tore you apart. Feel free to call me. Or stop by, day or night, if you want to talk."

An offer she didn't intend to accept this time. "Thanks, but I'll be fine."

Anne rushed back to the elevator and managed to catch a car before the doors closed her out. But she couldn't close out the decision weighing heavily on her heart after Hank's comment had sliced through her mind.

"He's got no one, Anne.... No one but you."

1983

In the country-club ballroom housing Dallas's most prosperous physicians, he stood out like a black diamond against a drift of snow. His stance exuded unmistakable confidence. His unkempt dark hair, faded jeans and sport jacket, sans tie, hinted at the unconventional.

Anne Cooper appreciated anyone who went against the norm in this setting. She detested these New Year's Eve snob-fest soirees. But the stranger across the way had made the obligatory event somewhat bearable. For the past half hour she'd pretended to socialize while covertly watching him, and playing the part of secret admirer suited her fine. Although her mother made an attempt at subtlety, Anne realized Delia Cooper's insistence that her daughter attend the annual shindig had to do with one thing only—introducing Anne to prospects with M.D. behind their names in the hope that she would eventually find one who suited her discriminating tastes.

"His name is Dr. Jack Morgan, Anne."

At the sound of the familiar voice coming from beside her, Anne closed her eyes briefly and muttered a silent oath. She should know by now that her mother qualified as a master mind reader. "I have no idea who you're talking about."

"The man you've been staring at since we arrived."

Anne saw no use in denying her interest. Only mild interest. "Actually, he doesn't look like a typical doctor. Are you sure he is?"

In her usual efficient fashion, delightfully refined Delia sent a wave at the hospital's chief of staff while murmuring through her compulsory smile. "Of course he's a doctor. Everyone here is a doctor. He's a first-year surgical resident. He graduated from medical school with honors—"

"Did you take his résumé at the door, Mother?"

Delia didn't seem the least bit irritated over the question. "Your father's mentioned him a time or two. He claims Jack's going to be a brilliant surgeon. The man also happens to be single, so this is your lucky day."

Lucky? Ha! Maybe if he'd been a tennis pro. For all of her twenty-three years, Anne had been steeped in the sanctity of medicine. Her father was a preeminent surgeon; her mother, a member of every medical auxiliary of acquaintance to God and man and even the inventor of a few; and she herself had become an R.N. She intimately knew the arrogance of physicians, the obsession, the insistence that the lowly folk bow and scrape in their presence. She bowed and scraped for no man.

Before Anne could issue a protest, Delia had her by the hand and was dragging her toward the doctor in question.

Anne stopped dead a few feet prior to the point of no return. "Mother, what are you doing?"

"I'm introducing you. Now, be nice."

"But I don't want—"

"Hush, Anne, and smile."

As much as Anne wanted to run in the opposite direction, as much as she wanted to dive beneath one of the pristine cloth-covered tables, she allowed her mother to lead her forward until she came face to shoulder with the mystery M.D.

Delia patted her blond bob, linked her arm through Anne's and then cleared her throat to garner his attention. "Good evening, Dr. Morgan. I'd like you to meet my daughter, Anne."

Considering his look of surprise, Anne could just

imagine what he was thinking—another matchmaking mother foisting her hapless daughter off on a prospective groom. Still, for the sake of civility, she offered a slight smile. "Very nice to meet you, Dr. Morgan."

He gave her hand a brief shake. "It's 'Jack,' and it's nice to finally meet you, too. Dr. Cooper talks about you all the time. I hear you work at the hospital."

The fact that her father had actually mentioned her shocked Anne. Bryce Cooper had never been the demonstrative-daddy type. "I'm a labor and delivery nurse."

"You're at the other end of the building," he said. "That must be why I haven't seen you before. I'm on a general-surgery rotation right now."

Without warning, Delia added, "I'll just leave you two young people to visit," before breezing away with a flip of one manicured hand.

Anne wasn't all that surprised by her mother's abrupt departure. She *was* surprised that Dr. Morgan hadn't made an excuse to do the same. Following a few moments of awkward silence, she said, "Your apparel definitely makes a statement."

He sent her a cynical yet still charming smile. "What? Screw tuxedos?"

Her laughter earned a curious glance from one of the medical matriarchs standing nearby, who was polishing her snobbish air. "I guess you could say that."

"I like what you're wearing. Nothing better than a little black dress."

His tone was suggestive, and that was when Anne decided it would be best to leave, before she began to make a few suggestions of her own. "Again, it was nice to meet you. Think I'll head home."

"Don't go yet," he said. "I could use the company."

"I'm sure you'll find plenty of company as the night wears on." From single women looking for the consummate catch, and she didn't fall into that category.

"I haven't run into anyone here I care to keep company with. Too much bowing and scraping."

Surely he hadn't really said *bowing and scraping*. "Excuse me?"

When a roving waiter passed by, Jack snatched two glasses of champagne from the tray and offered her one. "You know, kissing ass for the sake of appearances. I work forty-eight-hour rotations, and I can think of several things I'd rather be doing in my spare time than sucking up."

So could Anne, even if it meant curling up on the couch in her apartment and ringing in the new year alone. "I know what you mean. I'm only here because my mother asked me to come. I need to get a life." Wonderful. She'd just admitted she didn't have one.

He downed the wine in two gulps, then set the glass on the portable tray behind him. "This is going to sound crazy, but I really want to play miniature golf. There's a place on the interstate a few miles away. Are you interested in a game?"

She tightened her grip on the flute as if it were a life jacket capable of saving her from sinking. "Let me get this straight. We've just met and you want me to play miniature golf with you in the dead of winter while I'm wearing a cocktail dress and three-inch heels."

"It's not that cold."

"It's forty degrees out."

"If you don't own a coat, you can borrow mine."

Obviously he'd mistaken her for a fool. "Of course I own a coat."

"Then what's the problem?" When Anne didn't immediately respond, he added, "We only have to play one round. Of course, if you have other plans for the evening, we can do it some other time."

Faced with a situation that meant destroying her pride if she told the truth, she considered a small lie. Yet for some reason, either a lapse of sanity or unseen cosmic forces, she found herself saying, "Actually, no. I don't have any plans. But we barely know each other."

"What's your favorite color?" he asked.

"Red."

"Red's good. Now it's your turn."

Anne thought a moment. "What's your favorite sport, aside from miniature golf?"

"Baseball."

This might go somewhere after all. "I'm a rabid baseball fan."

"Great. Now, one more question," he said. "Why didn't you go to medical school?"

The question she'd been asked at least a thousand times. "You sound like my father. He's never understood why I didn't want to wield a scalpel and a mammoth ego. The truth is, I prefer the personal connection with patients, not to mention keeping doctors in line. You and I both know doctors are nothing without nurses."

He held out his hands, palms forward. "I guess I've touched on a sorry subject."

"You would be right."

He tried on an apologetic look, and it worked well. "I agree—doctors can't function without nurses. Okay?"

Suddenly she felt a little foolish over her semi-rant. "Okay."

"Go ahead and ask me something really personal."

Anne grabbed the opportunity to do a little fishing. "How many women have you propositioned tonight?" She watched for signs of discomfort in his demeanor, but found none. Then again, he could be very good at masking guilt.

"I'm taking the Fifth on that," he said.

Which probably meant he'd delivered too many propositions to count. "You don't play fair, do you? And that really makes me wonder if I should join you in that golf game."

"Are you worried I'd beat you?"

Anne's competitive nature planted a swift kick to her common sense. "That never entered my mind because it's not going to happen. I'm good."

"So am I. Better than most, in fact."

She downed the rest of her drink, ready to meet the challenge. After all, it was only a game. Mindless recreation. She could do mindless, even if she didn't do doctors. "Okay, you're on. And you're paying."

"Believe me, Annie, you're definitely worth the price."

She should have been insulted that he'd called her "Annie," a nickname she'd never cared for. She should rescind the offer and get away fast. But sometimes those "shoulds" weren't at all appealing. "Let's just see if you say I'm worth it when I kick your butt, Dr. Morgan."

Anne expected a comeback, but instead Jack studied her awhile before he said, "Do you want an honest answer to your earlier question?"

"That would be nice." She expected honesty from a man. In fact, she demanded it.

Jack surveyed the room for a moment, as if preparing to tell a secret, before he leaned close to her ear and whispered, "You're the only one."

CHAPTER 2

Delia Hayes Cooper hated only two things—raspberries and pompous asses.

At the moment, one sat in her untouched dessert plate and the other stood at the podium positioned in front of the banquet room. Her attention drifted away as Maxwell Crabtree, supercilious administrator of Dallas Regional, extolled the virtues of altruism to the group of volunteers as if he had personal knowledge of benevolence without the benefit of compensation.

Weary of the hypocrisy, Delia slid her chair from beneath the table and dismissed herself with a polite smile aimed at the dozen or so Pink Ladies, who regarded her with mild shock. Delia Cooper was never late to a luncheon, and she never left a meeting in the middle of a speaker's address. Today she had done both.

Let them think what they would about her departure, be it due to incontinence or the apocalypse; Delia didn't care. She had to get out of here fast before she gave in to the urge to grab a berry and lob it at the administrator's forehead the next time he mentioned commitment. But she was the consummate Southern lady, or had been since she'd crossed over into the realm of acceptable society from her youthful beginnings as a free spirit. That Delia of nearly forty years ago would not have hesitated to hurl a fruity missile at the speaker. Today that Delia no longer existed, at least superficially.

She slipped soundlessly from the room until she reached the double doors that creaked open like worn-out joints in winter. The doors closed behind her, but that did little to shut out Crabtree's booming oration. She made her way to the windows immediately across the hall and looked out over the crowded parking lot. Arms folded beneath her breasts, she shivered despite the fact that the temperature inside was comfortable enough. Outside was another story. The downpour that had begun early that morning hadn't let up, fueling her gray mood. She felt restless, disturbed on a soul-deep level, as if something ominous was about to happen. Her mother had labeled the intuition a gift. Delia considered it a curse.

Right now she wanted to be someplace balmy, kicked back on a sun-warmed beach, with a gimlet in one hand and a cigarette in the other—something she hadn't craved in at least three decades. No use wishing for what could never be. She was locked into a life of her own making, a comfortable life that included good friends and, most important, her only child and grandchild. A life that was safe, secure, necessary—and totally uneventful. Except for Anne's divorce.

If only Delia had been able to prevent it. If only she could somehow have convinced her daughter that she was making a terrible mistake. From the first time she'd seen Anne and Jack interacting on a day much like today, she'd known they were destined to be together, even if she had been the only one who'd acknowledged it at the time.

"He's good for her, Bryce."

As always, Delia had to wait an interminable amount of time for her husband to comment. Profile to her, Bryce continued to stare out the front window, a glass of Scotch in his hand, worry etched on his still-handsome face. A face Delia had enjoyed waking up with for much of her adult life, even though the demands of his career had infringed on a good many of their mornings.

Following a long sip, he finally said, "He doesn't have the sense to bring her in out of the rain, for God's sake."

Delia moved to his side and slid her arm around his waist. Jack and Anne were still playing a game of football in the front yard, soaked from head to toe from the downpour that had ruined the Sunday barbecue, and not seeming to mind at all. "They're young, Bryce. And in love."

"He told me they're just friends, so get your head out of the romantic clouds."

"Friendship is a wonderful place to start," she said. "We started as friends."

"I'm still not sure he's good enough for her."

"You said yourself he's gifted. 'Destined for greatness' is how you put it. Maybe your standards are just a tad high?"

"But that's the problem, Dee. Anne's always resented my absence from her life. She's not going to settle for anything less than all his time, and that's not possible. Not if he's going to be all he's meant to be."

"I managed fine, dear heart. Anne will, too. She's tough. And I suspect she'll learn that some sacrifices are simply worth it."

Bryce draped an arm around her shoulder. "She's her mother's daughter."

"She's your daughter, honey. Headstrong. Determined. She knows her heart, so we're going to have to trust her. And if she's lucky, she'll have what we have."

He shifted to face her and braced his palms on her shoulders, even deeper disquiet showing in his expression. "If anything happened to me, would you find someone else?"

"Nothing's going to happen to you."

"But if it does, you should find someone else," he said. "You shouldn't have to be alone. I'm serious about this, Dee."

Delia didn't care to consider a life without her husband. "If, God forbid, I do outlive you, I can't imagine finding anyone who'd have such a dearth of sense that he'd be willing to put up with me."

He smiled the smile that Delia had come to know so well, had come to cherish as much as she cherished him. She wished for Anne the blessings of that kind of a smile, the contentment of recognizing where you belonged and who you belonged with, the love of a good man. Anne deserved Jack's love. They deserved each other. And regardless of what the future might hold, Delia realized that she herself would never find anyone to replace her husband—

"You look real nice in pink."

Startled, Delia turned her attention from the window and the memory to the voice and its owner, who was standing a few feet away. With a full head of silver hair and first-class features, the man might have been labeled debonair had it not been for his tie resting loose and askew against his burgundy shirt. His navy suit was neat and nicely pressed, but definitely not Armani. More like outlet. She would guess him to be mid-fifties, and he appeared rather tall, but compared with Delia, everyone was.

Once Delia had established that he was in fact speaking to her, she sent him a tentative smile and told him, "Thank you," when she dearly wanted to mention that about thirty other women in the adjacent room were dressed in the same color smock. But good grace dictated she be kind. Besides, she couldn't remember the last time a man had paid her a compliment.

He forked a hand through his hair and returned her smile. "Hope you didn't take offense at what I said." His voice reflected the drawl many native Texans favored, a throwback to when Dallas hadn't been such a cultural melting pot.

"No offense taken, Mr.—?"

"Gabe Burks."

Delia lightly clasped the hand that he offered for a shake. It felt warm and dry, slightly calloused but pleasantly masculine. "I'm Mrs. Delia Cooper, Mr. Burks."

"It's just 'Gabe,' Delia."

Had she been alive, Delia's mother would have lectured the stranger for calling a lady by her first name without so much as an invitation. Delia found it refreshing.

"So you're married, huh?" Gabe asked.

"Actually, I'm widowed."

His expression brightened. "Yeah? Me, too. How long?"

"Almost eight years."

"Three for me. Cancer?"

People always assumed that had to have been the cause of her husband's demise. In reality, Bryce had worked himself to death. "Heart. He was very driven in his job."

"That'll get you every time. But not me. Not if I can help it. Life's too short to burn the candle at both ends."

Delia relaxed somewhat, intrigued by this man who claimed there was more to life than work. "Are you retired?"

"Nope. Not yet. I'm an attorney. One of the hospital's attorneys."

Bryce would be livid if he learned that his wife was socializing with the enemy—"swamp feeders," he used to call all attorneys. Oh, well. What Bryce didn't know wouldn't hurt him. Delia had never put much stock in the theory that a ticket to heaven included a pass with carte blanche to watch over surviving loved ones. At least, she hoped not.

Gabe inclined his head toward the banquet room. "Were you in the meeting?"

"Yes, I was, but my knee started cramping, so I came out here. That old arthritis. It acts up now and then, especially in this weather." She raised a hand to her chest, feeling a nip of guilt over handing Gabe Burks a lie. Sometimes lies were necessary. Better a lie than revealing her contempt for the keynote speaker.

"Actually, I left because I was about to fall asleep," Gabe said.

Total honesty. That brought about another flash of guilt in Delia. "Mr. Crabtree does tend to go on and on." He also tended to create havoc in Anne's life on a regular basis. The man had carried a torch for her daughter for years, and he continued to do so without Anne's encouragement.

"I take it you're a volunteer," Gabe said.

"Yes. I spend much of my time at the hospital." A sad commentary on her life.

"That's admirable. I'm a little surprised we haven't met, but then, I'm holed up in an office when I'm here."

Applause rang out from the nearby room, signaling the end of Crabby's speech. Delia felt obligated to say her goodbyes to friends before manning the lobby information desk for the afternoon—a reminder of how much she had conformed to proper behavior. "Well, I need to get on with my day, Gabe." His name rolled easily off her tongue, as if she'd known him for years, not minutes.

"Yeah, I guess I should go, too."

Neither of them moved for a long moment, until Gabe closed the gap between them with a few steps, catching Delia off guard. Yet she didn't feel the urge to move back, perhaps because she wanted to get a better glimpse at his eyes to further assess him. A woman could tell a lot from a man's eyes. His were a mossy green and reflected a certain self-assurance.

"Do you think you might like to have dinner with me sometime?" he asked.

"Me?" *Good grief.* Who else would he be talking to? Certainly not the wilting fern in the corner—unless in reality he had escaped from the psych ward. A possibility,

Delia decided. Why else would he be asking *her* to dinner, a total stranger and a grandmother—granted, a grandmother in the process of being dragged kicking and screeching into her twilight years.

"Just dinner," he said when she failed to respond. "Unless you already have a boyfriend, Delia."

How funny to have her name mentioned in the same sentence with *boyfriend*. She hadn't been involved with anyone since Bryce's death. Nor had she even considered something so ludicrous, until now. "I'm not seeing anyone at the moment."

His grin expanded, lighting up his eyes. "A woman as attractive as you ought to be fighting them off with a stick."

He was out and out flirting with her. Flirting with Granny Delia. In response, Delia patted her hair and then did something even more absurd. She giggled. Giggled like a sixteen-year-old girl standing in the high school hallway, not a been-around-the-block-more-than-once woman standing in the corridor of a high-tech teaching hospital.

A few people began to filter out the double doors, mostly other Pink Ladies, who sent curious glances her way. Delia could only imagine what this looked like—Mrs. Bryce Cooper, M.D., engaged in a conversation with a man who was more than likely a few years her junior. An attorney, no less. Yet except for the giggling, the scenario would probably appear completely innocent to most. Just a volunteer talking to a member of the team. Then why did it seem that people were whispering behind their hands?

Feeling the need to flee, Delia said, "I really have to go, Mr. Burks."

"It's 'Gabe,' and you didn't answer my question."

She caught a glimpse of loneliness in his eyes, the same loneliness probably mirrored in hers at times, though she'd learned to hide it well. Perhaps even a hint of desperation. She sensed his request was costing him a lot. What would it cost her if she agreed? Oh, to hell with it. She hadn't taken a risk in such a long time. What could be wrong about seeking companionship with a man? She was certainly beyond the age of consent. "Dinner would be nice."

"Can I call you later?"

Excitement as fresh and welcome as dawn hurtled through Delia. "Yes. You can reach me here until 5:00 p.m. Or I'm in the phone book under B. Cooper on Magnolia."

Nellie Mills, the medical center crier, picked that exact moment to rush up to Delia as if she had the demons nipping at her heels. "Can you believe it?"

Surely the main link to the hospital grapevine wasn't already privy to the dinner date Delia had made only seconds earlier. "Believe what?"

"You don't know about Dr. Morgan?"

She knew her son-in-law—*former* son-in-law—was supposed to be in the hospital, as always. She'd seen his name on the O.R. schedule while working in the surgery waiting room last week. Unless he'd never made it. A sickening feeling settled in her belly. "What about him?"

"He's in ICU. I saw the admission when I was manning the information desk this morning. He had a stroke two nights ago."

Delia's frame went stiff and her mouth went dry. "Are you sure?"

"Sure as can be."

A razor-sharp edge of anger over the pride in Nellie's voice sliced through Delia. She had to find Anne, and soon, in case she had yet to hear the news.

Starting down the hall, Delia had all but forgotten Gabe Burks until she heard him call, "I'll be in touch. Hope everything's okay."

She raised a hand in a brief wave without glancing back. "Thank you."

Delia cursed the fact that her nice calm world had been rocked without mercy today, just when things were beginning to look up. Cursed her intuition. And deep down, she knew nothing would ever be the same again.

"I came as soon as I heard the news."

Anne leaned against the open front door of her house for support and stared at her mother's compassionate yet somber face. The rain had yet to subside, but Delia looked warm and dry, and much too young for sixty-six, though she had survived the death of her beloved husband and the divorce of her only child.

Delia shook out her red umbrella, snapped it shut, then set it aside in the foyer while Anne closed the door and locked it as if she could lock out the world, the pain. Now she was reminded by her mother's sudden appearance of what she had tried so hard to forget. Anne wasn't surprised Delia had learned about Jack, nor did she question how she could tell that Anne needed her at that very moment. Her mother possessed a maternal sixth sense as deeply engrained as her ability to enter a room with poise and confidence even under overwhelming pressure.

Anne turned and trudged down the corridor to the breakfast nook, the place where they had shared their best mother-daughter chats over tea with milk and an occasional butter cookie, only mildly aware of her mother's prim footsteps behind her. She clicked on the fluorescent light above the breakfast table, washing the area in a harsh artificial glare that robbed the place of its homeness. Before, it hadn't seemed to matter that much, but today she longed for warmth and solace. If only she'd insisted on buying the brightly colored Tiffany fixture, the one Jack had deemed too prissy for the contemporary surroundings. It wasn't the only thing she had conceded to him. She had practically given up her soul, as well.

Collapsing into the oak barrel chair, she waited until Delia took a seat across from her. Then she let the tears flow, not bothering to hide them at all.

Delia clasped Anne's hand and wrapped it in her own. "It will be okay, baby girl." Her smile, motherly and forgiving, was the kind of smile Anne had hoped upon hope to present to her own daughter during a crisis. But lately her smile had been a charade due to the fatigue and frustration over not having enough hours to spend with Katie. A lonely smile that had grown only lonelier over the past few years.

Anne slipped her hand from between her mother's and wiped at her face with one sweatshirt sleeve. "I'm okay." She didn't sound okay. She sounded terrified, unsure—and she hated it. She longed to be as strong as her mother. As Jack. She never had been.

Delia fished through her black leather bag, brought out a small plastic packet and offered it to Anne. After taking a tissue, she sucked in a draft of air and released it on an uneven breath as her mother continued to study her, waiting for her to speak, she supposed. Delia had always been a good listener and a friend in times of need. Anne needed her now more than any other time she could think of.

"Did Max tell you?" Anne managed to ask through a rogue sob.

Delia sent her a look filled with disdain. "Maxwell Crabtree and I don't speak unless absolutely necessary, but I'm certain this probably thrills him to no end, considering how much he detests Jack. And that's not only because he's been pining for you for years between his marriages. He covets Jack's career. Did you know he couldn't make the grade in medical school?"

Anne wasn't sure she could handle any more surprises today, and she certainly didn't want to get into this now. "No, I didn't. And I don't care what you think of Max, Mother. He's remained my friend over the years. He's not cruel enough to wish ill will on anyone, even Jack."

"Is that how you found out about Jack—through Max?" Delia's tone sounded indicting.

"Hank told me." Anne preferred to keep her earlier conversation with Max under wraps. "How did you find out?"

"Nellie Mills caught me outside the hospital luncheon."

Anne couldn't imagine why her mother didn't spend her time someplace other than the institution that had been the center of her own husband's existence. The place that had stolen their weekends and deprived them of being a close-knit family. Just as it had Anne's married years with Jack.

But maybe her mother insisted on volunteering there to continue to connect with what had been her husband's life. Anne could relate to that in a very personal way. She could have taken a job elsewhere, yet she still worked in the same place whose hallowed halls her ex-husband graced. Or had until two days ago.

Fresh tears threatened Anne, so she left the chair, walked to the stove and grabbed up the teakettle to put on fresh water to boil.

"How is he, Anne?"

Anne clicked on the burner beneath the kettle. "Hank just called. He's out of surgery for repair of the aneurysm."

"Why aren't you there with him?"

"Because I'm no longer his next of kin, remember? Hank only phoned as a favor to me, not out of obligation." Her obligation to Jack had ended two years earlier with a simple signature. "Hank says he'll be okay if everything goes well the next forty-eight hours or so. But there's some paralysis in his right hand and leg."

"Oh, dear." Her mother's normally calm voice wavered. Anne couldn't stand it if Delia cried. Not the one person in her life who handled crises like a four-star general, including Anne's father's death.

"He'll get better," Delia said. "He'll go back to surgery eventually. Won't he?"

Now her mother was relying on her for optimism.

What a switch. Anne turned and feigned calm. "It's possible, but we just won't know for a while."

Anne faced the counter again and absently placed two tea bags in two matching green ceramic mugs from the set of four she and Jack had gotten when they'd married. None had been broken. She wished she could say the same for the marriage. And her heart.

The whistling teakettle startled Anne, but she managed to dole the water into the cups without making a mess. Balancing them in her trembling hands, Anne made her way back to the table to give her mother the tea while preparing for her questions.

"Have you told Katherine?" Delia always insisted on calling her granddaughter by her given name, Delia's mother's name. She'd claimed it was much more elegant than Katie.

"Not yet." Anne braced for the fallout, staring into her tea.

Instead of scolding, Delia said, "I'm sure you will when the time is right," then added, "but don't wait too long."

Anne raised her eyes from the teacup. Her mother's expression held no judgment, only sympathy. Delia was a master of sympathy. "I thought I would do it tomorrow." Suddenly, Anne felt like a teenager again, explaining why she hadn't cleaned her room.

And her mother responded in kind, like the disappointed parent, when she asked, "Why not now, Anne, while I'm here?"

"Because I don't know what's going to happen. If something should happen to him, then…" Anne let the words trail off, hating the thought of that *something*. Yet she couldn't write off the possibility that Jack could bleed out again, and this time it could be fatal.

Now Delia looked worried. "You don't really think—"

"I'm not sure what to think. I'm concerned." And scared, but she didn't need to voice that emotion. Her mother would already know.

Delia rimmed the cup with a neatly manicured nail. "I'm glad to hear you're worried about him. Things have been so bad between you two since the separation."

Divorce, Anne silently corrected. Her mother couldn't bring herself to say the word. "I still care about what happens to him, Mother." Trouble was, she still cared too much.

Anne sipped her tea for a moment, allowing its warmth to wash through her. All day she had been cold, moving through her shift in a state of shock until she'd asked to leave early. "Hank believes we should be actively involved in Jack's recovery."

"Of course we should. Jack has no one else."

A rerun of the conversation she'd had with Hank. But what did she expect from her overly loyal mother? "I have my own life now. I'm not strong enough—"

"I don't want to hear that, Elizabeth Anne. You're stronger than you realize. And you must help Jack recover, if only for Katherine's sake." Her mother's voice had risen a notch; not to shouting exactly, but pretty darned close for Delia.

Everything sounded so logical to Anne. But logic continued to evade her.

"I can help out," Delia added. "If I need to, I can cut down on my volunteering and help you take care of Jack. We owe him that much."

Anne's gaze shot to Delia, who still looked calm. "Owe him? Do I, Mother? He wasn't around when I needed him. When Katie needed him. When he finished the fellowship in California and we moved back here, he promised me he'd go into private practice. And what did he do? Sign on with the hospital as chief attending cardiothoracic surgeon, increasing his workload because of the added responsibility."

"Yes, he has a demanding career. But accepting that is part of the sacrifice of being a doctor's wife. You knew that when you married him."

And still she'd chosen to ignore it, because she'd loved him that much. "I guess I just wasn't as good at it as you were."

Delia shifted in her chair and showed the first signs of real discomfort. "The day you served Jack with divorce papers, he came to see me."

Anne tried to hide her shock. She wasn't certain she wanted to hear this, but she recognized her mother would continue despite her reluctance. "And?"

"He was devastated. You blindsided him. He'd had too much to drink, so he was open about his feelings. He didn't want the divorce, Anne."

"Great. He never talked to me about his feelings. He never protested, never fought. He just signed on the dotted line."

Delia leaned forward. "Did you give him the chance,

Anne? Best I can recall, you refused to speak to him after you threw him out."

"I was afraid he'd talk me out of it." Jack had been, and would always be, Anne's one true weakness.

"If he could do that, then you weren't ready to divorce him."

That brought Anne's chin up in defiance. No one, even her mother, would tell her what was best for her. Not anymore. "Come on, Mother. He's not the saint you make him out to be." The same sainthood Delia had bestowed on Anne's father, as well. Her mother had stood by her man, through countless absences and midnight calls, and she expected no less from her daughter, regardless of the consequences.

Delia sighed. "I realize he's not a saint."

"But you don't know everything."

"If you're referring to the other woman, I know about that, too."

Shock robbed Anne of an immediate response. She'd purposefully kept that information from her mother because it had seemed so sordid. It still did.

Before Anne could comment, Delia looked beyond her and said, "There's my other baby girl!"

Anne glanced up from her tea to see Katie climbing into Delia's lap. Sweet, sweet Katie, with her father's dark pensive eyes and her grandma's flaxen hair. The baby who had miraculously arrived after years of Anne's trying to become pregnant.

"Whatcha doin' here, Grandma?"

"I came to see my bestest girls," Delia said.

Anne smiled at Katie, a shaky smile. "Did you finish your homework, sweetie?"

"Yes, ma'am. All done. Can I play my computer game now?"

Delia studied Anne over Katie's head. Anne recognized that look, exactly what it was saying. *Tell her, Anne. Now's as good a time as any, Anne. Don't be a coward, Anne.*

Anne inched her chair a little closer. "Katie, I have something to tell you."

After taking a drink from Delia's cup of tea, Katie smacked her lips with satisfaction. "What?"

"Daddy's sick."

Katie set the cup of tea down and squirmed in Delia's lap. "Does he have the flu? A lot kids at school have it."

If only that were so. "No, sweetie, he's had something they call a stroke. It's made him pretty sick, so he's in the hospital."

Her daughter's eyes widened with comprehension and fear. "His hospital?"

"Yes. He's okay, but it'll take a while for him to get better."

Katie scooted out of Delia's lap. "I want to see him."

Anne reached for her and pulled her close. "You can't right now. They have him in a special place where they don't let kids in. He's still sleeping."

Tears welled in Katie's eyes, crushing Anne's heart. "Is he going to die?"

Drawing her daughter into a hug, Anne whispered, "No, honey. He's not going to die." If only she were as sure as she sounded.

Katie pulled back, her expression suddenly stern. "Are you glad Daddy's sick?"

Horrified, Anne tried to hug Katie again, but the girl would have none of it. She just stared hard at Anne, a few tears slipping down her cheeks. "Oh, no, Katie. It makes me very sad."

"You should be sad, even if you are divorced." Katie said the last word with clarity, with the tone of a child who knew all too well the reality of single parents and bitter battles.

Delia rested a hand on Katie's shoulder. "How about you go home with Grandma for the next few days, then we'll go to the zoo on Saturday. If Daddy feels up to it, I'll take you to see him after that."

Katie looked back at her grandmother, then leveled her gaze on Anne. "Daddy always takes me to the zoo. I want to go to the zoo with Daddy." Tears rolled down her cheeks in a steady, heart-wrenching stream.

Anne almost collapsed under the weight of her helplessness. What could she tell Katie? That her daddy might never get to take her to the zoo again? That he might never attend another soccer game or field day? Perhaps not even her wedding.

No, Anne couldn't tell her daughter those things. She had to tell her something that would allow her hope. Something to make her smile again. She could think of only one thing. That one thing would entail discarding latent bitterness toward her ex-husband. But if making the sacrifice of aiding Jack with his recovery meant giving her daughter some peace, she would do it for Katie.

"How would you like it if Daddy came to live here with us until he felt better?"

Katie's expression lit up, and so did Delia's. "Like before?"

Not exactly, but Anne wouldn't dare make that revelation. Not now. "Only until he gets well. He'll have to have lots of rest."

"Can he stay in the room next to mine? I could help take care of him."

Anne considered the stairs, how hard it would be for Jack to scale them at first, if ever. "No, he'd have to stay downstairs."

"In your room?"

Lord, she hadn't even considered that. The other bedroom was upstairs with Katie's. She supposed she could sleep in the guest room, but she would need to be nearby. She could sleep on the sofa in the living room and let Jack have the master bedroom. Or maybe she should arrange to have a hospital bed set up in the den. Already she was planning, and she realized the decision had been made for her.

"I'll figure that out later. First, Daddy will have to say it's okay."

"He will," Katie said with a child's confidence, as though all would be right with the world if she willed it.

Katie hugged Anne, Delia smiled, and one thought gripped Anne's heart. Jack was back in their lives—her life—if he agreed. If he lived.

CHAPTER 3

He awoke with a gasp as if surfacing from treacherous waters, held down by heavy limbs. Recollections came back to him in small frames, like some macabre B-movie with him in the starring role.

He remembered falling. Darkness. Pain. Flashes of Annie seeped into his consciousness. The dreams arrived as one patchwork journey into his past. Annie the way she looked back then. Katie as a baby. He was still running local marathons. Maybe even still in medical school. No—residency. He hadn't known Annie in medical school.

The visions made little sense, yet he found comfort in their familiarity. He wanted to go right on sleeping, fearful of the unknown. Terrified of what he might find when he came fully awake. But sleep wouldn't return, regardless of the fact that he kept his eyes tightly closed in an attempt to ignore the muffled voices, ignore other sounds he knew all too well. The nasal tones of an operator paging his colleagues. The hustle and bustle of the hospital halls. He recognized the sterile smells, the supercharged atmosphere. The place where he'd spent most of his waking hours in the past few years, but never like this.

He had no concept of time, no idea what day it was. Had he been asleep for minutes? Days? Weeks?

Jack searched his mind and vaguely remembered an eruption of activity after the initial confusion. Several times he'd wanted to ask what was happening to him, but he couldn't manage to form the words with any coherency. Hank had been there; he knew that for certain. He'd recognized several of the nurses hovering over him. Most had taken orders from him at one time or another. Now they ordered him around. Asked him his name periodically. What day it was. What year. He'd answered the best he could, but his mind continued to drift off to another place. A place to escape harsh realities.

The creaking of a cart somewhere in the distance caused him to open his eyes. He slowly scanned the functional room. Purple drapes, mauve-and-navy chairs. A TV perched on the stand mounted near the ceiling. He knew the territory like he knew every instrument he used in surgery. Like the back of his hand.

His hand. He worked his left hand into a fist, flexing it open and closed. Yet when he tried to move his right hand, it lay flaccid against his side. His right foot tingled, but he felt nothing above it.

He gulped more air into his constricted chest, trying

hard to push away the panic that threatened to consume him. He lowered his eyes to the needle in his arm, then followed the line as it trailed over the metal sidebars and up to where it attached to an IV pump. The equipment surrounding him was all too familiar. He just hadn't been on this side of the bed before.

As a physician, he should know the names of the medications they kept pumping into him, but he couldn't remember. Normally, he would be looking down on this scene—the narrow bed, the starched white sheets, the figure lying among leads and lines to sustain or relieve whatever malady had befallen him or her. But this time, he was the one lying helpless, surrounded by the miracle of modern technology. Half his body as dead as driftwood. Only half a man.

The door swung open and in walked Hank, a grim expression on his bearded face. Jack had seen that look before. He'd worn it several times himself, right before telling a patient's family that nothing more could be done.

Hank strode to the side of the bed and faked a smile. "Hey, bud, you're finally awake." He leaned over and checked the pump. "Do you know your name?"

Shit, Hank was treating him like one of his patients. "Morgan. M-m-miracle worker." It didn't come out quite right; his brain seemed short-circuited.

Hank chuckled. "Hell, the stroke didn't affect your industrial-size ego."

Jack tensed over the word *stroke*. His worst fears had been confirmed; yet he'd known all along that he'd suffered some sort of cerebral accident. A fried brain. The end of his career.

"What…d-day is it?" His throat was as dry as dead leaves in the winter, and it had taken him great effort to form the words. As if it really mattered what day it was. What was the use in knowing? He had no surgical cases to worry about. No strength. No will.

Hank set the metal chart on the rolling table and perched on the edge of the bed. "It's Saturday, Jack. You fell out around midnight on Sunday, after your transplant case. Do you remember any of it?"

"Some." He remembered the pain, the helplessness. That no one had been there to comfort him.

After clearing his scratchy throat, he pointed at the white pitcher on the table. "Water."

Hank poured a plastic cup full and handed it to him. After Jack took one sip, he asked the question nagging at him. "How bad?"

"An aneurysm. Nan Travers ordered you a nice buzz cut and fixed it. And if you don't have any more problems, you'll be good as new."

Jack sensed his blood pressure rising. Right now he didn't give a damn about anything. "Good as new, huh? What about the h-hand. The leg, Hank?"

Hank laid a palm on his shoulder. "Easy, bud. We'll take it one day at a time. Occupational therapy and physical therapy will work with you, get that hand and leg back up to speed. But you'll have to work with them, while you're here on the rehab unit and after you go home."

Home. Jack hadn't considered the apartment home. He had no idea how the hell he was going to get through this. He'd been alone for two years and he'd managed. He'd manage again, even if it meant wasting away by himself. Then no one would see his suffering, or witness his despair.

"Anne's here."

Jack stopped the cup halfway to his lips, then slowly brought it back down to rest against his chest. He no longer wanted water. He wanted whiskey. "Why?"

"She asked to see how you're doing. Talk to you."

Jack took another sip of water, which partially rolled from the corner of his mouth, before he turned away from Hank's scrutiny. "No."

Hank pushed off the bed and stood. "Be reasonable, Jack. She's worried about you. We're all worried about you."

White-hot anger bubbled up from Jack's gut. He sure as hell didn't want her to see him this way, all the proof she needed that he was too obsessed. Too driven. She'd find some way to blame the stroke on his work. She might not say "I told you so," but he would be able to spot it in her face.

He brought his gaze back to Hank. "Tell her...come back later."

"Can't do that, bud. She's on her morning break and she's damn determined. You know what Anne's like when she's determined."

Yeah, he knew what she was like. He'd lived with her long enough to know that when she had her mind set on something, she fought like a champion welterweight to get what she wanted. Okay, so he'd let her come in. Let her get her grins seeing him lying here like a limp fish. Then he'd tell her thanks for stopping by, now leave.

"Okay." He sounded like a damn bullfrog, a drunk one,

but this thing hadn't completely robbed him of his speech. At least he had that much left.

Hank slipped the chart off the table and tapped it twice on the bed rail. "Okay. I'll get her. I'll drop by later when I'm making my evening rounds."

"G-great." Just great.

Hank strode out of the room, leaving Jack alone to face his past. And when she walked in the door, he realized he couldn't run from the inevitable. She was dressed in her standard floral blue scrubs, a stethoscope draped around her neck. She'd cut her hair to her shoulders. He liked it better longer, not that his opinion mattered anymore.

Annie moved to the end of his bed and tried to smile. She'd never been good at hiding her emotions, and right now he could tell she was distressed. Hell, he must look worse than he thought.

She brushed back her gold-brown hair with one hand and said, "Hi."

He focused on her face. Her wary blue eyes held a cast of some unnamed emotion. Probably pity. He didn't like pity. "Nice weather…we're having, huh?"

She moved a bit closer and gave him a once-over. "You look better than the last time I saw you. So how are you feeling?"

"Like c-crap."

She raised a hand to her throat. "Well, that's to be expected for a while."

Enough of the small talk. He preferred to go back to sleep. Escape. Forget this nightmare. "Wh-what do you want?"

She looked surprised, maybe hurt. "I wanted to see how you're doing. See if you're up for visitors."

"You're here. You've seen me. You can…g-go."

"I meant Katie."

God, he didn't want Katie coming here, seeing him helpless and wasted. "I don't w-want…" He tried to calm down, but he almost welcomed the feeling of animosity. At least it kept him from thinking about his situation. "No. Not a good idea. For her to be here."

"She's scared, Jack. I had to tell her something. I think if she sees you're okay, then she'll be less worried."

"I'm n-not okay." Damn his stammering.

Anne stepped to the side of the bed. and laid a hand on his dead appendage. He couldn't even yank it back, away from her charity. All he could do was stare at their joined hands and hope she took the hint. Finally she pulled away.

She started pacing, her favorite pastime when her nerves got the best of her. "Look, Jack, we have a few things to discuss."

When she faced him again, he noticed the worry in her expression and chose to ignore it. "Support check's in the m-mail."

Anger flared in her eyes. "I don't care about your stupid money. I'm talking about your future. What you're going to do when you get out of here."

"Maybe I'll…take up gardening."

She fisted her hands at her sides. Annie was about to blow, and he couldn't even get out of her path. "This isn't a joke, Jack. You've got to consider your health. Your recuperation." She strolled around to the other side of the bed, appearing unsure. Very un–Annelike.

"What d–do you suggest, Annie?"

"I want you to consider coming to live with me and Katie during your recovery."

If that didn't bring on another stroke, then maybe he was out of the woods after all. At least for the time being. "What the...hell for?"

"Because you're going to need help. And we can help you. You don't have to decide now. I just want you to think about it for the next few days."

He didn't understand her motivation, why she was making such a crazy offer. He suspected Hank had had something to do with this. Maybe even Delia. "I don't need...any help. I wouldn't want you to p–put yourself out on my account, Anne."

"Quit being so damn stubborn!"

Annie had cursed at him. She was pissed, and he liked her that way. He liked her as pissed as he was over this whole mess. "You really want a vegetable...on your nice leather c–couch, Annie?"

In a matter of minutes, she recovered, erecting the emotional wall that had separated them for several years. She hadn't changed her attitude about him one whit, but what could he expect? "You'll get better."

"Just 'cause you say it's so...d–don't make it so. Thanks for the...offer. But no...thanks."

She shrugged and raised her hands all in one smooth move. "Okay, forget I asked. You hire someone to take care of you. And when you decide to stop feeling sorry for yourself, then maybe you'll be ready to see your daughter again."

When she spun on her crepe soles and headed for the door, a sudden fear gripped Jack. Irrational fear, yet too strong to ignore. He hated being at the mercy of everyone's idea of what was best for him, but if he let her leave, he might lose his port in the storm. Again. Although there was a lot of garbage between Anne and him, he knew he could rely on her if he had to. She was the connection to his daughter, and he couldn't survive without Katie in his life. He'd already given up too much.

"Annie, wait."

When she turned, her eyes looked red-rimmed and moist. Surely she wasn't going to cry over him. He wasn't worth it. She was willing to make a sacrifice, and he'd gone and hurt her. The way he'd hurt her so many times already. But what the hell was he going to do? He gave her the only response that made any sense.

"I'm s-sorry. Bring Katie. Tonight."

Now Anne stared at him, openly stunned. A long time had passed since he'd apologized to her for his shortcomings, and he had plenty. So many she'd never been able to forgive him, and most likely never would. "This probably wasn't a great time to discuss this, Jack. It's just that Katie cares about what happens to you."

"What a-b-bout you, Annie?" An unfair question, yet he had to know.

"Of course I care, Jack. I still consider you a friend, and you are Katie's father."

But not her husband, or her lover, and despite what she said, not her friend.

Not anymore.

1984

Anne had never believed for a second she would become friends with a doctor, much less go out with one. Twice.

For the past hour she'd tried to find something about Jack Morgan that she didn't like. Some hidden imperfection. Even the tiniest thing to discourage her. So far, she'd had little success. Of course, she could paint his persistence as a character flaw, and persistent he'd been since their New Year's Eve golf game, calling several times over the past week until he'd finally worn her down. But in all fairness, she couldn't fault him for a trait that she also possessed.

She'd unfortunately discovered they had a lot in common, including a love of nature, which was precisely how she'd ended up sitting in a small outdoor café on her day off, taking a break from the myriad tourists who had flocked to the zoo on a sunny January afternoon following a few days of freezing temperatures.

"Exactly how did you manage this little excursion, Doctor?" she asked.

"Easy. I bought tickets at the gate."

Considering his talent for teasing, she should have known not to expect a straight answer. "I meant, how did you manage to take the day off to entertain me?"

"I called in sick."

She looked up from her purple plastic souvenir cup to

find that his grin alone indicated he was lying. "You did not."

"It's my scheduled day off. Do you really think I'd call in sick when I run the risk of having to explain that to your dad, Annie?"

She bit back the urge to panic. "My father knows you're out with me?"

"Not unless you told him."

No, she hadn't told him, or her mother. "I decided not to say anything, just in case. I was afraid it might create complications for you." And for her. "I also don't want people believing there's more between us than friendship."

Jack frowned. "Are you worried some of my fellow residents might cry favoritism if they knew I was fraternizing with the chief's daughter?"

"Yes. Doesn't that bother you?"

"Not unless it bothers you."

"You say that now, but I doubt you'd be so cavalier about it if word got out."

"I'll deal with it if I have to." He pushed his own cup aside. "Want to go check out the gorillas now?"

"The gorillas can wait. First, I want to talk awhile longer." They'd been too engrossed in competition during the golf game for Anne to garner any intimate details, and he'd been in too big of a hurry during their previous phone conversations.

Jack leaned back in his chair and stacked his hands behind his neck. "Okay. Talk."

"You've never told me about your family."

His expression turned serious and hinted at sadness. "I

have a brother who's a banker. He's married and lives in Boston. My mother died two years ago from breast cancer. When I was eleven, my dad died from restrictive cardiomyopathy."

Like so many doctors she'd known, he'd been driven into medicine by personal experience, when she'd secretly hoped he'd been motivated by the money, prestige, power—all valid reasons for her to cling to the last of her resistance. "I'm sorry, Jack."

"So am I." He straightened, his hands clasped tightly before him on the table. "Back then, all I could do was watch him die. If I can prevent that from happening to someone else's family member, then the hell I go through to become a transplant surgeon will be worth it."

A transplant surgeon. No wonder her father held Jack in such high esteem. "Sounds like you have a long road ahead of you, educationally speaking."

"At least four more years of residency, then probably a couple of fellowships, with heavy emphasis on heart-lung transplantation. I could be looking at another ten years or so before I'm on my own."

Ten years of grueling training, long days and longer nights. He wouldn't have time for a serious relationship or a family. A definite negative to add to the pro-con list Anne had been compiling since they'd met. "And to think I'm worried about how long it'll take to get my master's."

"Your dad didn't mention you're in school."

"I'm not right now. I've only been out of college for two years, and I needed a break. But I plan to go back eventually, after I hone my clinical skills."

"Exactly how old are you, Annie?"

She was surprised he hadn't asked before now. "I turned twenty-three last September."

"You sure as hell seem a lot older."

Hadn't she been told *that* before? "I'm an only child, and only children tend to grow up fast. Plus I attended the best college-prep boarding school money can buy, so I've basically lived independently of my parents since the age of fourteen. How old are you?"

"I'll be twenty-six this summer."

She'd had him pegged to be at least four years her senior. "And you're already a surgical resident?"

"I graduated from high school at seventeen, immediately entered premed and knocked that out in three years. Following medical school, I did one year of internship before I was accepted into Regional's program."

"Wow. I guess that makes you some sort of child prodigy."

"Nope. That makes me determined. When I want something badly enough, I do everything in my power to get it. No holds barred. And that's why you're here with me now."

Anne supposed she should be flattered, but in a way she was uneasy. Uneasy over the look he was giving her at the moment—a look that had nothing to do with simple camaraderie.

A shrill, distress-filled cry drew their attention to a little girl pointing at a red balloon that had managed to drift to the top of the cabana roof covering the area. Jack immediately pushed out of his chair and, with little effort, grabbed the dangling string, then returned the prized souvenir to its distraught owner. When the child rewarded him with a vibrant smile and introduced herself as Sara, Jack knelt before her and asked her about her day. Anne looked on as he listened to the little girl describe her activities, as if he had all the time in the world. The young mother, a fussy toddler in her arms, appeared mesmerized by the man who had saved her daughter from a round of hysteria.

When Jack came back to the table, Anne couldn't help but smile. "Looks like you've done your good deed for the day, Dr. Morgan."

He gave her a no-big-deal shrug. "I like kids. In fact, I thought about specializing in pediatric cardiology, but then I realized how tough it would be to lose one."

The man was simply too good to be real. Surely beneath that white-knight exterior some serious flaws existed. He probably snored. He probably trailed dirty clothes through his apartment. He probably notched his little black bag with every sexual conquest. She didn't plan to be another notch or his good-time girl, available whenever he found a spare moment for her.

He favored her with the same winning smile he'd given the little girl. "So tell me, Annie, why did you decide to birth those babies?"

She couldn't resist teasing the teaser. "Listening to women in excruciating pain wail at the top of their lungs is a good form of birth control."

"You're not serious."

He seemed so disturbed Anne laughed. "Of course I'm

not serious. There's something miraculous about seeing a new life come into the world and hearing that first cry. The story doesn't always end happily. Sometimes babies don't make it, and a few times we've lost a mother. Those are the tough days, but at least that doesn't happen very often."

He mulled it over for a moment before reaching across the table to clasp her hand. "Now, see there, Annie? You enjoy bringing new life into the world, and I want to save lives. Just one more thing we have in common."

One more thing among many. They both had a passion for sports. They had the same taste in music—from classical to country. They both had a weakness for cheeseburgers with the works. They shared a certain chemistry that was almost palpable, even though they had yet to kiss. A large divide existed between friendship and something more, and she was beginning to move toward the "something more" side.

The all-too-familiar sound of a pager prompted Jack to release his hold on Anne, and sufficiently jolted her back into reality. His reality.

He withdrew the device from the holder clipped to his belt and sighed. "It's the hospital."

"I thought this was your day off."

He shoved the pager back into place. "Unfortunately, residency doesn't allow for a real day off."

The one thing Anne couldn't quite accept—his career choice—could be the one thing that would put an end to a relationship that otherwise had potential. He lived for his work, just as her father did, and if she stayed in Jack Morgan's life, she could be following in her mother's footsteps. Following in Jack's shadow—something she refused to do. But then, it was much too early to be seriously entertaining a future with him.

He pushed back from the table and stood. "Looks like our day's going to be cut short. But I'll make it up to you next time."

If there was a next time—something Anne would have to decide soon. "That's how it goes, I guess."

"Yeah. And it's a bitch."

Jack took Anne's hand, and although she considered pulling away, she simply couldn't. At least not now. Not until absolutely necessary.

When he led her down a path away from the exit, she gestured behind her. "That's the way out, Jack."

He pointed straight ahead. "And that's the way to the gorilla exhibit. The hospital will own me for the next two days straight. They can let me have at least another hour with you."

Jack gave Anne's hand a gentle squeeze, gave her another warm smile. But more disconcerting, he gave her hope.

CHAPTER 4

Delia was no stranger to hopeless situations, or seeing a loved one suffer. She'd kept a twenty-four-hour vigil over her husband some eight years before, only to face the heartbreaking decision to end life support and let him go. Yet that situation was very different from her son-in-law's. Jack was awake and still alive.

When Jack's gaze tracked to hers, she moved to the end of the hospital bed, braced one fist on her hip and said, "A fine mess we have here, but only a temporary mess."

"Maybe not t-temporary."

At least he could speak—a positive sign, Delia decided as she rolled the hospital tray aside, pulled up a chair and dropped into it. "Now, Jack, you're a fighter. You won't let this setback keep you down for long."

"S-stroke, Delia, not a setback."

"And people recover from strokes every day." She chose to save him from the story of her friend Alice, who'd suffered a stroke and amazed everyone by making a total recovery at the age of eighty-five. Jack didn't need an overdose of optimism. He simply needed a leaning shoulder and a nudge in the right direction after refusing Anne's offer to let her care for him.

"Does Annie know you're h-h-ere?" he asked.

She'd purposefully avoided telling Anne for many reasons, the first being that her daughter wouldn't approve of her meddling. "This is about you, not her." Only a partial truth. It was about both of them.

She scooted a little closer and took his right hand into hers—the hand that was as lifeless as his eyes. In a perfect world, she would have been in his place due to her age. Yet nothing about this situation—or life—was perfect. Far from it.

While Delia studied Jack in preparation for what she would say next, he stared straight ahead. Except for the absence of hair, he still looked the same, very much the handsome man who'd captured her daughter's heart and brightened all their lives for a long while. Before the light went out on a love that should have lasted a lifetime.

Perhaps reminding him of that love would serve as a good place to begin. "Do you remember the day you came to the house to ask Bryce's permission to marry Anne?"

"My mind's kind of…foggy."

His mind might be foggy, but Delia's role had become clear. She could serve as his memory for as long as necessary. "It's okay. You don't have to talk. Just listen."

She brought out those fond recollections of days past. Good days, before the bad. "You were so nervous when you were talking to us about the marriage. In fact, I've only seen you nervous three times in twenty-odd years. That day you were going to propose to Anne, your wedding day and the day Katie was born. Anyway, I remember Bryce telling you that he'd give his permission as long as you accepted Anne's faults, particularly her stubbornness."

Jack attempted a smile, but it only formed halfway. "She's not always r-right."

"But she's never in doubt." Delia laughed. "That's our Anne. Bryce also told you she had a long memory and that wasn't always a good thing."

She saw the flash of pain in his eyes and it gave her a much-needed sense of purpose. "I have a long memory, too, Jack. I remember how you looked at Anne from the first moment you met her. I remember that your love for her was so obvious, at least to me. But my best memory of you involves Bryce's funeral. You didn't stay with the other pall-bearers at the graveside. You came back and sat between Anne and me. Then you took my hand and you put your arm around Anne, but not before you touched her belly, as if you were comforting your unborn baby, too. It was such a precious moment, and I've never forgotten it."

When she glimpsed tears in Jack's eyes, Delia swallowed around the nagging lump in her throat. "You were a rock. So strong for everyone. You're still strong, Jack."

Though he successfully fought back the tears, Delia felt his sorrow as keenly as if it were her own. In many ways, it was.

"Not strong…now," he said. "I'm n-nothing."

"You'll never be *nothing*. You're a good man. This stroke hasn't changed that about you." She squeezed his hand, even though she recognized he couldn't feel it. "You told me once that Anne regretted the things she didn't say to her father before he died. She regretted not forgiving him for his absence in her life and failing to give him a second chance before it was too late."

Delia released a long sigh when his expression remained impassive. "She needs that second chance from you, Jack, whether she realizes it or not. You both deserve a second chance. Let her take care of you as you've always taken care of her."

"I wasn't t-there enough," he said before turning his face toward the wall.

"Yes, you were. When it counted most." After coming to her feet, Delia let go of his hand and leaned to kiss his cheek. "Think about it, Jack. That's all I'm asking. Anne needs to be needed by you, and you desperately need her. You need each other. You always have, but never more than now."

He stood alone in the middle of a room, alone and afraid. A stark hazy room filled with strangers. Not all strangers. Annie was there, at a corner table next to a window. He recognized the man seated beside her, but he couldn't remember his name. He did know he hated him. Hated the way he looked at Annie, the way he touched her, like he had the right. He wanted to go to them, but he couldn't move. He wanted to shout to the bastard that she belonged to him, but the words wouldn't form. Slowly he tried to lift one leg, take one step. Move forward. Move toward her. But he lost the battle. He'd lost her—

"Wake up, Doc. Time for a shower."

Jack's eyes drifted open to discover the Samoan R.N. standing over him, a man who had at least three inches on Jack and a massive frame that would rival a West Texas mountain. Despite his casual expression, shaggy hair and close-cropped goatee, Pete the Nurse looked ominous.

Jack's gaze roamed to the shower chair next to the bed—hell on rollers, with a seat that consisted of an open circle made to accommodate a bare ass. His bare ass, if Pete had his way. "Don't need a shower. I had a sponge bath…this morning." A spit-and-shine administered by a young nurse who'd had novice moves, and embarrassment written all over her face. She'd made quick work of her job and chatted nonstop. Enough humiliation for one day, Jack decided. Enough of everything. He wanted only to sleep. To escape from this hell.

Pete sighed. "Come on, Doc. Don't give me a hard time. Policy states everybody has to have a shower bath every three days." He put heavy emphasis on *every-body*—which meant, *We don't give a damn who you are.* Or were. Jack felt closer to a nobody than he ever had in his life.

Why couldn't they just let him wallow in his stink? Nobody cared anyway. "L-leave me alone. I'm tired."

It was obvious to Jack that Pete had no intention of leaving. The nurse just moved the damn torture chair closer to the bed. "Now we can do this one of two ways," Pete said. "I can get a lift—and we both know those are uncomfortable as hell—or I can just grab you up and set you in the chair."

As far as options went, Jack found neither appealing. But Pete continued to stand firm. "G-go away."

"Not a chance."

Jack wasn't so ready to accept defeat, at least where the chair was concerned. "Why can't I try standing in the sh-shower?"

"You could try, but if you fall, then my ass is grass. You'll sue the hospital and I'll be in the unemployment line. So let's just do it my way, okay?"

Maybe he would fall. More humiliation. "No lift."

Pete taped up the IV and hung it on a rolling stand, then in one smooth move slipped his arms underneath Jack and grabbed him up with little effort. Jack's dead arm dangled lifelessly at his side, his leg just as useless. He could imagine what kind of sick picture this would make—Dr. Jack Morgan in the arms of Pete the Mountain. He suddenly recalled the painting of the *Pietà* in his mom's dining room, a depiction of an emaciated Jesus in Mary's arms. Contrary to popular belief, even though Jack had held life in his hands, he wasn't God.

The back of the open-air hospital gown split, exposing Jack to the elements, sending a burst of cold air across his butt. At least he could feel the cool on the right side of his hip, and in some odd way he welcomed the sensation. But he didn't welcome the shower chair's hard plastic surface as Pete arranged him in it and rolled him and the IV pole into the bathroom shower. A shower not big enough for the all the equipment and both men. Somehow, Pete managed.

The effort of sitting up made Jack's stomach churn and threaten to expel what little he'd eaten for lunch—his first solid meal, if you could call cold soup and runny Jell-O solid. He fought the nausea, determined not to vomit all over the floor.

"I'm just going to take this gown off, Doc."

Jack didn't have time to prepare. As soon as Pete said it, he did it, unsnapping the gown's shoulders with proficiency and peeling it away. Now Jack sat in his birthday suit in a butt-exposing chair with a Samoan sadomasochist standing by. Thank God, Pete laid a towel over his privates. At least the nurse had left him that much dignity in a totally undignified situation.

After pushing the overhead faucet toward the wall, Pete turned on the water. Still, some frigid droplets bouncing off the tiled surface hit Jack on the face, awakening him to the fact he was completely helpless. Anger simmered in a deep dark place in his soul. He was wasted. Useless.

Pete busied himself with removing the paper from the bar of soap and gathering another towel and a washcloth. Jack sent him his best scowl, hoping the guy would get on with it. Once he'd tested the water, Pete pulled the faucet over him, thankfully angling it so it didn't drown him, and worked the soap into the washcloth, creating sufficient lather to bathe three men. "Heard your little girl's coming to see you tonight."

Jack wasn't surprised Pete knew. The hospital gab line was notorious for getting into everyone's business. Especially where he was concerned. And Annie. "Yeah."

"We'll get you all cleaned up and ready." Pete then

commenced soaping Jack down, raising his arms to wash pits, moving on to his chest, stopping where the towel draped across his lap. He offered Jack the washcloth and nodded toward his lap. "You've got one good hand. You wanna do this yourself?"

"Best idea you've h–had…all day, P–Pete."

"Okay. Go to it."

"You gonna…watch?"

Pete streaked a damp forearm over his chin. "Hadn't intended to. But I can't leave. I can just turn my back here and let you give the package a good scrubbing."

Jack laid the washcloth in his lap and held out his hand. "Soap?"

Pete handed him the bar. "Watch out. It's slippery."

"I can still do s–soap." Even if he couldn't speak without stuttering like an idiot. Even if he couldn't do surgery.

Just as Jack lifted the towel, someone called from outside the door. Pete pushed open the door to Melba, another hospital icon, who was changing the bedsheets. She smiled and asked, "How are you doing today, Dr. Morgan?"

Just peachy, he wanted to say. *Come in and join the party. Have a look at Dr. Jack Morgan, today's sideshow, while he scrubs his jewels.* Instead he simply said, "I'm g–great, Melba," with enough sarcasm to melt a steel O.R. table.

When the soap slipped from his fingers, Jack automatically leaned forward. Pete stopped him with a hand on his shoulder. "Whoa, Doc. I'll get that."

A teenage volunteer with a wide-eyed expression joined Melba at the open door, clutching a stack of magazines to her chest. Now Jack really felt like a circus act. At one time he'd thought to encourage Katie to volunteer at the hospital when she got older. A bad idea.

His anger threatened to combust. This was totally dehumanizing. But hadn't he treated his own patients the same way? How many times had he invaded someone's privacy for the sake of his schedule? How many people had he reduced to utter humiliation by holding a conversation while they sat on a bedpan? He swore if he ever got out of this mess, if he ever recovered enough to resume his career—and that was a big if—he'd never let it happen again.

Jack clenched his jaw and hissed, "Sh-shut the d-damn door, Pete."

Pete blinked as though he'd just woken up to reality. "Sure, Doc. Sorry." He closed the door with a hangdog look and studied the toilet while Jack finished washing.

"I'm done," Jack pronounced, realizing how much truth rang out in his words.

Pete helped him dry off, replaced the hospital gown with a clean one and rolled him back into the room. He maneuvered Jack out of the chair and into bed, readjusted all the equipment and monitors, then raised the side rails, leaving him feeling like a caged animal. Couldn't they see he wasn't going anywhere anytime soon? Except maybe home alone to wallow in his pity with a stranger attending to his needs. Unless he decided to take Annie up on her offer. Nope. Couldn't do that. He couldn't tolerate her sympathy on a daily basis. They'd both be miserable.

The loud reverberation of activity at the adjacent nurses' station traveled into the room. Jack would normally welcome the sound, but right now it clanked in his head.

He brought his attention back to Pete, who was finishing cleanup. "When you leave, sh-shut the door. Can't sleep with all the noise."

Pete gave him a quick salute. "Yes, sir." Then he left Jack alone to study the ceiling and wonder how in the hell he would ever survive this mess. How he would deal with the inability to take care of himself in very basic ways. Like now. He had to pee, which had become a major ordeal since they'd removed his catheter that morning. Fortunately some of the equipment still worked, or at least the plumbing. He shot a glance at the bedside table, determined to get the damn plastic urinal and do it himself. But the table was on his right side, out of his reach.

He tried to maneuver himself enough to retrieve it, skirting all sorts of tubes and lines, but to no avail. His body was too dead and the table was too far away. He pressed the button on the bed's metal arm with his good hand to summon the nurse, but it didn't work. Raising his head as far as he could, he noticed the cord curled on the floor like a hangman's noose, detached from outlet.

Goddammit! Trapped like a prisoner with no way to communicate. He considered yelling, screaming at the top of his lungs about the injustice, their incompetence. Rant like a madman who had totally lost his mind along with his ability to function normally.

He had lost everything. His dignity. His pride. So what good would shouting do? It wouldn't take away the pain, the loneliness. The loss. And he felt it all as sharp as a razor's edge.

But instead of shouting, he did the one thing no one would expect, not even him.

He wept.

CHAPTER 5

"*These have to be the most pansy-ass pajamas I've ever seen. What am I supposed to do with them?*"

Anne couldn't help but laugh over Jack's reaction, any more than she'd been able to resist purchasing the pj's earlier that day. "*How about wearing them?*"

"*I don't wear pajamas to bed.*"

That was news to Anne, considering she had no idea what he wore to bed. She hadn't been near his bed. In fact, after four dates, the man hadn't even kissed her yet. She was beginning to feel a bit like only his pal, or a pariah.

She yanked the top from his grasp and held it up. "*Just look at all the little blue stethoscopes. They're adorable. Who wouldn't want to wear them?*"

"*Me. I don't do adorable.*"

"*That's rich, Jack. I've seen your hula-girl surgical cap.*"

"That's not adorable. That's a conversation piece."

She feigned a dejected look. "You won't make an exception for me? I mean, I went to all this trouble to celebrate Groundhog Day...."

"Since when does Groundhog Day warrant a celebration?"

Since she'd begun to search for any excuse to see him. "That's not the point. The point is I brought you to the batting cage, bought your dinner—"

"Yeah. A great couple of tacos."

She patted his leg. "It's the thought that counts."

He moved closer to her on the bench and draped his arm around her shoulder. "Tell you what. We'll go back to my place, I'll model the pajamas for you, and then I'll take them off and you'll tell me what you prefer."

She leaned away and pointed a finger at him. "Aha! There's the Jack Morgan I've heard about in the hospital halls. The charming sex machine who's reportedly bedded half the staff."

"Don't believe everything you hear, Annie. When would I have had time to bed half the staff?"

"During your coffee break or in the on-call rooms?"

"I only have five-minute coffee breaks and I use the on-call rooms for sleeping."

"Why should I believe you?"

"Because you're the only woman I've been with, or cared to be with, in months."

"But not in a sexual sense." She hated the insecurity in her voice. Hated even more that she'd posed such a leading question.

"If you're asking whether I want to make love to you, the answer is yes. I think about it all the time."

So did she. "You haven't even kissed me yet."

"Do you want me to kiss you now, right here in front of all these Little Leaguers?"

She did. With all her heart, she did. "Not if it's going to em-barrass you. And not if you don't care to, of course."

"Oh, I want to kiss you, all right. And I will, on one condition. You take back these damn pajamas—"

"Honey, did you hear the nurse?"

Anne looked up from the newly purchased pajamas folded in her lap to find her mother staring at her expec-tantly. "I'm sorry. I guess I went somewhere else for a few minutes." Into the past—a place she didn't care to go. But she hadn't been able to stop the barrage of memories since Jack's stroke. "What did she say?"

"Jack's ready to see us now."

Anne wasn't sure she was she ready to see Jack, but she had no choice. She left the waiting-room chair, clutching the pajamas to her chest, and brought her attention to Katie, who was on her knees in front of a table, coloring a special picture for her daddy. "You wait here with Grandma, sweetie. I'll be back in a few minutes."

Katie glanced up, disappointment in her expression. "I want to go now. I want to give him this." She held up the brightly colored paper displaying a man and a woman with a little golden-haired girl between them, their hands joined, vibrant smiles on their faces. A depiction of the perfect family—the perfect family Katie had never enjoyed. Or at least that she remembered.

Anne smoothed a hand over her daughter's hair and

fought a few rogue tears. "I have to make sure Daddy's ready before you can go in."

Delia sat again and reached out her arms to Katie. "We'll just wait here until you're ready for us. Right, sweet girl?"

Katie climbed into Delia's lap and said, "Tell Daddy I love him."

Anne's heart took another nosedive. "You can tell him in a minute, okay?"

"Okay. But hurry."

When Anne reached the room, all her emotional strength seemed to disappear. She couldn't allow that to happen; otherwise she might suffer a meltdown the likes of which no one had witnessed to this point. Following a serious internal scolding, she knocked and, after a moment, received his permission to come in. She entered the room to find Jack sitting up in bed, his face still unshaven, and she wondered why no one had bothered to attend to it. Maybe Jack had refused. Considering his haggard expression, his listless eyes, that was a very real possibility. Yet Anne wouldn't let herself believe he'd given up. Not Jack.

She attempted a small smile. "Hi. We're finally here."

"Where's K-Katie?" he demanded as Anne approached the bed.

"With Mother in the waiting room." Anne held up the pajamas that she'd brought him. Navy-blue pajamas, not the ones with the stethoscopes. She'd taken those back all those years ago, even though she hadn't been able to take back the memory. "Thought you might want to change before I go get her."

Jack glanced down at his wrinkled beige hospital gown before bringing his attention back to her. "Something w-wrong with my attire?"

"Not your usual choice for bedtime wear, I'm sure."

"I don't wear anything…to bed. Remember?"

Yes, she remembered. In fact, she distinctly recalled cautioning Jack to wear something at night when Katie was a toddler and had often managed to find her way to their bed. That had been the only time he'd conceded to sleepwear, which had consisted of nothing more than worn jogging shorts. Jack had been a morning person in every sense of the word, including when he'd wanted to make love, so he'd always insisted that with his schedule, sleeping in the nude cut down on wasted time. Anne had learned to be a morning person, too, but she'd never abandoned her cotton gowns. She'd always viewed the undressing part beforehand as the best part, not wasted time. Just one of the many differences between her and Jack.

Shaking off the thoughts, she simply said, "I think Katie would feel more comfortable if she saw you in these instead of a hospital gown."

Jack shrugged. "Fine."

Anne backed toward the door. "I'll get someone to dress you. I'll just wait outside."

"I w-want you to do it."

"Me?" Her voice came out in a nervous squeak.

Jack smiled halfway. A cynic's smile. "What's the m-matter? It's not like you haven't…seen me before."

No kidding, but it had been quite a while. That

shouldn't make a difference. In the course of her nursing, she'd viewed naked men and women alike, all shapes and sizes, in every position known to God and man. And Jack wasn't a stranger. All the more reason she should be able to do this. Or perhaps that was the reason she felt so reluctant. "You're right. Besides, if you do decide to come home with us, this won't be the last time I help you dress."

"I didn't say...yes."

Anne afforded him another smile, hopefully one that showed her determination. She strolled toward the bed and summoned professional detachment. But it was hard to remain detached once she tossed back the sheet to reveal Jack's sculpted legs. A runner's legs. She had loved every inch of them, and she still admired the way his strong calves shaped them just right. Not overbearing; near perfection. Then she thought of his paralysis, the way the muscles would atrophy if he didn't take care to keep them worked. She would make him exercise. She would adopt the cause of keeping Jack's legs in good order.

Anne unfolded the pajama bottoms, reminding herself pride would probably prevent Jack from allowing her and Katie to care for him. And that would probably be best.

"See something...you like?" Jack asked, his voice laced with sarcasm.

Intent on ignoring his query, Anne took the pajama bottoms and began to slip them over his toes. His crooked toes. Thank heavens Katie had inherited her feet. "You know, Katie's teacher says she's the best student she has."

"Yeah?" His response held a note of pride—a very good sign.

"Yeah. She's going to recommend her for the Gifted and Talented program."

"K-Katie inherited her smarts…from you."

Anne halted the pajamas at Jack's thighs and stared up at him. "Oh, come on, Mr. Cardiac Surgeon. I'm not the one with the M.D."

When pain flitted across Jack's face, Anne mentally cursed her insensitive mouth. But he restored his expression to its familiar nonemotional state. "You aced c-calculus," he said. "I barely…passed."

Anne shrugged one shoulder and resumed the dressing ritual. "That's true. But you were better at P.E." She expected Jack to laugh at that one, but he didn't.

When she'd gone as far as she could without his help, she asked, "Can you lift your hips?"

"One side."

"That'll work."

Without raising the gown, she slid the bottoms up higher and accidentally brushed the territory she had once known so well. "Sorry," she muttered.

"Not a…problem."

But it was a problem, at least for her. She would have to learn Jack all over again if he eventually agreed to let her take care of him. As if she'd really forgotten one tiny detail. He had an athlete's body and a surgeon's stamina. She could never forget that.

So lost in her thoughts, Anne again contacted his groin as she positioned the other side of the pajamas. She started to apologize but decided not to call attention to her accidental touch, particularly since he seemed to have had no reaction to it.

"All done with the bottoms," she managed to say without looking at him, her tone overly jolly.

As she reached across his chest to unfasten the gown, he gripped her wrist. "Are you enjoying...t-torturing me, Annie?"

She snatched up the top and frowned. "I'm trying to dress you. I didn't know it involved any torture."

"You keep...touching me." His expression turned hard and mocking. "Maybe you're...testing me. To see if everything's in order. It's not, Annie. I may never...be able to...get it up again. But that would make you h-happy. A f-fitting punishment second only to...castration. Just rewards for my...cheating."

As much as his infidelity had hurt her, she would never wish that on him. "No, it wouldn't make me happy. I know how important it is to you." In order to remove the emotion from the situation, she prepared to spew her clinical expertise like Old Faithful. "A lack of erection, which is sometimes a factor after a stroke, could only be temporary. You can be optimistic that you'll recover all function, at least in that respect. Maybe not immediately, but eventually."

He pulled her forward, his lips hovering dangerously near hers. "C-care to help me find out if my erection...is functioning?"

Anne wrenched from his grasp. She wanted no awareness of him as a man. "In your dreams."

He gave her another half smile. "Yeah, that's the way it's been…lately, Annie. In my dreams. Just like back in the early…d-days, when we used to talk half the night and s-screw our brains out the other half. No…wonder I barely got through my residency. You distracted the hell out of me. You're distracting…me now."

She didn't have to acknowledge the memories, but she did. "For heaven's sake, Jack. You've just been through a critical bleed. How can you even think about sex at a time like this?"

He released a caustic laugh. "If I come home with you…we c-could make some more memories while… you're taking care of my *needs.*"

He'd spoken the last word with clarity, and his intent suddenly became all too clear to Anne. The sexual overtures, the crudeness, were simply a ploy to frighten her away. Dispose of her again like Monday's garbage. *I don't give up that easily, buddy boy.*

Anne affected indifference as she walked to the other side of the bed and slid one sleeve up his useless arm. "Sorry, Doctor, but my duties don't include bedroom therapy. And I strongly suggest you concentrate on regaining use of the rest of your appendages first."

Jack remained silent as she finished dressing him, but he continued to study her as if she were laid out under a microscope. As if he could see right through her waning control. After the last button was in place, she moved away from the bed and hooked a thumb over one shoulder. "I'll go get Katie and Mother, if that's okay."

He looked down at his lap, then back up at her. "All's

still…quiet on the home f–front. For now. Maybe… forever."

Anne was bent on ignoring the misery in his eyes and started toward the door. How could she handle him if he reentered her life? She probably wouldn't have to find out. He was too stubborn to agree, and that was okay. She would be better off if he had an alternative plan, hired someone to care for him. Katie would be disappointed, but Anne would make sure her daughter saw him often. Yes, that would be best. No one could argue that Anne hadn't tried to convince him.

She entered the hallway and walked a few steps until the waiting room came into view, then signaled her mother to bring Katie. She stopped a few feet from Jack's door and, when they arrived, knelt at Katie's level and pushed her hair back from her shoulders. "Just a couple of things, sweetie. Daddy's feeling better, but he's still not well. He talks slower, and his hair's gone because they had to shave it off to do the surgery. He also has some tubes in his arms to give him the medicine he needs."

"An IV," she said. "Daddy told me all about those when he brought me to work with him on summer break last year."

Anne hadn't even realized he'd taken Katie to the hospital during the week she'd spent with him. "That's good. Then you know what to expect."

"Can I hug him?"

Anne straightened and touched Katie's cheek. "Yes. He'd like that."

"Okay." With that, Katie rushed into the room.

As Anne started after her, Delia took her arm and tugged her around to face her. "She'll be all right," she said. "Katherine's a tough little girl."

"I know. If only I were that tough."

Delia brushed Anne's hair back from her shoulders exactly as Anne had done with Katie. "You are that tough, honey. But you're going to have to dig deep to maintain that strength. And you need to lead with your heart, not with your head."

At the moment, that seemed like an all-too-easy, and unwise, feat.

Delia trailing behind her, Anne entered the room, only to discover Katie had climbed into bed with Jack, the picture she'd colored of the perfect family in her grasp, her cheek resting against his chest. Jack stroked her hair with his good hand, his head tipped against hers, presenting the poignant portrait of a father holding the beautiful child who'd arrived in their lives after they'd all but given up.

When Jack leveled his gaze on Anne and she saw the threat of tears, the absolute love for his daughter, she battled back her own tears, quite possibly the first of many more from this point forward.

She witnessed another flash of sorrow in his eyes, then finally resignation.

"You win, Annie. I'll come…home."

CHAPTER 6

In a matter of hours, Jack would be coming home.

Anne had never been here before, in this bleak room that matched the dreary February day, or in this untenable situation. She wanted to pace, wanted to run. Wanted to forget the responsibility that had been thrust upon her. But the therapist seated across from her at the conference table, a luminous cheerleader's smile on her face while she laid out the plan for Jack's discharge, wouldn't let her. She'd introduced herself as Mindy Adams, Jack's team leader, as if this were some sporting event with Jack as the star player.

"Do you have any questions, Mrs. Morgan?"

"A few." Too many to cover in the ten minutes she had left before she had to resume her shift. "He's been in rehab for a month, when I was told he'd be here at least six weeks. A month doesn't seem like an adequate amount of time." Or enough time for Anne to prepare for Jack's arrival back in her life.

"The problem is he's not making much progress. The team feels that he would do better at home, with you and your daughter, particularly since you haven't been able to visit him."

The guilt hit Anne like an emotional wrecking ball. Since Jack had moved to the rehab unit adjacent to the hospital, she'd grabbed the excuse that she'd been too busy with work to stop by. Claimed that planning for his return to the house had prevented her from visiting him. In part that was true. For the past few weeks she'd been immersed in the preparations to make the house more handicapped accessible, according to the home-health-care assessment of what Jack would need to recover. She had also relied on her mother to take Katie to visit Jack.

But Anne saw no point in explaining that to a young woman with such limited life experience, in turn letting her know how painful the process had been. How frightening. How she couldn't bear to see Jack struggle, even knowing that she would face those trials for weeks, maybe even months. Or years. "You do realize we're divorced, Ms. Adams."

For the first time Mindy abandoned the upbeat demeanor. "I'm aware of that. But you must still care about him if you're willing to take this on."

"I'm doing it for my daughter's sake." When Anne realized how insensitive that sounded, she added, "And of course for Jack. As you've said, his being with Katie should help."

"I agree. But he'll need your support, too." She closed the chart and moved it aside. "It's not going to be easy, Mrs. Morgan. He's frustrated and angry. Completely uncooperative. The old saying about doctors making horrible patients is true."

Add that to Jack's inherent need for control, and it created more than its share of problems. No, this wasn't going to be easy. Anne recognized it could be the most difficult thing she'd ever done, second only to saying so long to seventeen years of marriage. "Has he made any strides at all?"

Mindy opened the chart and scanned it again, as if she had no idea about Jack's progress. Anne suspected the therapist was simply searching for a diversion, something she herself had done when confronting a patient's hard questions. "Actually, his hand and arm are much better. He has feeling in both. That's a positive."

Probably only one positive among many negatives, if Mindy's grave expression was any indication. "His leg?"

"It's not coming around as quickly as we would have liked. His balance isn't great, either, which is why he'll have to use a walker until P.T. feels he's ready for a cane."

His hand involved his career, and some might view the return of that mobility as a blessing. But if he couldn't stand for any length of time without getting dizzy, he couldn't operate. "Will the balance problem resolve itself?"

"Hopefully, but that'll take time. We're also concerned about his cognitive abilities. He's suffered some memory loss, although his aphasia has improved. However, he still stutters on occasion, particularly if he's angry. And I have to warn you, he's prone to spewing expletives. Not at all uncommon with a stroke."

Anne started to tell Mindy that that hadn't been uncommon before the stroke, but refrained. "I have done some research, and I've found that with comprehensive therapy, he could make a complete recovery."

"That's our goal," Mindy said, but the look she sent Anne was less than optimistic.

"Anything else I should know? Aside from the obvious challenges?"

Mindy closed the chart and stood. "I think we've covered everything. They'll keep to his regular rehab schedule today. He'll be discharged this afternoon around four."

Then he would be solely Anne's responsibility. She wasn't prone to panic attacks, but her chest tightened with the utter fear that this could lead to disaster. That she and Jack would only cultivate more resentment in such close quarters.

Anne came to her feet, pulled her stethoscope from her smock pocket and draped it around her neck. "Now that everything's settled, I'll get back to work."

Mindy pointed behind her. "He's in the P.T. room down the hall, fourth door to the left, if you want to observe him. You can watch from the window."

In other words, Anne didn't have to face him, at least not yet. Not until this afternoon. "I guess I could watch him for a few minutes."

Mindy picked up the chart and clutched it against her chest. "You don't have to do this."

"No, really. It's okay. If I'm a little late back to work, they'll understand."

"I meant in regard to his long-term care. We could still discharge him to a private rehab hospital for his recovery, or you could hire full-time assistance at his home. Then you could take your daughter to visit whenever it's convenient."

The therapist was offering her a way out, most likely due to Anne's less-than-enthusiastic attitude. But Anne didn't have the heart to turn back now, even if the road ahead might be paved with failure. "We'll manage fine." If only she felt as confident as she sounded. She wasn't. Not in the least.

When Anne followed down the corridor behind the therapist, she counted each and every door until they reached the sign indicating the physical therapy room.

Anne hung back, afraid of what she might witness. She didn't have a clue how Jack looked now, although her mother had mentioned he'd lost weight. Mindy gestured her forward to the narrow window, and she found herself once more on the outside looking in, and seeing a man she barely recognized.

The revered doctor who had once drawn a crowd at the drop of a smile sat alone behind a small table, surrounded by elderly patients enduring the rigors of physical therapy, yet seemingly unaware of their presence. Only stubble covered his scalp, revealing the slight scar etched above his left ear. His unshaven face was gaunt; his dark eyes, listless. He remained motionless except for his right pointer finger and thumb, which he touched together again and again with agonizing slowness.

Anne questioned if he was going through the mental motions of surgery, imagining he was still the respected physician, wondering if he would return to that status again.

One thing she did know—he didn't belong here, among people who were at least twenty years his senior. And in that moment, she acknowledged that despite the challenges ahead, he needed to be home with her.

"Welcome home, Daddy."

Regardless of his daughter's animated greeting, regardless that he'd lived here at one time, Jack didn't feel at home. Nothing about the living room felt familiar. Not the floral-print sofa or the matching club chair in the corner. Either his memory was completely shot, or Annie had tossed out all the old furniture, as easily as she'd tossed him out.

Katie wrapped a lock of her hair 'round and 'round her finger, keeping her distance. She appeared to be afraid of him, and he couldn't blame her. Right now he looked scary as hell.

She took a small step forward and rocked on her heels. "I made some peanut-butter cookies for you, Daddy. Do you want one?"

His gut pitched at the thought. "Maybe later." Or never. Food tasted like crap now, and he didn't care if he ever ate another cookie. Hell, he didn't care if he ever ate again.

Annie stood behind Katie and laid a hand on her shoulder. "I'm sure Daddy would be glad to help you with your homework a little later."

Sweet Jesus, if only he could. But his ability to comprehend written text was only one more thing that the stroke had taken away from him. Shame had prevented him from revealing that to anyone, even the therapists who had tried to force him to read, until they'd given up. "I'm tired, Katie. I just want to take a nap."

He turned his face away, hating the contempt in Annie's eyes. Hating that Katie looked ready to cry. Hating this whole scene.

"Why don't you go your room, sweetie," Anne said. "I'll be up in a minute to help you with your homework, after I get your dad settled in."

After she gave him a solid tongue-lashing, no doubt.

Following a moment's hesitation, Katie walked up to Jack and pressed a kiss on his cheek. "It's okay, Daddy. I know you're tired. I still love you."

He didn't deserve her forgiveness. He didn't even deserve to be her father, at least not now. "Thanks, pumpkin. I love you, too."

She smiled as though he'd presented her with a gold star. But then, it had always taken so little please her. And he'd never given her quite enough when it came to his time. Annie had been quick to remind him of that.

After Katie disappeared up the staircase, Jack waited for Annie's lecture. If she yelled at him, he could handle it. After all, he'd endured sermons on the benefits of rehab for the past month, most of which he'd ignored.

When Annie continued to stand there, her frame rigid, he asked, "Where do you want me?"

The look she gave him said she was considering several options, and the garage might be one of them. "I've set up your room in the den."

Just like a guest. Not surprising to Jack. For the past two years, he'd never gotten past the foyer when he'd retrieved

Katie for scheduled visits, per the terms of the divorce he'd never wanted. Not that he believed Annie would invite him into her bed. Their bed, dammit. The same bed where they'd made love. Where they'd attempted to conceive a baby for years. Where they'd fought and made up time and again. He definitely remembered the bed.

"Let's go," he said when Annie failed to move.

"Okay." She grabbed his bag from the floor near his feet and headed down the hall, leaving him behind, as she had two years ago. After struggling to rise from the sofa, he shuffled across the carpet, leaning heavily on the walker. He despised the thing, resented that he had to rely on it to get around.

Annie glanced back at him over one shoulder and finally slowed her steps. When he caught up to her, he followed her into the kitchen, a place he definitely remembered. The dinette where they'd shared meals as a family, but not as much as Annie would have liked. Countless times he'd called her to tell her he would be delayed, and many times he'd never made it home at all. Today the smell of peanut butter permeated the area, and resurrected a few memories that had been tucked away in his brain. Annie smiling at him over a cup of coffee; Katie perched on the counter, waiting to give him a morning hug. He also recalled the last argument that had begun here and ended up in the bedroom, where Annie had said she hated what he'd done to her. That she hated him. A memory he wished he could have forgotten.

By the time they arrived at the den, Jack was filled with an abiding sadness and an abundance of regret. He didn't know what was worse—remembering the good times or the bad, or not remembering at all. The sense of utter dejection only increased when he discovered that Annie had converted the den into the equivalent of a hospital room, complete with adjustable bed and portable bedside toilet. She'd even included an overhead shelf to hold the TV. He'd been reduced to handicapped-visitor status.

If he had the strength to hurl the damn walker, he would have, right through the window. "What, no cardiac monitors, Annie? The least you could have done was arrange for a m-morphine drip. I could use a few d-drugs to help me f-forget I'm a guest in the house where I used to live."

He noticed a trace of hurt in her eyes. "I thought you'd be more comfortable here than in—"

"Our old bedroom?" He let go a mirthless laugh. "D-don't worry. Even if I could walk, I wouldn't step foot in there again."

Ignoring his wrath, she gestured toward the bathroom. "I've had handrails installed and I bought a shower chair."

"Good for you."

Now *she* looked frustrated. "I'm only trying to make everything easier on you."

Easier on her, he decided. "P-pat yourself on the back."

He could tell she was fighting the fury, and losing. "Can the attitude, Jack. And please try to clean up your language. Katie shouldn't have to be exposed to that kind of talk."

He managed a shaky right-handed salute. "Yes, ma'am. S-speaking of Katie, she's waiting for you."

"Do you need help getting situated?"

He inched the walker to the bed, worked his way

around and sat on the edge of the mattress, the way they'd taught him. As much as he despised having to ask, he had no option. "My leg's a...problem."

She moved the walker aside, and when he lay back on the patchwork quilt, she lifted his legs onto the bed. Silently she unlaced and removed his cross-trainers, set them on the floor, then grabbed up the remote from the end table and offered it to him. "I assume you can still work this."

"I'll manage." Although he had a tough time distinguishing the numbers.

When she flipped a switch on a white box positioned on the bedside table, he asked, "What's that?"

"The monitor we had in Katie's room when she was a baby." She faced him and attempted a smile. "I found it in a box in the attic. It reminded me that every time she made a sound at night, you were out of the bed, checking on her. It's a good thing we were in the old house back then and you didn't have to climb the stairs."

He didn't remember any other house. He barely remembered this one. "The old house?"

She frowned. "The one we lived in until Katie was two. On Fallon Street."

He scraped his brain until a recollection broke through the fog. "It had a big backyard."

"Right. And a sidewalk."

"Yeah. A sidewalk. And trees. We had some good times there." That much he could recall, even if he couldn't scratch out all the details.

"Yes, we did." She sounded wistful, full of regret. "Mother will be by after dinner to visit while I go out."

Once more, his anger arrived, even though he had no claim on Anne any longer. "You and Max g-going out?"

"No." She folded her arms tightly around her middle. "I can't believe you'd bring up such ancient history, Jack. Max and I are only friends."

Maybe she wanted him to believe her relationship with Crabtree involved only friendship, but he knew damn well the jerk still wanted Annie. He also suspected that back in December, he'd had her again. The sorry memory of seeing the two of them leaving a restaurant together had returned a few weeks ago, and now came back to him in living color. "Are you sure about that, Annie?"

She sighed. "I'm not going on a date, Jack. I planned to go to your apartment and pick up a few of your clothes. I'll need a key."

He didn't like the thought of her in his apartment, although he didn't understand why that bothered him. "Let Delia go."

"Do you have someone living with you?"

"No."

"Then what is it you're hiding from me?"

Hell if he knew. He nodded toward the bag on the floor. "Outside compartment. The key's on the chain, next to my car key." That brought on another question he hadn't even considered until then. "Where's the Navigator?"

She crossed the room and riffled through his bag. "Still in the hospital lot."

In his parking space, a prime location reserved for doctors who had tenure. "Someone should drive it back to the apartment."

She turned to him and pocketed the keys. "I'll have Mother follow me over in the next couple of days. In the meantime, it's okay. The parking attendants know the situation."

He figured everyone at the hospital was well aware of his situation. They knew he was basically a cripple. Knew he wouldn't be back to resume his career.

"By the way, I got in touch with Bert," she said. "He's still in Japan, but he told me to tell you he hopes you get well soon."

Jack didn't welcome his brother's good wishes. With ten years separating them, they'd never been close enough to communicate more than once or twice a year. "Gr-great. Anything else?"

"That's it for now." Annie headed toward the door before facing him again. "Call if you need anything."

"I could use a drink. Got any bourbon?"

"No, I don't. And that's the last thing you need."

She didn't know what the hell he needed. No one did. Not even him. He did have to be courteous; otherwise he might find himself alone again, and that was one thing he didn't want, at least not yet. "Thanks, Annie."

"You're welcome, Jack."

Her dry tone told Jack he wasn't welcome at all, and he never would be again.

1985

She'd been caught in an impossible situation, carried away by emotions in lieu of logic. Now all unwise things must come to an end.

"I can't do this anymore, Jack."

As if he hadn't heard her, or had chosen to ignore her, Jack buried his face in her neck and slid his hand beneath the sheet, where it predictably landed on her breast. "You can't do what anymore?"

Anne rolled away from him to check the bedside clock. Now 6:00 a.m., he'd arrived on her doorstep an hour ago, using the key she'd provided to let himself in. For the past year, she'd grown accustomed to his early morning visits following his shift. She'd begun to feel like his concubine. His good-time morning girl.

After scooting up against the headboard, clutching the covers to her chest, she leaned over and flipped on the lamp. "I can't do this—" she made a sweeping gesture over the crumpled sheets "—anymore."

"You did it a few minutes ago, and I didn't hear any complaints."

Jack tried to win her over with a grin, but she refused to buy into his charm. "I'm complaining now. The only time we ever see each other is in this bed."

He shifted onto his back and stacked his hands behind his head. "That's not true, Annie. We've been having dinner at your parents' house at least twice a month."

"And that's another problem, Jack. Sometimes I think you're using me to impress my father."

When he turned his face toward her, Anne noted the first hint of anger, and prepared for more. "That's pretty screwed-up logic and you know it, Annie. This hasn't been easy, especially at the hospital. My fellow residents don't say it to my face, but I know damn well they believe your dad gives me special consideration because I'm involved with you."

"I'm sorry if I'm not feeling altogether sympathetic at the moment."

He bolted from the bed and snatched up his clothes from the floor, where they'd landed the minute he'd slipped into her room. "I don't need this, Annie."

Typical Jack. Run away when a confrontation is brewing. "I have to be more important to you than a quick round of sex whenever it suits your schedule."

He turned his back and redressed in his scrubs before facing her again. "We'll talk about this later. Right now, I'm going to go home, run a couple of miles, take a shower and get some sleep. In a few hours, I'm going to scrub in on a triple bypass, and if I'm lucky, I might actually get to do something besides observe."

And there was the crux of the problem, and the answer to her question. His career meant more to him than she did, just as she'd expected. Exactly as she'd known all along through experience with the other man almost in her life—her father. "You can take a shower here and forget the morning run. We can talk for a while before you go home to sleep."

He dropped into the chair and put on his cross-trainers. "First of all, I run to clear my head before I start the day. Second, my clothes are at my place—and that wouldn't be an issue if you'd agree to move in with me."

Same song, fiftieth verse. "You already know how I feel about that."

He stood and grabbed his keys from the dresser. "Yeah. No ring, no cohabitation."

"I've never said that."

"You didn't have to." After releasing a rough sigh, he sat on the edge of the bed. "Look, the next step should be moving in together. That way we'll know if we're going to work."

The words lodged in her mind, then in her mouth before she urged them out. "I'm not sure we're going to work, Jack."

Fury turned his expression hard, unforgiving. "What are you saying, Annie? Because I sure as hell can't read your mind."

"I'm saying it's over." And with the prospect of never seeing him again came the abject pain.

He stared at her a long moment, as if trying to comprehend what she'd proposed—the end of their relationship. "Fine." He pushed off the bed, and when he reached the door paused with his hand on the knob. "I knew from the beginning I might not live up to your expectations. But I never expected you'd give up on us so easily."

Then he was gone, out the bedroom door. Out of her life.

A stifling silence hung over the room, and so did the realization that he hadn't put up much of a fight. Any fight, for that matter. He hadn't said he loved her, either. But then, he never had.

Anne understood that he could never be what she wanted him to be. He could never give her what she needed—more of his time. In truth, she hadn't given up on the relationship because she hadn't felt there truly was an "us." But she had given up on Jack. She had no choice.

CHAPTER 7

Through the years, Delia had learned one thing about parenting—guilt was inevitable. You either doled it out, or received it on a regular basis. Tonight she happened to be the recipient.

After driving into a front-door parking place, she spotted Gabe Burks, her dinner date for the evening, seated at a booth next to the restaurant's wide-paned window. He wore an open-collar denim-blue shirt and a somewhat dejected expression, bringing on more guilt for Delia to digest along with the meal. She had kept him waiting for over fifteen minutes, but her intent had not been to be fashionable. Her tardiness had resulted from an ongoing debate over whether to cancel. Now she had all of an hour before she had to return to Katie and Jack so that Anne might attend to a few errands. An hour might be all she needed to establish that she shouldn't even think about dating a man at a time like this. A very nice man who'd called as well as spoken to her in the hospital corridors on several occasions. To this point, she'd put off his dinner invitation.

Why she'd agreed to this particular night was beyond her. Actually, it wasn't. She craved the companionship of someone who wasn't involved in Jack and Anne's life. Someone who could provide a sympathetic ear. If she was lucky, Gabe would be that someone, at least temporarily.

After drawing in the mandatory fortifying breath, Delia left the sedan and smoothed a hand down her lilac silk pantsuit—a bit of fashion overkill for the Sticky Rib, but she didn't own any jeans. She hadn't in a while now, something she would remedy soon, the one thing within her grasp among many that might stay outside her reach.

A shrill bell chimed when she pulled open the door, immediately drawing Gabe's attention as Delia made her way down the narrow aisle, past tables full of Friday-night family get-togethers. He came to his feet when she arrived and offered, "It's great to see you, Delia," along with his hand.

Delia cursed the little flutter in her belly, the twinge of excitement, the urge to outright twitter as she had that first day they'd met. She was entirely too old to carry on like the belle of the barbecue joint. "It's nice to see you, too, Gabe. I apologize for being late."

"Not a problem at all. I hope this is okay. You said nothing fancy."

"It's wonderful. I haven't had barbecue in ages." Nor

did she particularly care for it, but Gabe's company would be fair exchange.

She slid into the booth, opposite him, separated by a table covered in white butcher paper in preparation for a messy meal, even if Delia wasn't. She pored over the plastic menu for a time before asking, "What do you recommend?"

"Definitely the ribs."

Exactly what she'd feared. Picking her teeth in front of Gabe seemed somewhat unsavory. "I believe I'll just have the chef salad."

"Not me. I'm going for the full slab."

Gabe's grin aided Delia in relaxing. "Of course. You're a growing boy."

"Not unless you think fifty-eight makes me a boy."

Considering the difference in their ages, she might. A lanky young waiter saved Delia from having to make any revelations other than her choice for the meal. But after he left, an interminable amount of silence passed before she finally blurted, "Sixty-six." Before Gabe could respond, she added, "That's my age. Old enough to qualify for that monthly pension. Ten years past receiving the senior citizen's discount at the movies or for rental cars. Old enough to put a down payment on a retirement condo in—"

"I know."

Gabe's simple declaration stopped Delia cold. "What do you mean, you know?"

"I know how old you are, Delia. Mary in Administration told me. I knew before I ever introduced myself to you at the hospital."

He'd known all along and he was still interested in her? She wanted to question his sanity, or at the very least his motives. "But—"

"No buts. There're only eight years separating us, and truth is, no one would ever believe it by looking at you. You're a beautiful woman, Delia."

Now she wanted to question his eyesight. "Thank you."

He folded his hands on the table before him and leaned forward. "Since we have that issue out of the way, how's your son-in-law doing?"

Delia appreciated that he hadn't added *ex* to the equation. She appreciated many things about Gabe. "Not doing so well, I'm afraid. That's why I can't stay too long after dinner. Jack arrived home today and I have to make sure there's no bloodshed between him and my daughter."

Gabe frowned. "Was it bad? The divorce, I mean."

"Is there such a thing as a good divorce?"

"Amicable, yeah, but not that often. That's why I left family law to sign on as counsel for the hospital. The work I do involves a lot of paperwork, sometimes even tough malpractice law. But it beats watching people fight over who gets custody of the kids. Or the riding lawn mower."

Delia took a nervous swipe across the butcher paper. "I suppose you could say their divorce was apathetic. No real fighting after they made the decision. And that was the most difficult part of all—watching them give up. After everything Jack and Anne went through to be together, I find it all so unfair."

"So it wasn't one of those whirlwind courtships, huh?"

She released a small laugh. "Heavens, no. They married almost five years after they met. Jack was in the process of establishing his career throughout a good deal of the marriage. Anne needed more of his attention, and he couldn't seem to give her enough."

"I'd think she'd understand being involved with a doctor."

"Anne knew that all too well because her father was a doctor, and that was part of the problem." A problem Anne had had difficulty overcoming. Had never really overcome, Delia realized. And she probably never would.

Gabe reached across the table and clasped her hand. "You know, Delia, I've always thought some things happen for a reason. Even the bad things. You just have to have faith everything will work out."

When Anne walked into Jack's apartment—the threshold she'd avoided crossing to this point—she hadn't been at all surprised to discover functional beige furniture and no frills. She hadn't been the least bit taken aback by the orderly surroundings; she and Jack had both required organization in their personal space. But she had been shocked to find her picture on the bedside table, the photo of her holding Katie, the one he'd snapped after they'd brought their precious baby home from the hospital. And she'd been stunned to find herself riffling through his nightstand drawer as if she had permission, coming upon only birthday cards and crayon-colored artwork presented to him by their daughter.

After straightening the mess she'd made, she closed the

drawer, shamed by what she'd been seeking when she'd found the keepsakes. She was a sad, sad case, the ex-wife who couldn't resist invading the former husband's privacy, searching for signs of another woman, maybe even condoms, something that would indicate he'd gone on with his life without her. A wakeup call that although he had reentered her world a few hours earlier, they couldn't go back to the way it had been before all the destruction. Instead, she had found only bittersweet pieces of their past.

Shaking off her melancholy, Anne left the bed, crossed the room and opened the door to the walk-in closet. Jack's suits and shirts hung neatly on a rack to her left, his slacks on her right, and an assortment of cross-trainers stood in a row on the floor. Shelves inset into the far end of the closet contained precisely folded jeans and T-shirts, along with several running suits. Since his therapy would continue for probably quite some time, Anne decided to pack most of the casual clothes.

On that thought, she was hunting out some sort of duffel or suitcase when a flash of dark blue caught her attention. She raked back the shirts to find the bulky, cable-knit sweater he'd given her their first Christmas as a married couple, along with an apology because he couldn't afford to give her more. The same sweater she'd worn for years because she tended to hold on to those things she deemed precious. The same sweater she'd balled up and thrown at him when he'd told her he'd been with another woman.

She couldn't imagine why he'd kept it, or why seeing it hanging among his clothes made her heart ache like the devil. Jack wasn't one to hold on to anything for any length of time. At least, that was what she'd once believed. Only then did reality hit home—Jack's presence alone would not only revive old recriminations, but quite possibly emotions she couldn't afford to acknowledge.

Just temporarily, she told herself. Just for a while. And as soon as he was well and able to tend to himself, she would send him back to this place and once more resume her life without him.

As her gaze tracked to the top shelf, Anne spotted a black suitcase. She was determined to get on with the business of packing and get out of there fast, but when she noted a plain white box resting next to the bag, again her curiosity got the best of her. Though she somehow knew she shouldn't, she pulled the box down from the shelf, sat on the closet floor and opened the lid. More souvenirs from the past, most in the form of pictures taken during various events, including Katie's milestones.

Some recollections were best left buried, never to be brought out again, even on a rainy day. Even when those very memories served to remind her that not all the times had been terrible. Yet she continued to sit on the floor, sorting through the mementoes, the onslaught of reminiscences battering away at her mind, begging to be let in. Then she saw it—a napkin yellowed with age, the neat black script faded but still legible.

Holding it brought about an ambush of unwanted memories of that night over twenty years ago. A night that had sent her straight back into Jack's life.

1986

On the heels of her frustration, Anne stormed through the French doors that opened up to the veranda. And as he'd promised in the covert missive he'd pressed into her palm a few moments ago, Jack waited for her in the far corner, wearing a perfectly pressed black suit, looking much too handsome, and that only brought out more of Anne's fury. She resented his presence at the party hosted annually by her parents at their Highland Park home in honor of the hospital's residents. Resented that her father had put Jack Morgan on such a high pedestal that he would ignore his own daughter's request not to invite him this year. Resented that Jack would call her away from the festivities, expecting a response to his juvenile note passing. She planned to give him a response all right, and one he might not appreciate.

She strode up to him and waved the cocktail napkin in his face. "Are we suddenly in junior high again?"

He looked totally unfazed by her acid tone. "I wouldn't have to resort to passing you notes if you'd return my calls."

She wadded up the napkin and stuffed it into his breast pocket. "We have nothing to say to each other, Jack. It's over. It's been over a year."

"Maybe for you, but not for me."

"Oh, really? Until last week, I hadn't heard a word from you since that morning."

"We both needed time to sort things out. And during that time, I've realized a few things."

She backed away, hands raised as if to ward off the

words she instinctively knew could punch holes in her resolve. "I don't want to hear it."

He pushed off the railing and moved much too close for Anne's comfort. "You listen to me now, or later. It's your choice. But I'm not going to give up until I've said what I need to say."

She quickly checked her watch. "You have five minutes, then I have to go back in before Max starts looking for me."

Jack barked out a caustic laugh. "Crabtree only cares about politicking. He sure as hell doesn't care about you, not the way I do."

"You don't know what you're talking about, Jack. He's been a good friend. You're mad because I've moved on. It's an issue of pride. It's that old cliché—you don't want me, but you don't want anyone else to have me, either."

"If I had any pride left, I wouldn't be spilling my guts now, knowing that you're probably going to tell me to go to hell. And I've never stopped wanting you. Not one minute since you broke things off. More important, Crabtree will never be able to give you what I can."

She rejected the ring of truth in Jack's words. Rejected the return of awareness of him. "He gives me his time, Jack. That's something you weren't able, or willing, to do."

"I'm willing to try harder to make more time for you, as long as you'll give us another chance."

She'd heard that before. Both from him and from her own father. "Look, I know all too well what it takes to build a career in medicine, and I respect that you're driven. But I need more."

"You need to be with me. The rest will work itself out."

She needed to make a hasty departure, before she gave in to that nagging little voice telling her to give him one more chance. "I have to go back inside now. And regardless of what's happened between us, I still wish you well. Have a nice life, Jack. And a nice, successful career."

She turned, intent on walking away one final time, when he asked, "Do you love him, Annie?"

The unseen force that at times commandeered her common sense sent her back around to face him. "That's none of your business."

"Does he love you?"

"I don't see why any of this matters."

He moved closer until he stood immediately before her. "Does he tell you that you're beautiful? Does he make you freakin' breakfast in bed on Sunday after working trauma all night? Does he make love to you the way I do?"

God, she didn't want to hear this. Worse, she didn't want to acknowledge that Max had done none of those things. "Stop it, Jack." She was crying now, tears that had arrived without warning.

He hooked one arm around her waist and pulled her against him, held her tightly, whispered softly, "I love you, Annie. I know I've never said it before, but that doesn't make it any less true. And I only need to ask you one more thing before I let you go for good."

She clutched his lapels and lowered her head, sensing the words before they ever left his lips.

"Do you love me, Annie?"

CHAPTER 8

Nothing said "I love you" better than a book of memories.

Delia slid the white-leather photo album—a patchwork journey into the past—onto the coffee table's lower shelf. Jack sat silently beside her on the sofa, looking much too downtrodden for Delia to ignore. Anne's insistence on retrieving his clothes this evening could be the source of his less-than-pleasant mood. Add that to Katherine's refusal to come downstairs because of her father's absence from the dinner table, and you had a recipe for gloom. They all needed time, Delia decided. And quite possibly a little help from the designated meddling mother.

General conversation was the best tack to take, and letting Jack in on her little secret seemed logical to Delia.

Besides, she could use a sounding board, and her son-in-law had always served her well in that regard. "Guess what I did this evening?"

He centered his gaze on some unknown focal point across the room. "Attended a support group for families with gimps?"

She ignored his sarcasm and the bitterness in his voice. "I went on a date."

That garnered his attention. "With who?"

"He's only a friend. A man I met at the hospital."

"What about Bryce?"

Heavens, Jack's memory was worse than she'd thought. "Bryce died almost eight years ago, Jack. We talked about the funeral at the hospital, remember?"

Awareness dawned in his expression. "He had a myocardial infarction."

"Yes. His heart gave out right after he finished a surgical case." Exactly how Delia had predicted his death would come—Bryce spending his last day on earth doing what he loved.

"Bryce was a good man," Jack said, his tone wistful.

Delia hooked her arm through his. "Yes, dear heart, he was a good man. And so is Gabe, the man I had dinner with this evening. He's an attorney, if you can believe that. I want you to meet him soon. In the meantime, I prefer you not mention any of this to Anne."

"Mention what to me?"

Delia glanced up to find Anne standing near the sofa, demonstrating her knack for bad timing. "I'm cutting my hours at the hospital. I want to be able to spend more time with Katherine and Jack." Not exactly a lie; simply an omission of the whole truth.

Anne tossed her keys on the table and collapsed into the chair across from Delia and Jack. "That's not necessary, Mother. Jack's going to have plenty of help from aides and therapists."

"I'm going to be here to provide emotional support, Anne. That's what he needs."

"Where's Katie?" Anne asked, apparently bent on ignoring her own mother.

"I believe she's taking a bath right now."

She came out of the chair quickly. "I'll go check."

"Sit down, Anne. I have something to show you."

"Can it wait?"

"Yes, but I prefer it not." After Anne reclaimed her seat, Delia leaned over and lifted the photo album from the shelf. "Look what I found."

Anne appeared anything but pleased at the discovery. "That was in my bedroom closet, which means you were snooping around in my things."

Not exactly untrue. "I wasn't snooping. I was specifically looking for pictures, and if you recall, I was here when you stuck the album in the top of your closet." The day after Anne had demanded Jack leave, as if by hiding the album she could dispose of the memories.

"Anyway," Delia continued, "I thought that since Jack's having some problems with his memory, we could show him a few photos."

"Don't do this, Mother."

Ignoring Anne's protest, Delia opened the album and

inched closer to Jack. "Here are your and Anne's engage-
ment pictures." When neither Jack nor Anne responded,
she turned to the second page. "And your wedding photos.
Those red velvet bridesmaid dresses were lovely, although
I never understood why you two decided to marry so
close to the Christmas holidays."

"What does it matter now, Mother?"

Delia chose to disregard the question, and Anne's
glare. "That was quite a day, particularly when Jack came
into the church dressing room and ushered the wedding
party out so he could speak with you alone, Anne. I've
always wondered what that was all about." In reality,
she'd stood outside the door, eavesdropping, so she'd
known exactly what it had been about—Anne's apparent
case of cold feet.

Anne stood and began to pace. "You'll have to ask him."

"I don't remember," Jack said, although Delia suspected
that he wasn't being truthful, only determined to avoid a
confrontation.

"I'll never forget it." Anne stopped and braced her palms
on the back of the chair. "He thought I was going to back
out, so as usual, he brought out the ammunition and stormed
to confront the situation, verbal guns blazing."

"I d-damn sure didn't storm into the room, Annie. I
walked in, and I had every right."

Ah, so he did remember, exactly as Delia had assumed.
"Did Anne do or say something that angered you, Jack?"

Anne continued to walk the length of room like some
restive animal. "No, I did not. And that's the point. He had
no good reason to disrupt the wedding preparations."

"I had every r-right and you know it." His angry tone matched his expression.

Delia had definitely opened a nice can of night crawlers. But the benefits could very well outweigh the possible consequences. "Anne, what did you do?"

"I didn't do anything, Mother."

"She called me the night before," Jack said. "She told me she wasn't sure we were doing the right thing, and then she h-hung up on me."

Anne spun around and set her hands on her hips. "That's because you'd been out with your pals, drinking and doing God only knows what else. I wasn't going to hold a conversation with someone who was barely coherent."

"It was two-thirty in the morning, Annie. I wasn't awake, and you weren't m-making any sense."

Anne returned her hands to the back of the chair and clutched it in a death grip. "I was making perfect sense. You were too drunk to notice."

Delia leaned forward and took a sip of the wine she'd poured herself upon arrival. Consuming the entire bottle seemed very tempting at the moment. "Now, let me see if I have this straight. You phoned Jack the night before to call off the wedding?"

Anne shook her head. "I didn't do that."

"But you threatened it," Jack said. "I went to the church early to make sure you hadn't decided to s-skip town."

Anne pointed an accusing finger at him. "And then you bullied your way into the dressing room and told me you weren't about to blow a hundred bucks on a tuxedo and you definitely had no intention of sending back the gifts, particularly the coffeemaker."

"I also told you I was s-scared." A stark silence prevailed as Jack closed his eyes briefly, then looked away from Anne.

Delia sensed that he was scared now, too. Scared to relive those moments, to bare his soul and expose old wounds. She should probably be ashamed that she'd baited Anne and Jack into this conversation, but she wasn't. If this opened some lines of communication, then it would all be worth their momentary pain.

Delia took Jack's hand in hers and gave it a pat. "Obviously that did the trick, dear heart, as you both did manage to show up at the altar."

"He compared our wedding with sitting for the medical boards," Anne said, now somewhat calmer. "He told me that at least he could do those over."

"And that marriage didn't allow for a do-over," Jack added. "I also told you that I l-loved you enough to chance it."

Then Delia saw it, that unmistakable look between them, the silent sharing of the past, the recognition of the love that had existed not so long ago. A strong, solid love that should have sustained them. She was convinced it was still there, maybe little more than an ember, but with the right fuel, it could definitely ignite again.

Anne straightened and ran one hand through her hair. "You were right, Jack. Marriage doesn't allow for do-overs, and it's really a shame ours didn't take. I'm going to check on Katie now."

Then Anne was gone, practically sprinting up the stairs,

no doubt running from her momentary vulnerability to the man who'd been her husband, her life partner, for many years. Delia knew all too well that the adage about running but not being able to hide would remain true in this instance, until one of them finally acknowledged that their feelings for the other still remained.

"She hates me," Jack said.

"On the contrary, dear heart, I think it's the opposite."

At least, that was what Delia was counting on.

He'd managed to make it back to the bed, but that was as far as he'd gotten. He sat on the edge of the thin mattress, waiting to see if Annie might show up, and when she didn't come after a good half hour, he had no choice but to speak into the damn white box.

"Annie."

She arrived on the scene in a matter of seconds, dressed in a blue cotton robe, her damp hair hanging around her shoulders. "What is it?"

He slammed back his pride and swallowed hard. "I need some help."

"I'm sorry. I wasn't thinking. When you weren't in the living room, I assumed you'd already gone to bed."

"Kind of hard to do when you don't have any damn pajamas."

Annie strode to the suitcase that she'd deposited near the door and lugged it to the love seat. She rummaged through his clothes, then withdrew a pair of faded scrubs, which she held up for his inspection. "I couldn't find any pajamas, but I found these and two other pair you apparently pilfered from the hospital."

A green cotton monument to what he'd once been, and would never be again. "You trying to rub salt into the wound, Annie? Making me wear something that reminds me of my former career?"

She walked to the bed and laid the scrubs beside him. "I'm only trying to help. After all, you are still a doctor."

Not as far as he could tell. "I'll sleep in my d-damn clothes."

"Stop being ridiculous, Jack. Even Katie doesn't give me this much trouble at bedtime." She tried for a smile, but it didn't quite form.

"Where is Katie now?" For some reason he wanted her there. Maybe even as an ally. A reason to remember why he didn't just call it quits and go back to his own place.

Annie's expression told him that his own daughter couldn't care less about him. "She's already asleep—at least, I think she is. She did ask me to tell you good-night and she'll see you in the morning."

"She's mad at me."

"I don't think that's true at all. But maybe you should talk to her about it tomorrow."

He doubted Katie wanted to hear anything he had to say. Hell, she probably wished she'd never extended the invitation for him to come back home. He wished he'd never agreed, particularly when Annie said, "I'll help you take a shower."

He didn't want a shower. He didn't want her to see the underweight, washed-out man he'd become. "No, thanks."

"Are you sure, because I really don't mind at all."

"I'll take one in the morning. That's what I'm p-paying the damn aides for."

"Fine. But at least let me help you with your clothes."

To hell with hiding from Annie. If she wanted to watch him undress, then she'd just have to deal with the view. With his left hand, he reached around his back and pulled the shirt up and over his head. The simple act of undressing called for a lot of energy, but the expression on Annie's face when he finally got the thing off sapped him of strength.

"Oh, Jack." She ran her hands along his side, over his ribs, countable by sight alone.

Once upon a time he had welcomed her touch. But not now, when she touched him out of pity, absent of any desire for him. It didn't matter. He didn't feel anything but a burning sense of self-consciousness. And self-hatred.

"Are you trying to starve yourself to death, Jack?"

Ignoring the question, he grabbed the scrub top and slid it over his head with one hand. "Hospital food tastes like c-crap."

"Well, you're here now, and I can still cook. Can you manage with your jeans?"

"Yeah. I can…manage." Barely, and that was obvious when it took him a good five minutes to get his fly undone.

Annie just stood there, the picture of patience, waiting until he had his jeans around his ankles before she knelt and slipped them off. Without asking his permission, she worked the scrub pants into place and tied the drawstring loosely around his waist. Although she didn't say a word, he could tell what she'd been thinking—his legs didn't look much better than the rest of his body.

And right now he didn't care. He didn't care that he could no longer manage his morning run. Didn't care if his muscles wasted away like the rest of him. All he cared about was going to sleep, because that was the only time he could forget his sorry state of affairs. Forget that his future wasn't worth a plug nickel, that he'd never be able to hold a scalpel in his hand or maybe even do something as simple as read the sports page again. Worse, he might never be able to make love to a woman in the same way. But then, the one woman he wanted wouldn't be interested anyway. Annie.

"You're all set," she said, again donning a pleasant look that seemed unnatural.

He wasn't set for anything except a free fall straight into hell.

"Why is Daddy so mad at me?"

Anne flipped one of Jack's favorite banana pancakes over on the griddle before regarding Katie, who was seated at the kitchen island. "Daddy isn't mad at you, sweetie." He was mad at the entire world right now and, after three weeks, still frustrated. Still uncooperative. Anne had suffered the brunt of his fury, intermingled with his remorse and occasional muttered apologies. That was okay. She would gladly serve as a barrier to protect Katie from her father's hostility.

"Where is Daddy now?"

"With a lady who's here helping him take a bath."

Katie's eyes went wide. "He still can't take a bath by himself?"

"No, honey, he can't. He's too weak and too sick."

"He doesn't look that sick to me. He looks mean."

After stacking a couple of cakes on a plate, Anne slid the fare in front of Katie and edged onto the stool next to hers. "He is still sick, but he's getting better every day. He just needs some time. He'll get better even faster if you visit with him a little more."

"Okay, I guess." She grabbed the bottle of syrup and drenched the pancakes in it, exactly as Jack was prone to do. "Something happened at school yesterday."

Not so unexpected news to Anne. She'd sensed something had been wrong with Katie last night when she'd tucked her in. "What happened?"

Katie covered her face with her palms. "I can't tell you."

"Sure you can. You can tell me anything."

Finally she lowered her hands into her lap. "Jason Jennings tried to kiss me on the mouth. On the playground after lunch."

Great. A first-grade oversexed heathen. "What did you do?"

"I told him he had bad breath 'cause he eats tuna sandwiches for lunch, and then I ran away from him."

"Did you tell anyone?"

"Just Chelsea. She said I should slug him."

Anne didn't plan to encourage any kind of violence, but she certainly wanted Katie to know that defending herself was okay. "Tell you what. If he bothers you again, go find your teacher and let her handle it, okay?"

"Okay." She took a fast drink of milk and sat silent for a few moments before saying, "Where did Daddy kiss you the first time?"

"On a park bench."

Katie giggled. "No, silly. I meant, did he kiss you on the mouth or on the cheek?"

"I think he kissed me on the lips, but I don't exactly remember. Maybe he kissed me on the cheek first." How sad that she'd resorted to lying to her own child to avoid reminiscences. She recalled every detail of the first kiss, and it hadn't been on her cheek.

"Where were you when Daddy asked you to get married?"

"That was a long time ago, Katie." But not quite long enough to forget.

Katie lifted her chin, looked rebellious. "I know you remember. You just don't want to tell me."

Anne didn't want to dig up all those old, but good and never-forgotten memories. "Why all the questions?"

"Because I want to tell Chelsea about you and Daddy like she tells me about her mom and dad."

Chelsea's mom and dad were still married, so they had every right to share. But Anne didn't dare voice that. If handing Katie a pleasant memory helped dilute the pain of her parents' divorce, then so be it.

1987

With the March sun beginning to sink over the horizon, Anne tossed a pebble into the water and aimlessly watched the ripples until they disappeared. She'd grown tired of casting her line with no result, and she honestly wouldn't have cared to catch a bass even if they had been biting. She only cared that Jack had scheduled his day off to coincide with hers, bringing her to the small lake for a spontaneous fishing expedition.

He stood a few feet away on the sloping bank where she now sat, his baseball cap turned backward, his dark green T-shirt dampened by perspiration, his jeans looking as though they should have been tossed in the Dumpster years ago. And she'd never seen him look better.

For the past year, Jack had made an incredible effort to make her happy, and she'd been more than happy to make a few concessions, as well, including adjusting her schedule at the hospital, even working double shifts to be with him whenever an opportunity presented itself. They'd learned to talk more openly, to voice their dislikes and displeasures, and had even hinted at a future together—much to her parents' delight.

Although that consideration still frightened her a bit, Anne couldn't remember a time when she'd been more content, when she'd felt as if she'd arrived at a place where she truly belonged. Couldn't remember when she'd ever felt so much love for one person aside from members of her immediate family. Yet this was a very different love—the kind that made her ache whenever she thought about how close she'd come to losing it. To losing him.

After reeling in her line, Anne set the rod aside, came to her feet and brushed the dirt off her bottom. She picked her way through the briars growing along the path leading to him, ignoring the occasional limb reaching out to attack her bare ankles. She would literally walk through fire— or in this case fire ants—to get to Jack.

When she reached the clearing where he stood, still engrossed in casting his own line, she slipped her arms around him from behind and leaned her cheek against his back. "The fish aren't biting, and I'm bored."

He regarded her over one shoulder and smiled. "That's because you insisted on using a top-water plug instead of the purple worm."

"I liked that top-water thingie. It's a pretty lime-green. Besides, I don't see that your purple worm is doing you any good."

"True." He reeled in his line, turned and popped a kiss on her forehead. "I'm going to change my bait and see if that works."

Anne almost protested, almost demanded that they go home. Yet these moments of solitude, when the rest of the world went away, leaving only the two of them, were still too rare. "Fine. But it'll be dark soon."

He crouched before the tackle box. "Fish start biting at sundown."

She pulled several beggar's lice from the hem of her denim shorts. "You told me they bite in the morning, and that didn't happen, either. I'm ready for a break."

"We had a nice long lunch."

A lunch that had included making love on a blanket beneath a copse of thick trees while Anne had worried someone might see them. Jack had managed to convince her that the risk of getting caught would only heighten the excitement, which it had. Even now, even after all the times they'd made love, she couldn't quite quell her blush. "I'm getting hungry again. We could order in and have dinner in bed."

"I have something else I want to try first, and if it doesn't work, we can go."

So much for enticing him away with the dinner-in-bed strategy. Anne strolled around the area, kicking a few rocks aside while she surveyed the lake. She swiped an arm across her damp forehead, batted at a persistent fly, then scratched her knee where a welt had formed.

She turned to find Jack still kneeling before the open tackle box, and gave in to her increasing frustration. "By the time you're finished finding that perfect fly, it'll be morning again and I'll be covered in bug bites."

"I've found it." He stood and dangled the line before her. "What do you think?"

Anne couldn't think, not when she spotted the diamond ring clipped to the swivel. She stared at him, not bothering to hide her astonishment, although she relied on levity to stop the threatening emotional attack. "I'm far from an expert, but I'm fairly sure it's not common practice to use jewelry to catch a fish."

"I'm not interested in catching a fish, Annie. I'm interested in catching you."

Anne noticed his hands shook slightly as he attempted to unhook the ring, and she found that ironic since he was so skilled with a scalpel. But she couldn't deny that she was nervous, too. Nervous and surprised and scared and feeling a bit weepy at that. "It's not as big as I would've liked," he said. "But it's all I can afford right now. I'm hoping it's going to work for you anyway."

He moved closer and held up the ring. "Annie, I love you more than my Zebco reel, more than my Zeppelin albums. Will you marry me? And you better say yes, because I just used two *Z*s in a sentence, and when is that likely to happen again?"

She laid her palm against her throat, feeling the wild beat of her pulse. "Your Zeppelin albums?"

"Yeah. Hell, I'd be willing to sell them if you say yes."

Jack took her hand into his and slid the solitaire partially on her ring finger. "I've never proposed before, and I'm probably doing it all wrong, but I promise you, Annie, I might not be able to give you the world for a few years, but you'll always have me."

A sob caught in her throat. "Who would have thought you could be so poetic?"

"Pretty damn amazing what love does to a pragmatic guy like me. And I do love you, Annie. So what do you say?"

She waited for that moment of uncertainty, that fleeting fear of making a mistake, but neither arrived. She still didn't believe in love at first sight, but she knew his love was real. She also knew that she belonged with Jack, and always would. For that reason, she uttered the one simple word that sealed her fate.

"Yes."

CHAPTER 9

In sickness and in health....

Anne felt as if the vows she'd recited all those years ago had come back into play, despite the divorce. And she was beginning to believe Jack might never be completely healthy again.

For better or for worse....

Today definitely qualified as worse, Anne decided as she paused in the den's door to find the TV tray on its side by the chair and a pool of water on the carpet where the basin had landed. Apparently, Jack's first attempt at shaving had failed, bringing about another tantrum. For the past two weeks he'd routinely rejected putting any real effort into his therapy, but he had no problem throwing things with his good hand and kicking things with his functional leg.

Not bothering to afford Jack even a passing glance, she

walked into the adjacent bathroom, a litany of foul words running through her mind and threatening to spill out of her mouth. She'd grown weary of Jack's bouncing back and forth between trying to be too independent and acting like a spoiled brat. Yesterday he'd almost fallen in the shower after refusing any assistance from the aide. The day before that, one therapist walked out after he hurled the book she'd asked him to read across the room. Following that episode, Anne had requested that everyone charged with Jack's care take the weekend off—a decision she was already regretting.

After grabbing a towel from the rack, she drew in a few calming breaths and reclaimed what little was left of her patience before she headed back to clean up the mess. She set the tray on its legs, knelt to right the bowl and dabbed at the soggy pool. All the while she sensed Jack glaring at her, challenging her to yell at him. That seemed to be his intent of late—to make her angry. Well, she refused to scream and give in to his machinations. She was too frustrated even to offer a good scolding over his refusal to use an electric razor, because scolding him would simply do no good. Nothing worked with Jack these days. Not kindness. Not cajoling. Not even shouting, which she'd done one time due to frustration.

Leaving the towel spread out on the floor, Anne tossed the can of shaving cream and razor into the empty bowl, then stood before Jack, the metal basin propped on one hip. "Feel better now?"

He raised his gaze to hers, his eyes downtrodden, fatigue on his face. Anne saw no trace of anger, only a sadness that resonated in his tone when he said, "I can't shave, Annie."

At that moment he sounded like a little boy who'd announced he couldn't bat a ball out of the infield. In so many ways, he had become a child again. A middle-aged boy in a man's body, relying on her to make everything better. And she didn't know how to make it better.

Anne returned to bathroom, filled the basin with water and retrieved another disposable razor. She went back to Jack and set the supplies on the tray, then pulled a chair in front of him. When she noticed the thin trickle of red on the patch of cheek he'd managed to shave, she tugged the towel she'd tucked into his T-shirt away and dabbed at the spot. "You're bleeding."

"More than you know."

His voice held so much pain; his eyes showed so much dejection. She focused on treating the external injury, wishing she had a cure for the internal wound. "You've had worse cuts before, Jack."

"I'm dying inside, Annie."

She laid the towel in her lap and finally looked at him. "Don't say that, Jack. Please don't say that. You need more time. It's not even been three months since the stroke."

"Seems like three hundred."

In an effort to ignore her threatening tears, Anne concentrated on applying more shaving cream to his jaw. Then she lifted his left hand, wrapped his fingers around the razor and guided it to his chin. Together they worked their way over his face, the scrape of the razor across his beard the only sound penetrating the quiet.

When they were finished, she took the razor from his grasp and dropped it onto the table. "All done."

He caught her wrist when she started to stand. "Is this how it's going to be, Annie? You helping me with something as simple as shaving? That's not fair."

"I know that, Jack. Life's not always fair." Otherwise they would still be happily married.

"Not fair on you, I meant."

"I'll manage, Jack. For as long as it takes."

In sickness and in health…

For better or for worse.

Somehow Anne knew it would get even more worse before it got better.

"How's Jack doing?"

A question Anne had heard at least five times a day since Jack's stroke, and the answer was usually the same—and a blatant lie. "He's fine." But the person now posing the query would expect an honest answer, and he deserved one.

Leaning against the nurses' station, Anne looked up from the chart she'd been studying for the past few minutes. "You don't want to know, Hank."

"When I phoned him last week, he seemed okay. What's going on?"

Her only response was a slight sob as she held back the tears of frustration. Of utter helplessness.

Hank took her by the arm and guided her to one corner of the corridor, away from the chaos of the unit.

"Talk to me, Anne," Hank said, followed by a sincerely

sympathetic look that made Anne want to bawl louder than the babies being born in the delivery suites surrounding them. While young mothers brought new life into the world, Anne felt as though her life was coming apart.

She clung to the last of her composure and allowed the floodgates to open wide. "It's awful, Hank. He's not cooperating at all. We've been through at least a dozen therapists and aides in less than three months because he treats them so horribly, but he won't do anything himself. He barely eats enough to stay alive. When he's not lying around on the sofa, he's sleeping. I've tried to convince him to go outside and enjoy the spring weather, and he refuses."

She paused to catch a breath before continuing. "Katie's scared of him, and he lashes out at me on a regular basis. He also tries to bargain with me. If I leave him alone, then he'll leave me alone, which translates into he's giving up."

Hank withdrew a prescription pad from his lab-coat pocket, turned to the wall and scribbled something on the pad before facing her again. "This is for a mild antidepressant, one pill a day to take the edge off. But it might not be enough. In other words, he probably needs a good psychologist. I can recommend one."

Anne accepted the proffered paper and tucked it into the pocket of her smock, doubting one pill a day would provide the magic cure to Jack's apathy. "I've had trouble getting him to his follow-up neuro appointments. I can't imagine him agreeing to see a therapist."

"He might not have a choice, Anne. Use the pill first

and see if that helps. In the meantime, I can give you something, too, if you need it."

She didn't need a happy pill. She simply needed this nightmare to be over. "I'll survive. I just keep hoping…"

Hoping for what? That Jack would come to his senses and realize he was destroying any chance for recovery by drowning in self-pity?

Hank laid a hand on her shoulder. "Hang in there."

She was—from an emotional cliff. "I'll hang in there until I can't hang in anymore."

"Anne, Adams wants you ASAP."

Anne glanced at the unit clerk delivering the message, before regarding Hank again. "The boss is summoning me, so I guess I better go."

"Sure. And I'll give Jack a call and see if he's open to a visit from me and a few of the other docs. Maybe that would cheer him up."

"It's worth a shot." Although she doubted Jack would welcome any company, at least at this point in time.

After thanking Hank for his concern, Anne caught an elevator down to the first floor and sought out the nurse administrator's office, a strong sense of dread hovering over her as she walked the carpeted corridor. She stopped immediately outside the partially opened door and inhaled a fortifying breath before leaning inside. "Did you need me, Karen?"

"Come in, Anne. And close the door."

Anne complied, and when she noticed Max standing in the corner near the window, her sense of dread rocketed. "What's up?"

Without bothering to stand, sixty-something Karen Adams, champion of all nurses, gestured toward the chair positioned before her desk. "Sit."

Anne pulled back the chair and sank into it as if her muscles had melted.

When Max silently moved a bit closer to Karen's desk, Anne kept her attention leveled on Karen.

"First of all, I've invited Mr. Crabtree here for this discussion to make what I'm about to say more official," Karen said. "But right now we're keeping this conversation confidential."

Anne had a feeling this was much worse than she'd suspected. "I have several patients to tend to, so if we could make it quick, I'd appreciate it, and so would they."

Karen took a pen from the tin on her desk and turned it over and over. "It's been brought to my attention that you've been late quite a few mornings the past month."

"That's true. I've had a few problems at home." Problems as in her ex-husband's downhill slide.

"I know about Dr. Morgan's situation," Karen said. "And I completely understand how difficult that must be."

No, she didn't understand. No one would unless they'd lived it. "I promise I'll try to be more prompt from this point forward."

Karen glanced at Max before returning her focus to Anne. "That's not the only problem. Dr. Riggins has registered an informal complaint with Mr. Crabtree."

Anne had never cared for Carl Riggins, and the feeling was definitely mutual. "Let me guess. He's not happy because I interrupted his lunch last Tuesday to deliver a baby. My mistake for doing my job."

"He claims you missed decelerations on one of his high-risk patients," Karen said.

Anne's simmering anger began to boil. "The baby's heartbeat came back up without any problem. Besides, I had two other patients in active labor at the same time and we were short-handed. I was only out of the room for two minutes when the d-cells occurred, and the delivery went fine."

At least Karen appeared somewhat sympathetic. "Yes, it turned out fine, Anne. But that's not all. Nicole talked to me yesterday out of concern for you. She said that during one delivery, you handed her magnesium instead of Pitocin, which could have led to disaster had she hung it."

Anne had no real excuse for her carelessness, yet she struggled to find one out of sheer desperation. "The Pitocin and magnesium were right there together. Anyone could have made the same mistake."

"And those mistakes can cost lives."

Over twenty years of exemplary service to the hospital, and now her competency was under attack. "Okay, I admit it. Two errors in such a short period can't be excused. I promise to be more careful. Write me up and I'll face the review when necessary."

Karen tossed the pen aside. "I'm not going to write you up, Anne. But I am going to suggest you take a break. At least until you've had some time to deal with your personal issues."

Anne felt as if someone had slipped a rope around her neck and given it a tug. "How much of a break?"

"You have four weeks' vacation and another three weeks of accumulated sick leave. Now would be a good time to use them."

Now would be the worst time as far as Anne was concerned. "You're telling me that you want me to take an extended leave because I made a couple mistakes."

"You're distracted, Anne," Max said, the first words he'd spoken to that point. "Distractions create serious errors. You need to do this for yourself as well as your patients."

Both Karen and Max acted as though this offer was some kind of gift. Anne couldn't disagree more. Work had been her only saving grace, her deliverance from all things involving Jack. Her escape from watching him fade away. "This is totally unfair. By the time I can actually go back to work, Katie will be out of school for the summer. You can't force me to do this."

"I don't want to force you, Anne," Karen said. "But I will if I have to, even if that means suspending you without pay for two months. Wouldn't you rather keep a clean record and be compensated for your leave?"

She'd rather walk out on this miserable situation, away from Max and his pretend compassion. Away from Karen's look of understanding, which although genuine made Anne even angrier. Right now, away from Jack, if she had any choice in the matter.

She stood and backed toward the door before her temper reached the danger point. "I hope I don't receive a desperate plea to return when census is high and you need help, because I won't be answering the phone." That sounded utterly childish, but right then Anne didn't care.

She wanted only to get away, to take a drive. Have a drink, or several.

"Could you give us a minute alone, Karen?"

Anne bristled over Max's request. She definitely didn't care to talk to him, much less be alone with him. But when Karen rose from behind her desk and said, "Of course," Anne realized a reprieve wasn't in the offing.

Karen gave Anne's hand a gentle shake. "Good luck. I look forward to seeing you back at work in a couple of months. Hopefully things will be better for you then."

Anne looked forward to nothing. Not the mandatory break. For sure not her conversation with Max. Yet she was powerless to do anything other than tough it out. He was still the hospital administrator, in charge of her future, at least when it involved the job. As far as her personal life was concerned, that was none of his business.

After Karen closed the door behind her, Anne balled her hands at her sides. "I need to go home, Max, so get to the point."

He strolled around the desk and perched on the edge. "Why are you doing this?"

"You heard, Karen. I have no choice."

"I'm not talking about the leave. I'm talking about you taking care of him. You don't owe Jack Morgan a damn thing."

She should have known to expect this from Max, a man who'd viewed Jack as competition for her attention. A man who saw him as competition, period. "I don't owe you an explanation, either."

"You don't have to explain, Anne. You've always run

whenever he called. The thing is, your obligation to him ended two years ago when he screwed around on you. And here you are, in his life again, when you could be with me."

As if that were a prospect Anne would seriously entertain. "There's nothing between you and me, Max. We've been over this too many times to count."

"I didn't get that feeling back in December."

"That was a mistake." A mistake she'd made on her and Jack's former wedding anniversary out of loneliness, only to find that she'd still been lonely in Max's company, and in his bed.

"It wasn't a mistake," he said. "All you have to do is say the word, and we could have more of the same."

She had no desire to say that word. She had no desire to talk to him any longer. "Now I get it. This whole thing with Riggins was your idea. No doubt you were out with him on the golf course and he happened to mention me in passing. Then you decided that you'd make more out of this than necessary, forcing me out of a job and in turn forcing me to reconsider caring for my husband."

"Ex-husband, Anne. It didn't work the first time. It's not going to work now."

"That's so interesting, Max. You of all people doling out advice to the lovelorn. How many divorces have you been through now? Two?"

"Maybe my marriages didn't work because I wasn't with the right woman. It's time for you to finally come to your senses and realize we should be together."

He would be waiting until hell iced over before she

agreed to that. "Nothing's ever going to happen between us again, Max. Let it go."

"I'm not going to let it go. When you've had your fill of Jack again, you'll come back to me."

Not this time. "Unless you have something else to add in regard to my work, I'm leaving now."

He waved a hand toward the door. "Go. He's waiting for you. But remember, he ruined your life once. If you let him, he'll ruin it again."

He spent most of his free time alone, facing a fragile future, attempting to recall the past. Sometimes he laughed inappropriately, when nothing about his situation warranted humor. Other times he cried like a baby over something as stupid as a sappy commercial.

He'd learned to hide his emotions by remaining a recluse, trapped in the confines of his own living hell and a mind determined to malfunction. He rarely experienced even a shred of happiness, except in the presence of Annie and Katie. Even then, he didn't express that minimal joy. They saw nothing more than a shell of the man he used to be.

The door slamming jarred Jack's attention away from the program featuring the trials of trauma surgeons. A form of self-torture, he decided. A reminder of where he had been, and might never be again.

He raised his head from the arm of the sofa to check the clock above the fireplace. Annie had only been gone a couple of hours, so it couldn't be her. The speech therapist wasn't due for another half hour. The aide was currently making his bed, and unless she'd left without him noticing, he had no clue who had entered the house.

Probably another therapist trying to fix him, when he didn't care to be fixed. When he couldn't be fixed. He didn't give a damn about anything, aside from the fact he was making his former wife and daughter miserable. That misery was apparent on Anne's face when she strode into the room.

"Why are you home?" He regretted the question the minute it left his mouth. It sounded as though he didn't want her here, and nothing could be further from the truth.

"I've been asked…" She sucked in a deep breath. "Correction. I've been *forced* to take a leave of absence from the hospital."

This couldn't be good, but he had to ask anyway. "Why?"

She started her usual pacing. "It seems I've been too distracted lately, not to mention tardy to work the past month because someone in this house hasn't been cooperative with the very people who are trying to help him."

Of course it was his fault. Nothing new there. "I didn't ask you to hang around and supervise the help, Annie. That was your choice."

"You didn't give me any choice. If I didn't stay to make certain you behaved yourself, then we would've lost another aide. And frankly, I'm getting sick and tired of having to break in new workers every time I turn around."

He was sick and tired, period. "How long will you be off?"

"At least six weeks, which means I'll be here all day, every day, and if you think home health care's been tough, you ain't seen nothing yet." She pulled a bottle of pills from the pocket of her smock and set it down hard on the end table. "Did you bother to eat any breakfast this morning?"

Only because the aide had practically force-fed him a tasteless bowl of cereal the way she would a toddler. "Yeah."

"Are you sure?"

"If you don't believe me, go ask the woman who's in my jail cell, cleaning up after me."

"Her name is Betty, and she's a nice lady." Anne twisted the lid off the bottle, spilled a pink pill into her palm and offered it and the untouched glass of juice he'd left on the coffee table. "Take it."

"What is it?"

"An antidepressant. One pill a day, per Hank's instructions, starting this morning."

Damn Hank's interference. "I don't want it."

"I don't give a damn what you want, Jack. I'm at my wit's end with you. You've got to make more of an effort."

The venom in her voice told Jack she wasn't going to lay off him until he agreed. "And you think a pill's gonna make me do that?"

"Something has to give, or else..." Both her gaze and her words trailed off.

"Or else what?"

She set the pill and the glass on the coffee table before him. "Look, I know you're depressed. I know how hard this has been on you."

He didn't warrant her sympathy. He didn't want it, either. "You can't imagine how hard it is, Annie, being like this."

"No, I can't. But I do know that if things don't change

around here, if you don't try harder to get better, we're going to have to rethink this arrangement."

He managed to work his way to a sitting position, and even that made him tired. "Having me live here was your idea. Not mine."

A flash of anger passed over her face. "I see. Now it's my fault that you're not making any progress. My fault that you've alienated your child, not to mention the people who want to help you."

He shifted his attention to the carpeted floor beneath his feet. "I don't want anyone's help. I don't need it."

"Oh, yeah, Jack, you need help, whether you're willing to admit it or not. As far as I'm concerned, you have two choices. You make the effort to get better, or you waste away. But if you choose the second option, I'm not going to watch. More important, I'm not going to let you ruin my and Katie's life because you don't have the guts to get well."

Ruin her life *again*. Although she hadn't said it, he knew she was thinking it. Maybe he had ruined her life by not working harder at their marriage. In turn, he'd ruined his, too. As far as he was concerned, he didn't have a life in any real sense of the word. "You're right, Annie. You don't deserve my crap. You never have."

She gestured toward the table. "If you decide you want things to change, then take the pill. I'm not leaving until you do."

He didn't have enough energy to argue. He barely had enough energy to roll the pill into his left hand, put it in his mouth and swallow it with the juice. "Are you happy now?"

She didn't look at all happy. "I'm going to apologize to

Betty for whatever you've done to her this morning and then do some laundry before Katie gets home."

After Annie stormed out of the room, Jack centered his attention on the amber-colored bottle. Apparently, Annie trusted him enough to leave the medicine there. Trusted him enough to believe it would be in the same spot when she returned.

You only have two choices, Jack…

Wrong, Annie.

He had another choice, one that would save them all from the suffering this sickness had caused. The suffering that he was still causing everyone who cared about him.

Leaning forward, he slipped the pill bottle into his T-shirt pocket and reached for the walker. The process of making it to the master bedroom was slow, both from his lack of energy and the decision now weighting his soul. He felt as if he'd fallen into a dark void with no way out. He wanted out.

He paused at the bathroom door to garner a last look at the bed that he'd once shared with Annie—and he remembered. Sunday afternoons spent making love early in their marriage, when they'd taken the phone off the hook and shut out the world. And in later years, waking up in the morning to find Katie had crawled in between them sometime during the night, her tiny hand lying next to his face on the pillow, her blond curls a tangled mess.

He couldn't dwell on those memories now; the days that were long gone. Days he couldn't get back.

He inched his way into the bathroom, closed the door and set the walker aside. Using the wall for support, he slid to the white-tiled floor and emptied the bottle's contents beside him. He began to count pills, and felt as if he was calculating the remaining minutes of a life that was no longer worth living.

One…two…three…

His short-circuited brain wouldn't allow him to move past ten, but he did know he had enough medication to provide his escape. He didn't have a pen or paper, and even if he did, he couldn't write a damn note—or at least, one that made sense. He had little choice but to hope Annie would understand why he'd arrived at this decision.

As he contemplated the path he'd taken to this point, he briefly questioned if anyone would miss him, if anyone would even care once he was gone. If they would consider his demise a loss, or good riddance. None of that mattered. He wasn't afraid of dying. He was more afraid of a future that seemed as useless as his hand and leg. Right now he welcomed the prospect of falling asleep and never waking up.

If he was going to do it, he had to do it now, before Katie arrived home. Before Annie came looking for him, if she even bothered to look for him at all. By the time she did find him, he would be unconscious. When she finally realized what he had done, it would be too late, and she would be free.

He couldn't hurt her anymore.

He managed to scoop up the first of the pills in his left hand and, as he closed his eyes, willed away the doubts, the image of Annie telling Katie that her father wouldn't be around anymore, of Delia bearing the brunt of his family's distress. He tried to shut out the memory that abruptly came to him. Without success. But he couldn't ignore the words they had spoken to each other so many years ago.

Promise me…

1992

Years ago he'd learned that surgery and sentiment didn't mix. He'd convinced himself that he'd built an adequate emotional fortress to counteract the tragedies that had become so commonplace in his line of work. But tonight he'd begun to realize that despite all his valiant efforts, his humanity wouldn't always stay hidden.

Still, he'd waited until he'd left the hospital to analyze his feelings. Waited until he'd gone home to Annie.

After shedding his lab coat and dropping it onto the threadbare sofa, Jack passed through the kitchen on his way to the bedroom, finding the single place setting still on the dinette table, symbolizing all the dinners he'd missed in the past four years—and all the disappointment he'd caused his wife. He'd dragged her to California, thousands of miles away from her family, to take a renowned fellowship to fulfill his dreams, while she'd put hers on the back burner. They'd settled on the overpriced cracker-box apartment because that was all they could afford between Annie's job and his limited salary, most of which went to pay off his loans.

He'd vowed that when they returned to Dallas in a couple of years, little by little, he would make it up to Annie. He'd eventually buy her a decent house, a dependable car, and one day give her what she wanted more than anything—a baby. At the moment, he could only give her a few hours of his attention.

He found her in bed curled on her side, the space nearest to the door reserved for him, her eyes closed in sleep. The book she'd been reading lay open on the night-stand, next to the lamp that she always left on for him. Leaning one shoulder against the door frame, he took a few more moments to watch her. He surveyed her slender hand resting on his pillow, his ring on her finger, the modest wedding set he'd given her because he hadn't been able to afford something more elaborate. But in classic Annie fashion, she'd said she didn't care about owning a larger diamond; that one was perfect.

She was perfect, and every bit as beautiful as when he'd met her eight years earlier. Still everything he'd ever wanted in a woman, and a hell of a lot more.

Her mouth twitched slightly, bringing the crease of a dimple into view before her eyes drifted open. As she focused on him, she smiled as she always did when he came home to her. "Hey, there."

He walked to the bed, perched beside her on the edge of the mattress and rested a hand on her leg. "Hey, babe. Did you get the message about the delay?"

She scooted her back up against the headboard and stretched her arms above her head. "Jenny from the Surgery desk called to let me know you'd be late. We're becoming really good friends. I told her we should do lunch tomorrow in the cafeteria."

He felt damn guilty that he couldn't be a better friend to Annie. "That sounds like a plan."

She studied him a long moment. "Is something wrong, Jack?"

"I'm tired."

"I'm sure you are, but something else is bothering you. I can tell. I'm willing to listen if you're willing to talk."

He didn't want to talk right then. He wanted to make love to her, absorb her warmth in an effort to ward off the cold.

He stripped out of his clothes and climbed into bed beside her. She lifted her gown over her head and tossed it away, demonstrating without words that she recognized what he needed before he had a chance to voice it. Although he knew every soft sound she would make before she made it, knew how she would feel even before he was inside her, tonight memorizing all the details he'd once taken for granted was important.

"I love you, Jack," she told him. "I'm here."

But he couldn't seem to get close enough to her, even though they were as close as they could be.

In the aftermath, he laid his cheek against her breast. Even after spending most of his waking hours listening to beating hearts, he found something comforting in hearing the sound of Annie's.

She sifted her hands through his hair, over and over until he was on the brink of sleep. "Talk to me, Jack."

He kept his eyes shut and muttered, "About what?"

"About the case. Were there complications?"

"No. It went great." And it had, without a hitch. At least, the transplant itself.

"Then tell me what's bothering you. I'm not going to let you sleep until you do."

Exactly what he'd expected from her. Exactly what he needed—the understanding that only she could give him. "The donor heart came from a young mother of three." A woman the same age as Annie.

"Oh, God, Jack. What happened to her?"

He rolled onto his back and centered his attention on the faded ceiling. "She put a bullet through her head, but she didn't get the job done immediately. Her husband decided to withdraw life support and donate her organs." A decision Jack wasn't sure he could make if he had to face losing Annie, regardless of a dismal prognosis.

"Is this the first time you've had a donor that resulted from suicide?" she asked.

"No. But for some reason, it bothered me tonight. And that pisses me off, because I've always kept things in perspective."

Annie shifted to her side and draped her arm over his chest. "You're only a man, Jack. A good man who still has the capacity to feel things. And it's your compassion that makes you such a good doctor, not just your skill."

He pulled her closer. "It's just such a damn shame, someone that young reaching a point where she doesn't see any other way out."

"It's hard for me to understand it, too. But I guess you wouldn't know what it's like to be in that place unless you've been there."

A place Jack never intended to go, and a prospect he never wanted to encounter with Annie, either. "Promise me you'll never do anything that desperate."

She raised her head and stared at him. "Why would you even think that, Jack?"

"Being married to me hasn't been easy. I understand you're lonely because I'm not here enough."

She smoothed a hand over his jaw. "I realized when I married you it wasn't going to be easy. But I'm willing to make the sacrifice because I also know there will come a time when it will be easier. And most important, because I love you that much."

"I love you, too, Annie." More than she would ever know. More than he could ever express.

"Now you promise me something, Jack."

"Anything."

"Promise you'll never leave me…"

When the closed bathroom door caught Anne's attention, every ounce of her intuition screamed something was terribly wrong. She deposited the laundry basket on the bed, crossed the room and rapped her knuckles on the door. "Are you in there, Jack?"

She received no response, so she knocked again. Called to him again. Slowly she tested the knob, despite the sense of trepidation. It opened easily, providing some measure of relief. But that relief was short-lived when she discovered Jack sitting on the floor, legs sprawled out before him, his back to the row of cabinets beneath the vanity, the walker lying on its side not far from the tub to her right.

He'd somehow fallen—Anne's initial assumption… until she saw the open bottle on the floor next to his leg. The empty bottle.

"Oh, God, Jack. What have you done?"

He stared off into space, his red-rimmed eyes devoid of emotion. She dropped onto her knees before him and pressed her fingertips against his neck, felt for his carotid artery to check his pulse, which thankfully appeared steady, though that meant very little if he'd only recently ingested the pills.

She framed his face in her palms, forcing him to look at her. "How many did you take?"

When he didn't answer, she tightened her grasp. "How many, Jack?" Her voice held an edge of hysteria, sounded shrill and panicked.

"I didn't take any."

She grasped his shoulders and shook him. "Swear to me you're telling the truth."

"Look in the trash can if you don't believe me."

Anne grabbed the chrome basin and peered inside—and was relieved to find the pills lying helter-skelter in the bottom. She dumped them onto the floor and made sure they were all there, then ladled them up in her hands and tossed them into the toilet.

She collapsed onto the floor beside him and rested her arms over bent knees, suddenly aware she was shaking. "I thought you'd—"

"Downed the bottle. I wanted to do it. I almost did. But I couldn't."

What might have been sent a chill up Anne's spine. "Why would you even consider taking your life, Jack?"

"Because I'm tired, Annie. I'm tired of seeing you sad and knowing I'm the one who's causing it. I'm tired of having my own daughter look the other way when she sees me. I'm sick of being sick."

After crossing her legs, she held his hand to hers and rested it on her thigh. "I know you're tired. I know how tough this is on you. And I'm sad because you won't help yourself."

When he finally looked at her, Anne saw a pain so intense it stole her breath. "I can't do it, Annie. Not without you. For God's sake, don't leave me alone again."

Then he laid his head in her lap and began to tremble, cried mournfully, released soul-shattering sobs that echoed in the otherwise silent bathroom.

Anne did all she knew to do, all she could do—held him as he wept and let her own tears fall. "I'm here, Jack," she crooned over and over, as if he were a lost little boy, not a man who had always been so strong and so sure. The man she had relied on for so many years to quiet her own sorrow.

"I'm not going to leave you alone, Jack. I promise."

CHAPTER 10

Delia wasn't quite ready to leave the comfort of Gabe's car, or his company as they sat parked along the curb at the end of Anne's driveway. But duty to her daughter had given her little choice in the matter. "I'm so sorry we've had to cut the evening short, Gabe. But Anne sounded so worried that I—"

"You don't have to explain anything to me, Delia. I understand."

She realized all too well that he did. She'd known that about him for some time now, during their numerous dates and conversations when she'd bemoaned the continuing problems confronting her beloved family. Not once had he tuned her out or turned her away, even when she'd had to put off being with him to spell Anne for a few hours several times a week.

Delia clasped the handle, yet failed to open the door. "Call me tomorrow morning and we'll reschedule the movie."

"I could wait for you here while you see what's going on."

She shook her head. "That's not necessary. Besides, this could take a few hours." Or all night, depending on the current crises that Anne had refused to detail over the phone.

She saw the first signs of frustration in Gabe's expression, which he covered quickly with a slight smile. "Okay. Call when you're ready for me to pick you up."

"You live across town, Gabe. Driving all the way back here doesn't make any sense."

"How are you going to get home, then?"

"I can phone a cab if I have to. Or walk the two blocks."

"No way, Delia. You're not going to go traipsing around the neighborhood in the middle of the night."

"A virtually crime-free neighborhood, might I add."

"There's no such thing in this day and time. It won't be any problem for me to pick you up. I can find a place nearby to hang out until I hear from you."

Delia knew the perfect place for Gabe to hang out. A place not far away. Her place. She withdrew her set of keys from her purse and offered them to him. "Go into the backyard and unlock the kitchen door. You'll have thirty seconds to disarm the security system. The code is six-seventeen."

He grinned. "Your birthday."

The man didn't forget a thing. "That's correct. Feel free to make yourself at home."

"Then I guess I'll see you when I see you."

An idea struck Delia that had been gnawing at her for the past two weeks, once she'd realized that the vintage years hadn't killed her desire. She wasn't normally a risk taker, but this one she was determined to take in the near future. As far as she was concerned, the near future was now. "Since it probably will be late when I'm ready to leave, I see no good reason for you to drive all the way back to your place until morning."

He inclined his head and gave her a questioning look. "Are you suggesting I spend the night with you, Delia Cooper?"

She rested a hand on the string of pearls at her throat. "Well, yes, I am." Her confidence began to wither and wane. "Of course, I'm not necessarily suggesting that we have to…you know, sleep in the same bed if that's not what you want."

He reached over and touched her face. "I've wanted that for some time now. Question is, do you really want it?"

Heavens, she wanted it more than she'd wanted the award for Volunteer of the Year. "Actually, I have been thinking about it quite a bit lately, and yes, I'm ready for the next step." She released a nervous laugh. "I only hope I haven't forgotten how. It's been a while."

"For me, too." Gabe leaned his head back against the seat and chuckled. "I'm pretty sure you haven't forgotten a thing. But on the off chance you have, I'll be glad to guide you every step of the way."

Gabe leaned to kiss her, and Delia recognized she should feel badly that she was considering sleeping with

Gabe when she should be focused on supporting her daughter. But she didn't feel badly at all—not yet.

Delia patted Gabe's cheek. "I'll see you in a while, then. Hopefully not too long a while."

"I'll be waiting."

She slid out of the car and rushed up the walkway to get this ordeal over with so she could get back to Gabe. And just when she'd thought she'd avoided a visit from the guilt monster, the thing arrived with the force of a tempest when Anne answered the door, her face streaked with tears.

Delia kept her concerns to herself as they walked through the foyer. Once they had settled side by side on the living room sofa, a mound of crumpled tissues littering the coffee table before them, she draped her arm around Anne's shoulder and waited for her fresh onslaught of tears to subside before she asked, "What happened, dear heart?"

Anne withdrew another tissue from the pocket of her robe and dabbed at her eyes. "It's Jack."

No real surprise to Delia. "What about him?"

She listened patiently as Anne recounted the events of the day, beginning with her leave of absence. Patience turned to horror as Anne explained that Jack—a vital man once full of life—had contemplated suicide.

"Oh, Anne, I knew he was depressed, but not enough to consider something like this."

"I should have known. I've been so angry with his attitude that I ignored all the signs. I thought he was just being stubborn, and maybe even punishing me."

"Of course that's not what he's doing. He's sad. You can't blame yourself, Anne."

Anne brushed away another tear. "I was fairly hard on him earlier. I told him to either get with the program or get out."

Oh, dear. "Where is he now?"

"In my bed. He's been asleep most of the afternoon. I decided it would be best if he stayed there all night so I could watch him."

"Is Katherine in bed?"

"No. She's at her friend Chelsea's. I thought it would be better to have her out of the house even if it is a school night. Just in case."

In case Jack should try something else, Delia realized. "That probably is best."

Anne hesitated a moment, wringing the tissue so hard it began to fall apart. "It was horrible, Mom, seeing him so torn up inside."

Delia pulled her closer. "That's because you care about him more than you're willing to admit. And because of that, you will be there for him. Just as he was there for you when it counted most."

Anne tossed the tissue onto the table among the others. "We've been through this before, Mother. He wasn't there when I needed him to be."

"That's because you've forgotten." She smiled. "When you decided to have a baby, I remember Jack saying that he felt as though he'd turned into a baby-making machine. You wore him out. But he never gave up, even when you wanted to."

"I realize that."

Delia wasn't certain she did. "When things didn't work

out with little Jacob, Jack was there to comfort you when the rest of us had no idea what to do or say."

She sensed Anne didn't want to think about—much less talk about—the baby born to a seventeen-year-old patient of Anne's with no job, no husband and no prospects. The precious little boy presented to Anne and Jack by the same young woman, only to be taken away three months later because the mother had a change of heart.

"And don't forget he spent every night with you following your hysterectomy," Delia added. "He made sure he brought Katherine to visit you every day, even though it was against the rules."

"I know, Mother."

"If you'll let go some of your resentment, Anne, you'll be able to recall all the times he supported you, not the late nights and missed events."

"But I can't let go of the fact he cheated on me," Anne said.

"Infidelity is a warning sign that something's not right with a marriage, honey. Besides, you were staying with me when it happened. For all intents and purposes, you and Jack weren't together."

Anne looked away. "It still hurt, Mother. Knowing he'd turned to someone else."

For years Delia had held on to a dirty little secret that she'd been too ashamed to tell her daughter. Now seemed an appropriate moment to bring out the information, if for no other reason than to illustrate no one was perfect. "Your father and I managed to get past infidelity issues in our marriage."

Anne's gaze snapped to Delia, her eyes saucer-wide. "Dad cheated on you?"

"Actually, no. I cheated on him."

"Mother, I'm not believing this."

"Believe it. You were five, and like Jack, your father was working wicked hours. We were living in Chicago then and you'd just started private kindergarten. At the time, I had no real hobbies and very little social life. I craved attention, and someone came along who could give that to me."

"Who was he?"

"A neighbor." A rugged, common man very unlike her husband. "He worked nights at a factory, so I would spend afternoons with him, before you came home from school. That lasted about two months before I ended it and told your father."

"And he forgave you?"

"Eventually. We had a rough patch for a few months, but at least the lines of communication were open. From that point forward, our marriage grew stronger. He became more attentive—I became better at expressing my needs. We never spoke of it again."

Anne mulled that over a moment before she said, "But your situation is different. Jack's the one who cheated, not me."

"And you're the one who shut him out."

Anne's mouth dropped opened a split second before the anger set in. "So you're saying his cheating was my fault."

"I'm saying that you were both at fault. You're too quick to hold on to resentment, and Jack's not one to express his feelings. The most important thing is that you try to forgive him now, even if you need more time to forget."

"You have to accept that our marriage is over, Mother. We can't go back to the way things were."

If only she could convince Anne to move forward. "Regardless, he still needs you now, and you've shown that you still care enough about what happens to him to help him recover. Are you willing to continue to make that effort?"

"I'm not sure I can after what happened today." Her eyes misted again. "I didn't think he could break my heart more than he already has."

Delia smoothed a damp strand of hair from Anne's cheek. "A heart that still loves is fragile, honey."

"I need to check on Jack, and you need to go home. It's getting late."

Yes, Delia definitely needed to get home…to Gabe. But she also needed to make certain her daughter was okay, or as okay as could be expected. "I could stay longer, if you'd like. We could have some coffee."

Anne shook her head. "I don't need caffeine. I need sleep."

"All right. If you're sure." Delia came to her feet and headed to the kitchen. "I have to use the phone to call my ride." For once, she'd wished she'd embraced technology and bought a cell phone.

Anne followed closely behind her. "I didn't realize you weren't in your own car."

There was quite a bit Anne didn't realize. "Someone dropped me off."

"Who?"

Delia snatched the phone from its charger and began to dial. "A friend."

"Ingrid?"

"No." When Gabe answered, Delia simply responded with, "I'm ready now," then hung up, something for which she would have to apologize later.

Leaning a hip against the counter, Anne stared her down. "What are you not telling me, Mother?"

Delia dismissively flipped a hand in her direction. "All right, if you must know. He happens to be a man."

Anne looked as though her mother had announced she'd befriended an alien. "Who is this man?"

Oh, someone I picked up in the local tavern. You know, the little bar down the street. I showed him my sagging cleavage and he followed me home like a Labrador retriever. "He's someone I met at the hospital."

"A doctor?"

"An attorney."

Anne's hand immediately landed on her throat as if she were choking. "Mother, do you know what Jack would think about—"

"I've already told him, dear. He was fine with it."

After grabbing a dishcloth from the sink, Anne wiped the cabinet with a vengeance. "Great. You told your ex-son-in-law before you told your own child."

"Have you considered that your reaction now is a good indication why I decided to wait?"

"I'm happy if you're happy, Mother."

"You're such a horrible liar, Anne."

"I'm not lying. I am a little concerned." Anne paused gripping the cloth. "I don't want you to get hurt."

Delia patted her cheek. "I'm a grown-up, Anne. And Gabe's a good man."

"Gabe, huh?"

"Yes, that's his name." She pointed behind her. "And I'm sure he's probably waiting for me."

"One more question, Mom."

Delia wasn't sure she could handle one more question. "Okay."

"Are you and this Gabe…" Anne's gaze slid away. "Are you and he—"

"Sleeping together?"

"Exactly."

"Do you think I'd really tell you if we were?"

"Probably not."

"Actually, the answer is no, we're not intimate." At least not for another few minutes or so.

Anne's shoulders relaxed. "Okay, then. I'll show you out."

When they reached the front door, Delia turned to Anne. "Are you okay, honey?"

"I'll be fine now. And I really appreciate you stopping by and putting up with me."

"That's what mothers are for."

Anne peered out the narrow window flanking the door. "Can I meet him?"

Delia wasn't in the mood for introductions. "Why don't we all have dinner soon."

"Just let me know where and when."

"I will." After Gabe pulled up to the curb, Delia opened

the door, then kissed Anne's cheek. "Try to concentrate enjoying your time off with your daughter and husband."

"Ex-husband, Mother."

As if Delia really had to be reminded. "You should go check on him now."

"And you should run along and have fun with your new friend."

That was exactly what Delia had planned, although getting naked with a man for the first time in years might not qualify as "fun."

A flash-fire heat rose to Delia's cheeks, sending her out the door and straight into a situation she wasn't certain she could see through. No. She would see it through. For this one night, she would forget that she was past her prime. Forget that Anne and Jack still had a long road ahead. And remember that she was still very much a woman who craved intimacy. Gabe would be her touch-stone, her respite from the loneliness.

When he heard Anne enter the room, Jack feigned sleep, although he'd slept most of the afternoon, mildly aware of Annie's presence as she'd sat in the chair next to the window, pretending to read a magazine. He knew why she'd been there and what she'd been doing—making sure he didn't do anything stupid. She'd watched over him like a guard dog, motivated by some sense of mis-placed obligation, when all he'd given her was a good scare and a whole lot of grief. Again.

The bathroom door closed, and only then did he open his eyes. He listened to the muffled sound of running water and realized she was taking her shower. He knew she would spend a good five minutes brushing and flossing, applying moisturizer to her face, lotion to her legs and arms. He knew she would be wearing one of her favorite cotton gowns, maybe even the one he'd given her on the last birthday they'd celebrated together.

For so many years, he'd taken her routine for granted. He'd missed the little details, the smell of her, the feel of her. The way she would kiss him good-night before fitting herself against his back, her arms around him.

The bathroom door opened, sending a stream of light across the bed and setting Annie in shadows. He remained very still and waited. Waited for her to oust him from their former bed and send him back to his prison.

When the mattress dipped behind him, Jack released the breath he didn't know he'd been holding. He listened to the sound of her respiration, longed to roll over and take her in his arms. But he knew better than to wish for something he couldn't have. Not now. Maybe not ever.

He heard her soft sigh, felt her arm slide around his waist. Then she took his hand in hers, the one that had failed him for the past few months.

With every ounce of strength he could muster, with a determination that had been absent since the stroke, he called on all his concentration and squeezed her hand, letting her know he was going to try harder—for her.

CHAPTER 11

Following a succession of annoying doorbell chimes, Anne peeked through the peephole to find a slip of a woman standing on the porch, her hair pulled back in a braid, a duffel slung over one slender shoulder. Anne had met most of Jack's therapists, but she didn't recognize this one. If in fact she was a therapist. Had it not been for the streak of gray in the lady's hair, Anne might have believed the woman was a member of a high-school drill team, selling candy for a fund-raiser.

After Anne opened the door, the stranger stuck out her hand and gave Anne a wrestler's shake. "I'm Shelly Garza from home health care, and you must be Mrs. Morgan."

The former Mrs. Morgan, she wanted to say, but settled for, "Call me Anne."

"Anne it is. Can I come in out of the rain now?"

"Sure." Anne stepped aside and, after she closed the door, faced the miniature therapist. "You haven't been here before, have you?"

Shelly slipped off her jacket, balled it up and crammed it into the bag still hanging on her arm. "Nope. I guess you could say I'm the last line of defense. Usually I get handed the worst of the worst, which is why I'm here. In fact, they would have sent me two weeks ago, but I've been on vacation."

Worst of the worst would be an adequate description of Jack, and if Shelly was all she claimed to be, Anne wished they had sent her sooner. "Are you P.T. or O.T.?"

"Mostly O.T., but I'm trained in both. I'm an over-achiever."

Thankfully the woman had that in common with Jack, or at least the Jack before the stroke. "Then you'll be heading the team from now on?" Anne asked.

"I'll be in charge of overseeing every aspect of Dr. Morgan's treatment. Since he's been pretty rough on most of the staff, I figure he might respond better to only one therapist."

Anne could only hope that would be the case. "Actually, Jack's made a bit more progress the past couple of weeks." While she'd gauged every move he made, watched him like a hawk, kept every pill out of his reach and prayed when he'd flatly refused the psychologist but promised never to pull a stunt like that again.

"Good for Dr. Morgan," Shelly said with a large dose of sarcasm. "In my opinion, he's not making enough progress. I plan to change that immediately."

Anne had the feeling that despite Shelly's small stature, she could be the right person for the job. "Follow me and I'll introduce you to him."

She walked the therapist through the house, making small talk along the way, none of which earned a response. Once they'd reached the den, Shelly entered without formality and approached Jack, who was stretched out on the hospital bed, watching some game show. "Dr. Morgan, my name is Shelly Garza. For the next few weeks, I'll be your therapist, your mother, your warden and your cheerleader. I won't be tolerating any excuses."

To avoid Jack's reaction, Anne leveled her gaze on the lengthy black braid traveling down Shelly's back.

Shelly set the duffel down and moved closer to the bed. "First of all, I'm going to call you Jack. Second, I have to know that you're willing to work. Otherwise I'm out of here and you're on your own."

Anne realized Shelly was nothing if not direct. And stern. Maybe Jack needed stern. After all, patient prodding had done little for him to this point.

Jack turned off the TV with the remote and draped his legs over the edge of the bed. "I'm working at it, but it's taking a damn long time to see any results."

Shelly braced her hands on her hips. "Tell me something, Jack. When you left med school, did you immediately walk into the O.R., grab up a rib spreader and tear into a pericardium?" She regarded Anne over her shoulder. "I was premed until I learned I held a certain disdain for doctors." She turned back to Jack. "Well, did you spring from the womb with a surplus of surgical skill?"

Anne noted the intimation of anger in Jack's expression, heard it in his voice when he said, "Hell, no."

"Then don't expect to recover overnight, especially since you're already behind." She checked her watch. "It's almost ten-thirty. When did you have your breakfast?"

"At eight."

"Fine. Do you like spaghetti?"

"He hates it," Anne offered.

"Jack, do like spaghetti?" Shelly asked again, letting Anne know she wasn't a part of the conversation.

"As long as it's Annie's spaghetti," he said.

After all these years, Anne had always believed he'd preferred steak over her spaghetti. "Really?"

He sent her a crooked smile. "Yeah. Really."

"Why didn't you tell me that, Jack? I would have made it for you."

He answered with a one-shoulder shrug.

"Well, now we all know Jack likes spaghetti," Shelly said. "Anne, make some for lunch. Jack and I are going to go to work. We should be done with this session by the time you're finished cooking."

Now that Anne had her marching orders, she left the room, feeling somewhat disturbed by Ms. Garza's gestapo tactics. But if they worked, more power to her. Anne only hoped Jack didn't demand Shelly leave before Anne had the water boiling and the sauce simmering.

He stared at the plate piled high with pasta, his muscles aching, his head reeling and his appetite all but absent. He had a good mind to tell his current taskmaster where she could shove the spaghetti. In fact, he had no idea why he'd even said he liked spaghetti, when it was his least favorite food. But with Annie sitting across from him, eyeing him expectantly, and aware that she'd gone to all the trouble of making him lunch, he decided to cooperate. He couldn't let her down again. Not after what he'd put her through two weeks ago.

"First of all, pick up your fork and try twirling the spaghetti around it," Shelly said. "You're not going to be graded, so I won't count off for screwups. I just want to see how well you manage."

When Jack snatched up his fork in his left hand, she wagged a finger at him. "No cheating. Use your right hand."

Damn her for making him do this. Damn all the pious therapists who thought they knew what was best for him. He didn't care if he ever used his right hand again, and they couldn't seem to grasp that concept any more than he could get a solid hold on the utensil.

Still Annie continued to study him, and for that reason alone, he transferred the fork to his right hand. His grip had improved, but his dexterity still sucked.

What the hell. If he ended up with most of the meal on the floor, maybe then Shelly Garza would leave him alone. He slowly wound the spaghetti around his fork, and watched the majority of it drop back into his plate.

"Try again," Shelly said. "You don't have to take a big bite. The trick is to work that wrist."

Annie stood and went to the stove, returned with her own plate of food, spiraled the spaghetti onto her fork, then tipped it until the pasta was hanging in strings. She lifted an eyebrow, smiled at Jack, then slurped a noodle into her mouth, and the sauce dripped down her chin and onto her pink T-shirt. He knew what she was up to—giving him permission to make a mess. So he did. He lifted his own fork and sucked the noodle into his mouth. Loudly.

Shelly glared at him, then turned her attention to Annie before pushing her chair from the table and slapping her palms on her thighs. "Okay. I can tell the two of you are into playing right now, and that's okay." She pointed at Annie. "I don't care if he ends up wearing most of it—just don't cut it up for him." She stood and asked, "Do you have any weights around here, Jack? As soon as I think you've gained enough strength, we're going to pump you up."

He regarded Annie. "Do I?"

She looked alarmed. "They're still in the garage. But isn't that a little radical?"

"I'm not going to make him bench-press a hundred pounds," Shelly said. "We'll start slowly, with two-pound hand weights, and go from there. Tomorrow, I'll begin weaning you off that walker, something that should've happened weeks ago."

Jack had to admit the prospect made him wary. The thing had become his crutch, his only insurance that he wouldn't fall on his ass. "Great. Anything else you want me to do? Maybe climb a ladder and change lightbulbs?"

Shelly didn't look at all amused; not that he cared. "It's a thought, but we'll save that for next week. I do want you eating as much as you can. I'll check with the nutrition-ist and come up with a better plan to put some weight on your body before you lose all your muscle mass. That means even more high-calorie foods and energy supplements." She turned back to Annie. "Make him milk shakes or brownies or something."

"I can do that," Annie said. "But I can't force him to eat."

Jack wished they'd stop talking as if he wasn't in the room. "I'll eat. But when I weigh three hundred pounds, it's on your head."

"Yeah, right." With that, Shelly picked up her bag, said goodbye and told them she'd be back tomorrow.

"She's pretty unorthodox," Annie said as soon as the therapist had left the room.

"She's a bitch. A sadist. She nearly killed me."

"She does have your best interest at heart, Jack. We all do. Look how far you've come with your speech therapy. You're not missing a beat with your words now. And your memory's coming back, too."

That wasn't always a blessing, and talking normally wouldn't help him operate again. Not to mention he still couldn't comprehend written text to any real degree—a secret he'd managed to keep from everyone, even though he figured he'd roused a few suspicions when he'd refused to read. "Score a few points for Jack. He's not stuttering like a moron anymore and he remembers what day it is now."

Annie's punishing stare could melt the silverware. "You promised me you'd be more cooperative, Jack."

He shoved his plate away and slumped in the chair like a whipped dog. "I've been trying, Annie." For her. Only for her and Katie. Not for himself.

Annie dabbed her chin with a napkin and tossed it

aside. "You did shock me with the spaghetti thing. If my memory serves me correctly, we swore off all pasta when we moved back from California."

Then it hit him, the reason he'd claimed he had a fondness for spaghetti. The meal symbolized good memories and good times. A point in their lives when they hadn't had a pot to piss in, but they'd had each other. All they'd needed back then. "You're right. You made it at least three times a week."

"Because it was cheap," she said. "And because I wasn't the best cook in the world."

Jack laughed, earning him a look of surprise from Annie. "Remember that time you tried to make that pesto sauce?"

She momentarily covered her face with her hands. "It was horrible. Not even close to being edible." She sighed. "But you ate it anyway."

Time for true confessions. "Actually, when you went to answer the phone for your weekly chat with Delia, I took it out back and fed it to the neighbor's dog."

"You didn't."

"I did. Luckily he survived."

She rested one elbow on the table and supported her cheek with her palm. "What was that dog's name? Skippy?"

"Scruffy. The owner's name was Skip."

"That's right. He was one weird guy."

"Yeah, he was. But what did you expect from a proctology intern?"

Annie smiled. "You brought home a bottle of wine that night of the pesto disaster."

"Yeah, a cheap bottle. We downed the whole thing. I

remember you being pretty damn drunk." He remembered a lot more than that.

Her smile faded into a frown. "I remember you weren't exactly sober, either."

"I wasn't so drunk that I don't remember that little striptease you did in the kitchen."

That sent Annie away from the table, plate in hand. She began to wash the remnants of her lunch into the sink, keeping her back to him. "I must have been really drunk, because I don't remember that at all."

She was either lying or she'd made a conscious effort to forget. He'd just have to jog her memory. "We didn't even make it into the bedroom. We got busy right there on the kitchen floor."

When she came back to the table to retrieve his plate, Jack caught her wrist. "We used to be damn good together, Annie. What happened to us?"

She sent him a regretful look before tugging out of his grasp. "We changed, Jack. We stopped talking, stopped making love. It happens to a lot of couples."

As far as Jack was concerned, they'd never been just any couple. They'd been in sync, completely committed to each other.

He wanted that back. He wanted her back. And that was probably way too much to want.

The doorbell rang at the same time the kitchen timer sounded to signal that the double-fudge cake was done. Katie climbed down from the stool and proclaimed, "Grandma's here!" with the exuberance she always displayed when Delia visited, though it hadn't been all that frequently the past month.

"Wait a minute, Katie," Anne called before her daughter bounded away. "Don't mention the surprise."

Katie pretended to zip her lips before rushing off to greet her grandmother.

After removing the pan from the oven, Anne flipped on the coffeemaker and retrieved three green ceramic mugs from the cup tree. She could hear the commentary for a televised baseball game filtering in from the den, where Jack waited for her to summon him. Tonight was somewhat of a special occasion, not a birthday or holiday but significant all the same. An accomplishment a very long time in coming.

"Something smells good in here."

Anne turned from the counter to find her mother and Katie walking into the kitchen, hand in hand. She crossed the room and gave Delia a solid hug. "I'm really glad to see you, Mom."

Delia smiled. "And I'm glad to see my girls, too. I should apologize for being so scarce lately. We've lost a few volunteers, so I've been doing extra duty."

Anne surmised that was only a convenient cover for what her mother had really been doing in her spare time— the new man, whom they had yet to meet. "Katie, why don't you visit with your dad for ten minutes or so, until the cake cools? We'll have our dessert in the living room."

Katie said, "Okay, Mama," followed by a wink that she didn't bother to hide.

"What's going on, Anne?" Delia asked as she climbed onto a bar stool.

Anne withdrew four dessert plates from the cabinet—the good china with the tea-rose pattern, which she'd received during her wedding showers. "Nothing's going on, Mother. We're about to have dessert and a nice visit. That's all."

When Anne faced Delia again, she immediately noticed her mother was staring off into space, her smile wistful. "Maybe I should ask what's going on with you."

Delia appeared taken aback by the query. "I don't know what you mean."

"You're practically glowing. I haven't seen you this happy since they appointed you president of the library board."

Delia toyed with the emerald broach pinned on the lapel of her white blazer, the one Bryce had given her on their thirtieth anniversary. "I am happy, Anne. I didn't know I could be this happy."

"Does this have to do with your friend Gabe?"

"As a matter of fact, it does."

Anne sat on the stool beside her, posing a question she'd considered asking for a while now, yet fearing the answer. "Is it serious between you two?"

"I suppose you could say that. We've been spending quite a lot of time together." Delia sighed like a smitten schoolgirl. "I truly feel alive for the first time in years. I've also discovered that I still have certain needs and desires, if you catch my drift."

Anne had caught it, all right, and she wanted to throw it back. She held up her hands to ward off any forthcoming revelations. "Okay, Mom, that's probably too much information."

"What's wrong, Anne? Did you think an old widow like me wouldn't be interested in sex?"

"I'm not sure I want to hear this right now." Or ever, for that matter.

Delia straightened her shoulders and lifted her chin. "Good grief, Anne. I haven't done anything illegal—unless they've changed the laws and made having an orgasm at my age a felony."

"Mother, please—"

"It's an experience to be savored. And with no worries about birth control, I'm completely enjoying it."

Anne was thankful she hadn't poured the coffee yet; otherwise she probably would have anointed the ceramic floor tile. "I'm glad you're enjoying yourself, Mother. Now, can we change the subject?"

Delia narrowed her eyes, no doubt preparing to take her best shot. "You're jealous."

Of all the crazy things for her mother to assume. "I am not."

"Yes, you are. And you should be. You could use a good roll now and then, too."

Since when did her mother refer to lovemaking as a *roll*? Since she'd started sleeping with a mystery man; that was when. "Sure, Mom. I have so many prospects lining up at my door I'm surprised you managed to get into the driveway."

"No need for the sarcasm, Elizabeth Anne. Besides, you have one man in your house. A very virile, extremely handsome man who isn't a stranger."

"You're suggesting I have sex with Jack?" she whispered.

"It's not like you haven't done it with him before."

Of all the nerve… "I'm going to do no such thing. And even if I did want to, I'm not sure that he could."

Delia tapped her chin with one neatly manicured nail. "I didn't realize that the stroke might have affected him in that way. Have you asked him about it? Better still, have you perhaps tried to get some sort of reaction out of him? Or have you forgotten how to do that?"

Anne slid off the stool and returned to the coffeemaker. "I have no intention of doing any such thing." No intention of asking Jack or trying to find out if he was still functioning sexually, even though she certainly hadn't forgotten how to manage that. She remembered it quite well, thank you very much.

"It's only a suggestion, dear heart. You're lonely—he's lonely. You're living together—"

"And we're divorced." Anne grabbed a knife from the block and took out her frustration on the cake. "Go have a seat in the living room. I'll bring the cake and coffee."

"Make plenty of coffee. I want to be fully awake when I leave, since Gabe's waiting for me at the house."

Anne didn't bother to comment or to turn around until she heard footsteps heading down the corridor toward the living room. Her mother had unnerved her so badly that twice she'd almost dropped pieces of cake on the counter before setting them safely on the plates. She pulled two serving trays from the bottom cabinet, one for the cake and another for the coffee, and poured Katie a glass of milk.

After she had everything in place, she called to her daughter. "Come here a minute, sweetie. I could use your help."

Katie rushed into the room. "Is it time for the surprise?" she asked, twirling a strand of hair 'round and 'round her finger.

"Not yet. I need you to carry the tray with the cake. Can you manage that?"

She gave Anne a get-real look. "I'm not a baby, Mother."

Anne ruffled her golden hair. "Of course you're not. Now, let's take this to the living room and then you can get your dad."

She handed Katie the cake tray, picked up the one with the coffee and milk, and followed Katie down the hall. Once in the living room, they found Delia seated on the sofa, speaking softly to someone on her newly purchased cell phone, exhibiting that same dreamy expression no doubt inspired by the new man in her life. Anne realized how odd that seemed, her mother actually dating someone. Sleeping with someone, for heaven's sake.

When Delia caught sight of her daughter and granddaughter, she said a quick goodbye, closed the phone and shoved it in her purse, as if she'd been caught with contraband. "That looks wonderful, my sweet girls."

Katie carefully slipped the cake tray onto the coffee table, then turned to Anne. "Can I go get Daddy now?"

"Yes, you can go get Daddy," Anne said as she set the coffee tray down and sat next to her mother on the sofa.

Anne went about the business of doctoring her coffee with too much sugar, until she simply couldn't stand the suspense any longer. "Was that the lawyer?"

"Why no, honey. That was the postman. I'm sleeping with him, too."

Oh, but dear Delia was determined to shake her up tonight. "That isn't funny, Mother."

"Lighten up, Anne. All that sexual frustration has you much too tense."

Ignoring the comment, Anne handed her mother a cup of coffee, black, as she'd always taken it. "Not another word, or I'll phone Nellie and tell her you're having sex with the hospital's attorney."

"You wouldn't dare."

"Watch me."

The sounds of muffled voices and shuffling footsteps effectively halted the conversation. When Jack entered the room, Anne regarded her mother to gauge her reaction, and an obvious reaction it was. Delia's mouth dropped open momentarily before it formed a smile. "Oh, my sweet boy, I can't believe it!"

With Katie serving as his escort, Jack slowly walked into the room, his right leg still dragging as he used only a cane for support.

"Surprise, Grandma!" Katie said when she guided Jack to the chair across from the sofa. "Daddy can walk almost all by himself."

"He sure can, honey," Delia said. "You look absolutely wonderful, Jack. You're hair's growing back and you've even put on some weight."

He put the cane aside and settled back in the chair. "I'm getting there."

"He's working very hard," Anne added. "He has a new therapist, who's done wonders for him."

"She's a mean heifer," Katie said as she handed Jack a

plate, then sat on the floor next to his feet, her own plate balanced precariously in her lap.

"Katie, that's not nice," Anne scolded, although she knew that her daughter hadn't come upon that phrase all by herself. "Shelly's helping your father."

"Shelly's trying to do in her father," Jack said.

Delia rose and set a cup of coffee on the end table next to Jack before returning to the sofa. "As long as it's working, honey, then I'm certain you're tough enough to handle it."

"Cake looks good, Annie." Jack cut a large bite and shoved it into his mouth.

"And he's using his right hand," Delia said. "What a wonderful, wonderful surprise."

As they ate their dessert and drank their coffee, the conversation—thanks to Delia—soon turned to the infamous long weekend Jack and Anne had spent with her parents on South Padre Island. Of course Delia couldn't resist telling Katie about how Anne's face had become a nice shade of green on the deep-sea fishing excursion, or how she'd gotten so sunburned Jack had started calling her Scarlett. Fortunately she hadn't mentioned catching them together in the shower. But Anne didn't care that she'd become the brunt of all the jokes, then or now. She enjoyed the familiar banter, the reminders of better times when they'd functioned as a real family, not perfect by any means but still a loving unit.

Almost two hours of nonstop conversation passed before the reality of a school night set in. "Katie, it's getting late," Anne said. "You need to get ready for bed."

Katie stuck out her bottom lip in a pout. "Do I have to?"

"Yeah, you have to, kiddo," Jack said.

Katie stood and frowned. "I still have to read to someone."

Delia placed her mug on the table. "You can read to me, honey."

Anne came to her feet. "I'll do it, Mother. I wouldn't want you to keep your friend waiting any longer."

"I'll do it, Annie."

They all leveled their attention on Jack simultaneously, yet no one spoke until Katie asked, "Do you want me to bring my book down here, Daddy?"

"No." He grabbed the cane and pulled himself up from the chair. "I'm going to go up the stairs."

Anne ran head-on into a wall of fear. "Are you sure, Jack? You haven't tried the stairs yet. And you're still off balance every now and then."

"I can do it," he said with conviction. "Katie, you wait for me at the top, because it'll take me a while."

"Do you need my help?" Anne asked.

"No."

She saw no sense in offering more assistance or issuing another protest, even if a possible disaster waited in the wings.

Both Anne and Delia followed him to the bottom of the staircase, while Katie hurried to the top and stopped at the landing. With his left hand braced on the banister, his right clutching the cane, carefully Jack managed the first step.

"You can do it, Daddy," Katie called from above him. "I know you can."

"You're doing great, Jack," Delia said as he took the second step.

Anne could only stand silently by, watching and praying. And remembering...

"Annie, come here quick."

She imagined a disaster, not a milestone. *"What is it?"*

"Look what she can do. Come to Daddy, Katie...." A baby step, then two...

"Come to me, Daddy. You're not going to fall."

One more stair. Slowly. Slowly.

"Come on, pumpkin. Daddy won't let you fall...." And he didn't. He never had.

A tight knot formed in Anne's throat as she silently cheered Jack on, wanting desperately to walk behind him in case he did fall, yet knowing that this was the next step in his recovery. A major step toward Jack's return to normal. Exactly what she'd been hoping for. Then why did she suddenly feel so melancholy?

When he finally reached the landing, Katie squealed, Delia applauded and Anne exhaled.

"I can't believe he did it, Mom."

"I can," Delia said. "He's a remarkable man."

Anne couldn't agree more.

The effort of scaling the stairs should have made him dog-tired, but a strong sense of euphoria hit him the minute he stretched out on his daughter's white canopy bed, Katie beside him, reading to him like a pro. That euphoria dissolved, though, when Katie paused and pointed to one word. "What's that, Daddy?"

Trouble was, he didn't know. He recognized the letters, but the word looked foreign. "Why don't you try to sound it out."

"If you tell me what it is, I'll remember. My teacher says she only has to tell me something once and I remember."

Jack couldn't remember how letters should be lined up to make sense. He'd mastered the intricacies of a heart, and now he couldn't comprehend a second-grade reader. He saw no way to remedy the situation except to tell Katie the truth, pride be damned. "Since I've been sick, I'm having some trouble reading."

She looked crestfallen, as if her hero had lost his magical ability to fly. "You forgot how to read?"

"I didn't really forget. My brain doesn't let my eyes see the words right."

She took his hand into hers and laid it on the book in her lap. "That's okay, Daddy. I'll teach you."

He didn't know what he'd done to deserve his daughter. "You'd do that for your old dad?"

She nodded and smiled. "Try this sentence first," she said. "It's easy."

"A grof—"

"Frog, Daddy."

He stumbled on the next word, as well, yet Katie patiently coaxed him until he finally got it right. She rooted him on to success, laughed when he mistook "boy" for "yob," although she thought that was a better word to describe some kid named Jason who'd tried to kiss her. Jack imagined a future full of boys pursuing his little girl, and although he didn't like to think about it, he knew it was inevitable. Particularly if she grew into the woman her mother had always been. And still was.

It took ten minutes for Jack to read three complete sentences, and two minutes for him to realize how blessed he was to be in the presence of his daughter, who passed out no judgment, only praise.

And there, in Katie's world filled with stuffed animals and soft innocence, the child became the teacher; the surgeon, the pupil.

Anne abruptly sat up in bed, thrust from sleep by the sound of a shout. Or maybe it had been a groan. She knew only that it had originated from the monitor on the nightstand, and that Jack could very well be in trouble.

She bolted from the bed and sprinted through the house. When she made it to the den, the stream of light from the bathroom spilled over the bed, allowing her to view Jack seated on the edge of the mattress, head in hands.

She crossed the room and dropped beside him. "Are you okay?"

"I had a nightmare." He kept his head lowered and rubbed his palms over his face, as if trying to erase the images. "I couldn't move, but I felt like I was still awake. I'm okay now."

His less-than-confident tone led Anne to believe he wasn't okay. "It could be some sort of sleep paralysis. Or you could be too tired to sleep well. You did quite a bit today, with the two therapy sessions and Mother's visit. And then the stairs and helping Katie with her homework. How did that go, anyway?"

"She's one smart kid. She could probably teach me a thing or two."

Anne didn't like the dejection in his tone. "Do you want me to stay for a while? Just until you fall asleep?"

He finally looked at her. "You don't have to do that."

"I don't mind." And she honestly didn't. She wouldn't be able to rest unless she was assured he was all right. "Now, lie down and make some room for me."

After Jack stretched out on his side, Anne curled up in the place that he'd made for her and faced the door, his chest against her back. Only then did she acknowledge how little space separated them. "I didn't realize this bed was so narrow."

"Yeah. Now I know why we've never slept in a twin bed together."

"Oh, yes, we have. At Mom and Dad's when we moved back from California. Before we found the house."

"I remember now. In your old room. You nearly beat me to death."

She reached back and playfully slapped at his arm. "I did not."

"Yeah, you did. You stole all the covers and half the time you had your feet all over me."

He'd had his hands all over her many a night. "You could have slept in the other twin bed."

"The sex was too great to do that."

He could have said her mother's blueberry muffins had been great, the proximity to the hospital had been great. Did he have to mention sex? "Really? I don't recall."

"Liar."

"Okay. I guess it was pretty good."

"Only pretty good?"

It had been exceptional—something she didn't want to consider right now. "Speaking of sex, my mother told me tonight she's having it with her new boyfriend."

"Good for her."

"This is my mother we're talking about, Jack. I don't like to think about her having an intimate relationship."

"With someone other than your father, you mean."

"No. Just the whole concept of my mother having sex with anyone makes me really uncomfortable."

"At least someone's getting some action."

Anne wasn't sure if that was a proposition, and even if it was, she didn't dare answer it.

"My arm's going numb, Annie."

Alarmed, she lifted her head from the pillow they shared and looked back at him. "What do you mean?"

"I mean, it's crammed against your back and it's going to sleep."

She settled onto the pillow. "You should know better than to say something like that to a nurse."

"Sorry. I didn't mean to scare you."

"Apology accepted." In a fit of compassion, she tugged his arm forward and draped it over her hip. "Better?"

"Yeah. Much better."

Maybe for him, but not for her. She felt oddly nervous, maybe even excited in some bizarre way. She debated getting up and shutting off the bathroom light so she didn't have to look at his hand, which rested precariously close to her lower abdomen. But that wouldn't matter. She would still know it was there. She would still wonder what he would do if she inched her bottom closer to him until they were in full contact. Wondered whether he would turn away if she rolled to face him. Whether he would even be able to respond normally to any overture she might make.

This was all her mother's fault, planting ideas about sex in her head. Insane ideas about taking up with Jack where they'd left off, when they'd still made love regularly and their problems had been only minimal.

Anne decided then and there that being in bed with her past was a bad place to be, particularly when she recalled how good it once was. How good it had been for many years.

Apparently going so long without a man's touch had impaired her judgment. She vowed to ignore the memories, ignore Jack. But every move he made, even the slightest shift of his weight, unearthed the desire for him that she'd worked two years to destroy.

Silly, silly Anne, wanting something that would provide only a temporary escape from the reasons you're no longer married.

She should get up immediately and go back to her room, before she did something really stupid. But when she heard the sound of Jack's steady breathing and knew he slept, she experienced relief and, sadly, disappointment. Still, she saw no reason to leave right now. After all, she planned to be gone before dawn, because Jack and morning had once proved to be a lethal combination.

1994

When Jack tore back the shower curtain, Anne dropped the bar of soap on the tile floor, narrowly missing her big toe. "What are you doing?"

He stepped into the tub without hesitation, turned her around and claimed the spot beneath the spray. "I'm taking a shower with you."

She yanked the curtain closed. "You're naked." Which would top the list of the lamest things she'd ever said.

He snatched the soap from the floor and handed it to her. "During the five years we've been married, have you ever known me to bathe fully clothed?"

No, and it also happened to be morning; therefore she highly doubted he had only bathing in mind. "All you intend to do is shower?"

He pulled her against him and gave her substantial proof of his intent. "What do you think?"

"I think my mother and father—"

"Aren't an issue. Your dad went fishing before dawn, and your mother's still asleep."

"She won't be for long."

"Hey, it was your idea to go on this vacation with them. A free vacation, I might add, which is all we can afford at the moment. Besides, I can't practice getting you pregnant if you won't let me near you."

She rolled her eyes. "You've got to be kidding, Jack. Lately we've been acting like a couple of teenagers over-dosed on hormones, and in my parents' house, no less."

"Look at it this way, Annie. There may come a time when I'm too old to do this kind of thing, and I don't want to regret that I didn't grab the opportunities while I had them."

He did have a point, in every sense of the word. "What if my mother hears us?"

"Delia already knows what's going on with us. Last week she stopped me before I left for the hospital and asked if I could get you to be a little quieter."

Anne dropped the soap again, this time grazing her toe. "She did not."

"Oh, yeah, she did. I told her I had no control over your habit of making a lot of noise during sex. Then she told me she meant when you got ready for work in the morning."

Heat traveled up Anne's neck to her face. "I hope she hasn't discussed this with my father."

Jack raked one hand through his damp hair. "Come to think of it, Bryce did look at me kind of strangely in the O.R. a few days ago when I mentioned how much I appreciated them letting us use the extra bedroom until we found a place of our own."

Anne didn't even want to imagine what her father might be thinking—or her mother, for that matter. "That's all the more reason we shouldn't be doing this."

He slid his palms down her back and up again. "That's all the more reason we should. It's kind of wicked."

And she was about to dance with the devil himself. Not that Anne was in much of a mood to complain about it. Since their return from California, Jack had been extremely attentive. And he was definitely paying quite a bit of attention to her now.

She had to admit, making love in her parents' condo and in their house was an exciting taboo. The risk of discovery fueled that excitement, which was perfectly okay with her as long as—

"Anne, dear, do you mind if I use your sunscreen? I can't seem to locate mine."

Anne slapped her palm over Jack's mouth. She should flog him with a wet towel for not locking the door. "Sure, Mom. Take it with you. I have another bottle."

"Thank you, honey. I'll see you at the beach. Oh, and good morning, Jack...."

CHAPTER 12

"It's morning, Mommy."

Anne's eyes shot open at the sound of Katie's voice. *Mortified* would best describe her feelings when she noticed her daughter standing at the door, wearing her favorite pink pajamas, looking extremely baffled.

She sat up in a rush, as if the bedsprings had exploded beneath her. "What time is it, sweetie?"

Katie twirled a lock of hair around her finger. "Almost eight. I'm going to be late for school. How come you didn't wake me up?"

Because Anne had inadvertently fallen asleep in Jack's arms. "I forgot to set the alarm." She climbed off the bed and stood. "Get dressed and I'll meet you in the kitchen."

Katie brought out the smile she reserved for Jack. "Hi, Daddy."

Anne glanced back to see Jack still on the bed on his side, bent elbow and fist supporting his jaw. "Morning, pumpkin. Did you sleep okay?"

"Uh–huh. The doorbell woke me up, so I let Shelly in."

Oh, great. Just what Anne needed, the therapist making huge assumptions. "Where is Shelly, Katie?"

"In the kitchen. Bye, Mommy and Daddy." Katie grinned before rushing away.

Anne walked right out the door behind her without affording Jack a second look. For some reason she felt as though she had done something naughty, when in fact the only thing naughty had been her thoughts.

She passed through the kitchen, where Shelly was manning the coffeemaker. "I'll be back in a minute," Anne called before heading into the bedroom. She stripped out of her gown and slipped on an oversize T-shirt, knit shorts and a hideous pair of white flip–flops. After brushing her teeth and running a comb through her hair, she returned to the kitchen, praying she didn't have to answer any questions about why she'd been in bed with her ex-husband.

"I overslept," she told Shelly, who handed her a cup of coffee.

"I figured that much when Katie answered the door."

Anne went for a packet of artificial sweetener and tore it open. "Jack's probably in the shower. He should be out in a few minutes."

"Just like every morning," Shelly said.

"Right." Anne stirred her coffee and immediately flipped the spoon onto the floor. After muttering an apology, she picked it up and tossed it into the sink.

"Are you okay, Anne?"

"I'm a little tired. Jack had a nightmare last night so I ended up sleeping with him. I mean, actually sleeping, not anything else."

Shelly smiled, a sly one. "Hey, what you and Jack do is none of my business. Although it would be a positive if he's not experiencing any erectile dysfunction."

"I really wouldn't know. You'd have to ask him."

"I will."

"You will?"

"The primary brain tends to work better when the secondary brain is also functioning."

Anne couldn't stifle a laugh. "An indication good blood flow has been established."

Shelly returned her smile. "You betcha." The therapist's expression grew solemn. "Katie told me she's been teaching Jack to read."

That was more shocking than getting caught in bed with Jack. "I beg your pardon?"

"Last night, when he helped with her homework, he told her he was having problems reading. He probably has acquired dyslexia. That explains why he's been so resistant to work on anything that involves the written word."

Anne couldn't believe that he'd been in the house for weeks and hadn't informed her. "I had no idea. But then, Jack's got a lot of pride." She wondered when the suffering would end for him, when this stroke would stop wreaking havoc. "Is there a chance he'll recover his reading ability completely?"

"The dyslexia could very well resolve on its own with

some help," Shelly said. "I think having Katie assist him is a great idea. Children aren't prone to pass judgment, plus it gives Katie the opportunity to be proactive in her father's recovery. And then there's that special bond between fathers and daughters. I have two girls of my own, both teenagers, and they prefer their dad to me. Of course, he's a pushover when it comes to them."

Anne couldn't deny that Katie had always been a daddy's girl. "He made it all the way up the stairs by himself to help Katie with her homework."

"He's been practicing when you've been out," Shelly said. "He wanted to prove that's he trying to get better."

He had definitely proved that last night. "Since he's taking care of all his personal needs now and he seems to be getting stronger, how long before he's able to live independently?"

Shelly seemed troubled by the query. "Physically, he could probably manage it now. Emotionally, that's a tough call. He still needs your support in that regard. Are you considering asking him to leave?"

"That's not what I meant." Anne's declaration came out a little more forcefully than she'd intended. She tempered her tone and added, "I only want to make sure he'll be okay when I go back to work."

"I'm sure he'll be fine."

Katie entered the room like a house afire, backpack in place, her hair piled into a lopsided ponytail. "We have to go now, or I'm going to be really late."

"Get a juice box to take with you." Anne walked to the pantry, retrieved a breakfast bar and tossed it to Katie, who grabbed Anne's hand and practically dragged her to the door, barely allowing her time to snatch up her purse and keys from the table in the foyer.

Once they were settled into the car, Katie said matter-of-factly, "Moms and Dads are supposed to sleep together, right?"

Not divorced moms and dads—something Anne didn't care to discuss with her daughter right now. "Put on your seat belt so we can go."

Perhaps she wasn't being totally fair to her child by not responding. Because of her lack of denial, she might even be providing Katie with false hope, leading her to believe that Jack would be a permanent part of their lives from this point forward. Living in the same house, waking up together every morning as a family.

That wasn't in the cards. But the future seemed as hazy as the currently overcast skies, and Anne could only think about the here and now.

When Jack heard the patio door slide open that evening, he kept his attention trained on the low hedge-row lining the deck. It was good to be outside. Anywhere but in the house—his prison.

He heard the scrape of a lawn chair and glanced to his right to see Annie taking a seat beside him. She stretched her legs and laced her hands together on her abdomen. "I wish you'd let someone know when you're going to disappear. I searched everywhere for you."

No doubt the master bathroom was first on her list. "Sorry. I had cabin fever."

"I understand. But I was worried."

"You don't have to be. I'm okay."

When Annie remained silent, Jack assumed she was content to just listen to the night sounds and appreciate the warm spring weather, as he had for the past half hour. But when he afforded her another quick look, he could tell she was troubled about something. "What's wrong, Annie?"

"You should have told me about the dyslexia. I hated hearing it from Shelly."

"I was hoping it would go away on its own before anyone found out."

"But you told Katie."

Jack couldn't ignore the hurt in her voice. "Not because I wanted to. I had to explain why I couldn't help her with her reading."

"I'm glad you're letting her help. Knowing she can do something for you gives her a sense of accomplishment."

If Annie only realized how hard that was. Letting down his guard, letting his child know that he wasn't the father he used to be. "She's a special kid."

"She's just like you."

He shook his head. "Not in the least. She's you in a smaller package."

"If you say so." Annie tipped her face up and surveyed the stars. "It's a nice night. I'll have the service remove the pool cover in a week or two, when it's warmer. Swimming might be good therapy for you."

If he could figure out how to kick with only one functioning leg. "I haven't been swimming since I moved out." The memory arrived as sharp as jagged glass, and he wanted to share it. Whether she wanted to hear it remained to be seen. "I remember when we had a fight one night and I came out here to swim a few laps to work off some steam."

Jack expected her not to acknowledge the recollection, but she surprised him by saying, "And I came out here to continue the argument. You pulled me into the pool. I still had on my work clothes."

"But not for long."

She started to smile, but it faded. "Don't you have a pool at your apartment?"

Annie's avoidance at its finest. "Yeah, there's a pool. And too many people using it at once."

"Lots of bikini-clad coeds, I'm sure."

"I haven't noticed."

"That's a good one, Jack."

In reality, he hadn't. In fact, he hadn't even bothered to visit the damn apartment pool. "Dinner was great tonight."

"Thanks. I'm glad you're eating more."

"I'm glad you decided not to fix spaghetti every night."

She laughed softly—music to Jack's ears. "Your hair's really beginning to grow," she said.

He streaked a hand over his scalp. "My hair's almost all gray."

"It looks nice."

She looked nice, even in the ragged pair of cutoff sweats that he would have thought she'd thrown out by now. "Where's Katie?"

"She's at Chelsea's birthday party. They're supposed to bring her home around nine."

At one point, before their final goodbye, before the

divorce, having Katie out of the house would mean having their own party. That seemed like a long time ago to Jack. Two years *was* a long time when you missed someone as much as he'd missed his wife. He still missed her, even though she was rarely far away from him these days. At least in a physical sense. "The days pass way too fast, Annie. Before we know it, Katie will be in college."

"Let's not go there. I'm having enough trouble accepting she's in primary school."

Jack was having trouble staying grounded with Annie so close, but still so far away in many respects. Last night he'd pretended to sleep, but he'd stayed awake for hours, remembering the times they'd made love. God, had he remembered, even if his body hadn't followed his mind's lead.

Annie leaned forward and pressed a palm against her lower spine. "My back is killing me."

With every move she made, she was killing him. "Did you lift something?"

"No. It's that horrible hospital bed. The floor would have been more comfortable. How have you managed to sleep on it every night?"

In fits and starts. When bad dreams didn't wake him. When thoughts of what might have been didn't haunt him. "I'm getting used to it."

She stretched her arms above her head and then relaxed against the chair. "You know, I've been thinking. We could return the bed to the medical supply company. You could stay in our old bed and I could sleep in the guest room upstairs."

Our old bed just about said it all. "I don't want to kick

you out of your room, Annie." He wanted to be there with her, even if only to hold her.

"It would be a temporary situation," she said.

Until he moved back to his own place. That went without saying. "Whatever you prefer."

"What do you want, Jack?"

He wanted to kiss her. He wanted to know if, given the chance, he could feel something again. Anything. "It's a big bed. We could sleep in it together. I'm not going to jump you in the middle of the night."

Her discomfort showed in her inability to look at him. "I'm going to have a beer. Do you care for one?"

A beer might numb him, and right now, numb sounded good. "Yeah, I'll have one. But when did you stop drinking wine?"

"When I started drinking beer."

After she headed into the house, Jack decided the backyard had lost its appeal. He grabbed his cane, straddled the lounger and tried to stand, but soon realized that sitting down was a lot easier than getting up. After two attempts, he managed to come to his feet without falling on the wooden deck.

He pulled open the door and found Annie standing at the kitchen counter, flipping the top off his favorite lager. She still looked incredible, even though he knew she'd point out the lines around her eyes, the effects of gravity on her body, none of which Jack had noticed at all. As far as he was concerned, she was the same Annie Cooper who'd driven him to distraction more than once. She was doing it now. And he wanted to do something about it.

Bent on taking a chance, he hobbled across the room, propped the cane against the cabinet and positioned his palms loosely on her hips.

"Did you get tired of being outside?" she asked without turning around.

He pressed his face against her hair and recognized the scent of the same shampoo she'd used for years. "I'm tired of being alone, Annie."

She uncapped the other bottle of beer, set the opener aside, but still didn't face him. "I know what you mean, Jack. But sometimes you're alone even when you're with someone."

He slid his hands up her waist. "You asked me a minute ago what I wanted. I want you to really look at me for a change. Look at me like I'm a man, not some freak who needs pity."

Slowly she turned and leaned back on bent elbows, putting some distance between them. "I don't feel sorry for you, Jack. I'm just sorry that this happened to you. I know you believe that I think you somehow deserved it, but you're wrong."

"Is it wrong that I want to kiss you right now?"

She kept her gaze connected with his, but he could tell she fought looking away. "That would be wrong on so many different levels I couldn't even name them all."

He reached around her, grabbed the bottle of beer and downed a swig before placing the bottle back on the counter. "Are you afraid you're not going to like it if I kiss you? Or are you more afraid you will?"

Exactly what Anne feared—that she would like it and

she'd want more than only a kiss. Yet when he continued to look at her the way he always had when he wanted her, she became that foolish young woman who would do anything for him. Accept anything he was willing to give her.

He leaned closer, leaned into her, trapping her against the counter. As if they'd developed a will of their own, her arms went around his neck, an open invitation for Jack to have his way. And he did, resting his lips lightly against hers before he settled there.

All the old feelings rushed in on her then, those emotions that she hadn't been able to deny since the day she'd met him. She was vaguely aware of the taste of beer on his tongue, but more aware of her own reaction. She could go on this way indefinitely, kissing Jack and believing that if she kept her eyes closed, kept her heart shielded, she could see this for what it was—plain and simple need. Yet there was nothing simple about it.

Anne finally managed to wrest herself away and lowered her head. She didn't understand why she was crying now, why she had even allowed this.

"God, I'm sorry, Annie," he said as he lifted her face with one hand. "Making you cry was the last thing I wanted."

"We can't do this, Jack. I can't do this." She swiped a palm over her damp cheeks to rid them of the tears, wishing she could rid herself that quickly of the remnants of feelings that she'd tried so hard to ignore. "I understand your need to prove you're still a man, but that doesn't make it any easier on me."

He tipped her chin up, forcing her to look at him. "I'm

only trying to prove one thing. We still have feelings for each other, and if you deny this, then you're lying to yourself."

The front door slamming sent Anne away from Jack. She sat at the dinette, finger-combed her hair and attempted to appear casual. When Katie walked into the kitchen and frowned, Anne realized she hadn't fooled her daughter in the least.

"How was the party, sweetie?"

Katie came to Anne's side and dropped a bag full of favors onto the table. "It was okay. I didn't like the pizza."

Anne gently laid a hand on her shoulder. "I'm sorry. Do you want me to fix you a snack before you get ready for bed?"

"I'm not hungry." Katie brought her attention to Jack, who still had his back against the counter, arms folded across his chest. "Were you and Daddy fighting?"

"We were having a talk." Sharing a kiss. An unwise kiss. She turned Katie around and patted her on her bottom. "Now, scoot upstairs and get your bath."

"Are you going to read with me, Daddy?" she asked.

"Sure, pumpkin," he said. "I'll be up in a minute."

"Okay." Katie headed off, but not before giving them a questioning look, indicating that her concerns were still alive and well.

Jack grasped his cane and inched toward Anne with slow, stalking steps. "This isn't over, Annie." He stood behind her while she studied the wood grain in the table as if she'd never noticed it.

When he slid his palm down her arm, then brushed a

kiss across her cheek, her defenses went on high alert. "Don't, Jack."

"Don't what, Annie? Kiss you again? I'm not going to—at least, not now. But I can't ignore what happened, and neither can you."

Unfortunately he was right. "We'll talk about it later."

"Fine. What bed do you want me to sleep in?"

"Mine. I meant, ours." Her subconscious was apparently bent on sabotage. "Sleep in the master bedroom, and I'll go upstairs."

"You know, there's another solution."

Considering his wily grin, Anne wasn't sure she welcomed his solution. "What would that be?"

"I could get the chain saw and split the bed down the middle. Or you could sleep on the mattress and I could sleep on the box spring. I'm pretty good at taking beds apart."

The onset of silence and Jack's somber expression told Anne he had dredged up another memory. He confirmed her conjecture when he asked, "Do you ever think about him, Annie?"

She closed her eyes for a moment before leveling her gaze on him again. "Every now and then, I do. Sometimes I even wonder…"

"What he looks like now. If he's okay." He rubbed a hand over his nape and sighed. "So do I. And that's the one thing I've always hated—that I couldn't protect you from that loss."

She rested her palm on his arm. "It wasn't your fault, Jack. It wasn't anyone's fault."

1997

Since they'd returned Jacob to his birth mother two days earlier, Anne had spent most of the time mourning the loss, despising the unfairness of it all. She hadn't gone back to work. She'd only briefly left the bedroom. And Jack had barely left her side, even though she believed he hadn't felt the pain as deeply as she had. This could have happened at any time, he'd told her. Maybe even a year from now, which would have been much worse than three months, he'd said. Typical physician's logic. But he had been there to hold her, to dry her tears, to serve as her touchstone since the teenage mother named Liza had changed her mind and re-claimed her child.

Tonight when Anne reached for Jack and found only an empty space beside her, she dragged herself from the bed to seek him out. When she saw the light filtering into the darkened hallway, she recognized that he had ventured to the room that she'd been avoiding—a pale blue nursery decorated with teddy bears in baseball uniforms. The place that now signified shattered dreams.

She paused in the open door to find him standing in front of the spindled crib set lengthwise against the opposite wall near the window, his back to her, arms wide, hands braced on the top railing. An open toolbox rested at his feet, a few screwdrivers and wrenches scattered about on the floor nearby, and next to the toolbox, a cardboard box filled to the brim with the baby items they'd lovingly purchased three months ago in preparation for the arrival of their son.

Their son. But he hadn't been theirs, and never would be. And now Jack's actions served as a painful reminder of that.

Anne padded into the room and stopped a few feet away, her arms stiff at her sides. "What are you doing, Jack?"

"I couldn't sleep, so I decided to take down the crib. I thought it might be easier on you if you didn't have to walk by here every day and know…"

Jacob's never coming back.

He didn't have to voice the words for Anne to understand what he'd meant to say.

"Anyway, I haven't gotten very far." Jack straightened his arms and lowered his head. "I guess I didn't realize it was going to be so damn hard."

When she touched his back, Jack turned to her, tears in his eyes, the first Anne had ever witnessed. He wasn't one to cry; he never had been. And only then did she recognize that all those times she'd believed he hadn't made enough effort to connect with Jacob, he'd really been protecting himself so he could protect her. Preparing to let him go, as Jack had somehow known all along they would have to do. But he'd given her what she'd desired—a child—with no argument, and in the process he, too, was suffering.

Yet when she should be comforting him, he held her close and said, "I love you, Annie. It's going to be okay. We'll have our baby someday."

In that moment, she truly believed they would.

CHAPTER 13

"**H**ey, Daddy!"

Katie kissed his cheek before skipping out of the room, leaving Jack and Hank seated on opposite sides of the sofa, in the den that had been returned to its former state. All the furniture was back in its proper place, the hospital bed exchanged for a wide-screen, high-definition TV, a gift from Delia—and a not-so-subtle attempt at making sure he was there to stay for a long while. Something else to add to Annie's list of things to be pissed off about.

"You sure have a talent for clearing a room real fast, Morgan."

Jack sent Hank a prime go-to-hell look, even though his friend was right. A little less than an hour ago, three of his former colleagues, who had come to watch the

Saturday-afternoon baseball game, had cut out before the end of the seventh inning. "No one wanted to be here in the first place, Hank. This was all Annie's doing."

"Not so, Jack. The guys were happy to be here."

"Don't try to bullshit me. Barry wouldn't look me straight in the eye. John couldn't wait to get home to Lucy—and we all know they should've split years ago. Doug kept checking his damn watch."

Hank removed his baseball cap and bent the bill back and forth. "All right, maybe they weren't exactly comfortable, but when we were joking about you turning fifty next year and you said you'd be glad to make your forty-ninth next month, you forced them to face their own mortality. If something like this happened to you, it could happen to them, too."

Something like this. "It was a time bomb going off in my brain. A freaking aneurysm, not some communicable disease."

Hank propped his heels on the coffee table and slumped in the sofa. "So how are you and Annie getting along these days?"

Not a subject Jack really wanted to broach. "She's avoiding me."

"What did you do to her?"

"I kissed her last week." Jack felt like a kid again, confiding in his best friend about his Friday-night date and getting to first base.

"Oh, yeah? Did she knock the crap out of you?"

She'd responded more than he'd expected. More than he'd hoped for. "Not yet, but she might if I try something again." And he had considered it. Several times.

Hank planted his feet on the floor and shifted forward. "Look at it this way. If she hasn't kicked your sorry ass out and she didn't slap you when you got amorous, then maybe she just needs a little extra persuading. It's worth a shot."

"I'm not sure I can even get it up." Okay, he'd said it and the ceiling hadn't crashed down on his head. Hank hadn't laughed at him, either, but he did appear uncomfortable.

"That's why they make those little pills, Jack," he said. "I can write you a script if you want. Never hurts to have a little help."

The last time Hank had prescribed him pills they'd almost done him in. Not that Hank knew about that. Jack had only told him that he hadn't liked how the antidepressants had made him feel. "Great. I take a pill and then have to make a trip to the E.R. after sustaining a four-hour erection."

Hank chuckled. "We should all be so lucky."

Jack didn't think he'd ever get so lucky again, at least with Annie, and she was the only woman who mattered to him now. She was the only woman who'd ever really mattered to him. "I'll just wait for nature to take care of it first. I can't see wasting good money on pills if I have a hard-on and no place to go."

"Suit yourself, but Ruthie kind of likes the new medicated me." Hank put his cap back on and stood. "Speaking of Ruthie, I need to get home. She's got a to-do list for me the size of the Constitution."

Jack grabbed his cane from the floor and hoisted himself up. "I have to get rolling, too. We're going to dinner with Delia and her new boyfriend."

"Delia has a boyfriend?"

"Yeah, some attorney who works for the hospital."

"That's a good thing. You might need him in your corner when you decide to go back to work."

If he decided to go back. If he was able to go back. "As long as I'm medically cleared, it shouldn't be a problem."

"Crabtree's going to be a problem, Jack. He hates you with a passion, although I've never understood why."

Jack knew why—Annie. "I'll handle Crabtree when the time comes, but I doubt I'll have to deal with that anytime soon."

"That reminds me. How's the hand coming along?"

Jack made a fist. Not a tight one, but still a fist. "It's better, but my fine motor skills need more work. My therapist is hell on wheels, and if she had her way, I'd be performing surgery and running marathons already." Only, his body wasn't completely cooperating. At least he could read the newspaper again, thanks to the combined efforts of Katie, Annie and Shelly, though he sometimes had to spend over an hour to get through the first section.

"Just keep working hard, Morgan. Before you know it, you'll be fighting Gentry for O.R. space again."

"Gentry can kiss my ass."

Hank slapped him hard on the back. "That's the old Jack we all know and despise. And while you're at it, you should try wooing Annie a little."

"I don't think she'd appreciate any wooing."

"You might be surprised, Morgan. You know she still loves you."

Jack knew no such thing. "That's history, Hank. It's over between us."

"You don't want it to be over. You never have. And my guess is, neither does she. You're both scared shitless of messing up again, but once you get past that fear and jump back in, everything will fall into place."

If only Jack could believe that, then he'd make twice the effort to convince her to give them another chance. "Since when did you start handing out the psychobabble, Steinberg?"

"Since I met two people who are so damn stubborn they've both lost sight of what's really important. Each other."

Jack hadn't lost sight of that at all. He also recognized that he'd been a major factor in their marriage's demise. But if what Hank had said was true, that Annie might eventually come around, he'd climb a sheer cliff on one leg, with his good hand tied behind his back, just to have her in his life again. Permanently.

As soon as they entered the crowded European bistro, Anne immediately caught sight of her mother huddled with her current suitor in a corner table, looking as if no one else in the restaurant existed. Anne never gave much credence to envy, but she had to admit she experienced more than a little at the moment. At one time, she and Jack had acted that foolhardy in this very establishment. Yet that had been many, many years ago. Unfortunately she had another, not-so-pleasant, memory of this restaurant that hadn't involved Jack. One she was definitely determined to forget.

Anne kept her steps slow, allowing Jack to keep up with her as they worked their way through the maze of crowded tables and harried waiters. As soon as they reached their own table, Delia presented an overly pleasant and somewhat self-conscious smile. "It's so good that both of you could join us," she said. "Anne, Jack, this is Gabe Burks."

When the man stood, Anne was admittedly taken aback by his height as well as his superior looks. No wonder her mother had been acting like an infatuated adolescent. Anne took his offered hand and shook it gently. "I'm glad to finally meet you, Gabe."

"I'm glad, too." He turned to Jack, hand extended. "Dr. Morgan, it's good to meet you."

"It's 'Jack,'" he said as he gave Gabe's hand a shake. "I don't stand on formality where Delia's friends are concerned."

Anne was pleasantly surprised when Jack pulled back her chair, something he hadn't done in years. She muttered a quick, "Thank you," and claimed the seat across from her mother and Gabe, with Jack settling for the chair to her left.

"You look very handsome tonight, Jack," Delia said.

Anne had noticed this the minute Jack had walked into the living room wearing her favorite navy suit and red-patterned tie, the one she'd given him the Christmas before the divorce.

"And, Anne, you look wonderful, dear heart," Delia said, before bringing her attention back to Jack. "Doesn't she look wonderful?"

Jack sent Anne an appreciative smile. "She looks great in red. She always has."

Anne had always known he liked her in red, which gave her pause. She questioned if she'd somehow subconsciously chosen the dress for that reason. No, she wouldn't go that far. It happened to be her favorite dress, too.

"Where's Katherine, Anne?" Delia asked.

"At her first sleepover," Jack said. "Her social calendar is more loaded than my appointment book. Or maybe I should say former appointment book."

Delia leaned over and patted his right hand, now resting on the table. "I'm sure it will be filling up again very soon."

Anne snatched the cloth napkin from her plate and draped it on her lap. "I probably should call Katie and see how she's doing."

Jack rested his left arm over the back of her chair, as if he and Anne, too, were a couple. "I keep telling Annie that we should wait for when Katie's in high school and boys are involved to worry."

Delia laughed. "You're right. That's definitely when you should worry. And it's not only about the boys. It's also about the booze. Anne knows all about that."

Anne didn't like the direction this conversation was heading. "I didn't give you any real trouble, Mother."

Delia flipped a diamond-bedecked hand in her direction. "You must have forgotten the time you and Melanie raided the liquor cabinet and made some kind of vodka concoction. Then you filled the bottle with water, thinking we wouldn't notice. Best I can recall, you were rather ill that evening."

Her mother could have gone all night without

bringing that up. "That was the only instance I remember being that drunk." With the exception of "pesto" night.

"You got pretty wasted after the wedding," Jack said.

Obviously it was put-Anne-in-the-hot-seat time. "You can't get wasted on three glasses of champagne."

"You did," Jack said. "Not that I complained about it."

"Women plus alcohol equals a lack of inhibition," Gabe chimed in, then winked at Delia.

If this kind of talk continued, Anne might be tempted to walk out. She opted to switch the topic to something that didn't involve her and drinking; otherwise Mr. Burks might begin to believe his girlfriend's daughter was a common lush. "Jack had a nice gathering with some of his friends this afternoon."

"Did you watch the new television, honey?" Delia asked.

"Yeah, we did," Jack said. "It's great."

Anne didn't think it was so great at all, but she didn't care to enter into that fray again. "Tell me, Gabe. How are things at the hospital these days?"

He shrugged. "Same old stuff. I'm ready for a vacation."

Delia exchanged a quick look with Gabe. "Speaking of vacations, I have something I want to ask the two of you about that very thing. A proposition to make, actually."

Surely her mother didn't intend to invite them on a group outing. Anne definitely wasn't ready for that. "I'm on vacation now. I won't have any time left to take a trip."

"I wasn't going to ask you to go on a trip, Anne," Delia said. "I was going to ask if you or Jack have any objections to us taking Katherine to Disney World the first week in June."

That seemed just a bit too convenient. Leave Jack and Anne alone and see what came up. "I had planned to take Katie on her first trip to Disney World. Not that I don't appreciate the offer."

"But you just admitted you don't have any vacation time left," Delia said. "I would hate to think Katherine might miss out on having a real vacation this year."

When the waiter arrived for their drink order, Anne hoped her mother would let the vacation idea go. But Delia consulted Jack. "What do you think about us taking Katherine on the trip?"

"I don't see any good reason you shouldn't," he said. "As long as it's okay with Annie."

Anne had two choices—argue the point and look like a harpy in front of the new boyfriend, or agree and regret it later. "Let me think about it."

Delia smiled. "Of course, honey. We would also be willing to let Katherine bring a friend."

"Good idea," Gabe said. "She'd probably prefer hanging around with someone her own age instead of a couple of old fogies."

Delia elbowed him in the side. "Speak for yourself."

Anne noticed the glance the two shared, and recognized something serious was brewing between them. "Jack and I will let you know in a few days."

"Please do," Delia said. "We only have a couple of weeks to finalize the arrangements to get the best accommodations."

When the waiter returned with a bottle of Chardonnay and attempted to fill her glass, Anne declined, using the excuse that she was driving. But she'd given up wine since last December, for a reason no one knew. A reason no one would ever know.

After the wine had been poured for everyone else, Delia requested that the waiter give them a few more minutes before taking their orders, then held her glass aloft. "To family. May we all have good health and many more good memories."

Jack touched his glass to Delia's. "I'll definitely drink to that."

Jack said very little on the drive home, and Anne chalked his silence up to fatigue. After all, this was the first time he'd been out of the house, aside from doctor's appointments, since the stroke.

Yet the minute they pulled into the driveway, he asked, "So what did you think of Gabe Burks?"

Anne shut off the ignition and settled back in her seat. "It doesn't matter what I think. He apparently makes my mother happy." So happy that Delia was practically giddy.

"I like him, even if he is a lawyer. But I have to admit, it's strange seeing her with someone other than your dad."

"She deserves to have a man in her life, Jack. I'm okay with it."

"Are you okay with your mom and Gabe taking Katie to Florida?"

Katie accompanying her grandmother on a fairy-tale vacation wasn't the problem. Anne being alone with Jack was. "Tomorrow I'll ask Katie if she wants to join them.

If she does, I'll call Mother." She hid a yawn behind her hand. "I'm tired. Let's go in now."

"Too tired to stay up awhile longer to talk?"

Anne questioned whether talking was all he intended. She questioned even more what she would do if he had other ideas. "I guess I can stay awake a few more minutes."

She left the car and rounded the hood to help Jack out, only to find he'd managed himself. Each day brought positive signs that he was recovering. It should have made Anne happy, yet she felt almost sad, although she didn't plan to analyze that until much later, if ever.

She followed Jack through the house, noting he was walking much faster than he had in the restaurant, and with purpose. Once inside the den, she kicked off her heels and sat on the couch, curling her legs beneath her. Instead of joining her, Jack hobbled to the entertainment center and switched on the stereo.

As the music began to play, Anne felt as if she'd been launched back in time.

"God Only Knows…"

She'd first heard the song as a child, when her mother would bring out her favorite Beach Boys albums on Saturday afternoons. But Jack had never been a fan. "I thought you didn't like this."

Jack faced her with a solemn expression. "But you do, and that's what counts." He walked to the sofa and held out his left hand. "Dance with me, Annie. I realize I wasn't that good at it before the stroke, but I'm game, as long as we don't try to fox-trot and you don't expect me to dip you."

She mentally cataloged all the reasons she shouldn't get that close to him, but he looked so hopeful she couldn't bear to let him down, even if it meant dropping her guard.

After pushing off the sofa, Anne set his cane against the cushions and said, "You don't need this when you can hold on to me." She wrapped one arm around his waist, guided him to the middle of the room and moved much too easily into his embrace.

She couldn't count the times she'd listened to this song, and wondered what she would be without him. She couldn't count all the dances they'd shared, but she recalled a few. On a warm summer night their first year together, they'd swayed beneath the stars during an outdoor concert, even when no one else was dancing. At the wedding reception, they'd danced to this very song for the first time as husband and wife, believing they would always be together.

She also recalled Jack dancing with the other girl in his life, the one they had created together. She'd woken up one night to find Jack gone from the bed and three-month-old Katie missing from the bassinet they kept nearby. She'd come upon father and daughter in the living room, Katie resting securely in Jack's arms as he carried her around the room, singing a sweet lullaby off-key. Yet the baby hadn't seemed to mind. She had simply stared at him, as if mesmerized by this man called Dada—her first word.

As Jack held Anne close, she realized she'd forgotten how safe she felt in his arms, how much she had cherished his strength. She'd let bitterness rule her memories, harden her heart to all the good days and good memories. But tonight she recalled them all.

When she lifted her head from his shoulder and looked at him, she realized she was inviting a kiss. An invitation she should probably decline, but she didn't have the will or the want to. She wanted the kiss as much as she wanted to forget all the obstacles they still had to clear.

He molded his palm to her face, lowered his head and touched his lips tentatively to hers. He was asking permission, and she granted it. She banished her worries and allowed herself the pleasure that kissing Jack had always brought her.

All too quickly, the song ended, and so did the kiss. Jack studied her eyes, as if searching for answers she wasn't sure she could give him. "I need something to believe in, Annie."

"You have to believe in yourself, Jack."

"It's not enough. If somehow, some way, we can get back what we had, then I'll try that much harder to get well. To be everything you need this time."

Anne was still too afraid to believe, but slowly, slowly, she was beginning to hope. "I'm scared, Jack."

"So am I. Scared that I might screw things up again. That I might never be able to make love to you in the same way again. But I'm not going to give up."

Rarely had he ever admitted that he was afraid, even after the first time he'd flown solo during surgery in his residency days. "I need time to think about this," she said, and she would think about it, most likely all night.

"That's all I'm asking, Annie." Jack moved back and, without her help, worked his way to the sofa to retrieve his cane before facing her again. "The next step is up to you." Then he disappeared without another word.

If only she were brave enough to take that step. If only she could trust him. She had trusted him with all her heart and soul. When other promises had been made, only to be broken.

1998

Anne surveyed the Bay of Naples from their villa's balcony, committing all the sights to memory—the red-tiled roofs, the jagged shoreline, the majestic view of Vesuvius framed in shades of blue and orange, complementing the setting sun. She hated the thought of leaving this magical place, but tomorrow they would board a plane for Dallas. Go back to their lives, their work and the problems they'd left for this temporary retreat from reality.

When Jack's arms came around her, Anne leaned back against him, absorbing his strength, cherishing the newfound closeness between them, physically and emotionally. "We have to talk about dinner," he said. "Or we can just stay in bed."

"We've been in bed all day, Jack. You wouldn't even let me out for another shopping excursion."

He tightened his hold on her, as if he worried she might decide to go shopping right now. "Admit it, Annie, you had a lot better time with me, and what we did today didn't cost a thing."

She looked back at him and smiled. "You're right. I really didn't want to lug home souvenirs, anyway."

"It's a shame we have to go tomorrow," he said, echoing Anne's sentiments.

"But as they say, all good things must come to an end."
She paused for a moment, released a sigh. "What if we
never have a baby, Jack?"

"It could still happen. If it doesn't, we can adopt."

"I can't go through that again." And she couldn't, even
if infants were readily available, which they weren't.

Jack turned her around and rested his palms on her
shoulders. "Listen to me, Annie. We can't give up, not yet.
And if it's not in the cards for us to have kids, then we'll
have to rely that much more on each other."

"But you're gone so much these days, Jack. It's hard to
rely on you when you're not around."

"I'm going to lighten my schedule when we get back.
I'm going to make sure we spend more time together."

"Promise?"

"I promise." He kissed her gently. "You mean a lot
more to me than my job, Annie, even though I know that's
sometimes hard for you to believe."

"I want to believe it, Jack. I really do."

She saw the sincerity in his eyes, heard it in his voice
as he said, "Even on the days I've played a role in saving a
life, when I've held someone's heart in my hands, it's never
measured up to loving you, Annie. Nothing about my
work can measure up to all the years we've had together.
Our future means more to me than anything. You mean
more than anything. You always will...."

CHAPTER 14

For the first time since the stroke, Jack had begun to focus on the future.

He doubted anyone would be shocked to learn that his first unaccompanied driving excursion would lead to the hospital. Annie wouldn't be astonished, either, but she'd probably be pissed, and this was the reason behind his covert departure before she got home from work. His return to the setting that had been his refuge for the past two years seemed a logical place to begin his expedition back into the real world.

As he passed through the lengthy corridor leading to the medical offices, several colleagues greeted him with surprise, as if they'd witnessed the Second Coming. And although they'd tried not to be obvious, all had noticed his cane. Regardless, that cane could get him where he needed to go much faster, even if he hated his continued dependency on it.

He keyed the code to the privacy door and stepped inside, immediately experiencing a strong sense of familiarity, of comfort. He stuck his head in the employee lounge, where the staff took afternoon break, and did nothing more than say, "Hello," before traveling down the hall that led to his office.

When he entered the room, pure adrenaline rushed through him. Nothing appeared to have been moved in his absence—at least, as far as he could tell. Katie's first-grade picture still sat on the corner of his desk beside the small ceramic jar Annie had bought him in Faenza, a souvenir from their trip to Italy ten years ago.

He belonged in this place, but he wanted to be back as the surgeon, not the visitor. And for the first time since the stroke, he was starting to believe he would be back. Maybe not in a few days. Maybe not even in a month. But he would be back. Many memories of his previous life had returned, one at a time, with a few of the pieces still missing—particularly his ability to recall the names of all the surgical instruments. He figured that if he could get them down, then the details of the actual procedures might follow.

With that in mind, he crossed the room and pulled a book from one shelf, a volume he'd owned since the beginning of his career. Basic, easy to read and virtually self-explanatory. He sat behind his desk, but then set the book aside. He'd take it home and study it later, when no one was around, not even Annie. Particularly not Annie. Things had been going well between them, and with Katie now in Florida with her grandmother and Gabe, he planned to pick up the pace and hope for the best. Hope that his body wouldn't fail him. Hope that if he lost everything else, including his job, that he could at least make love with Annie again.

When the rapid knock sounded, Jack suspected word had gotten out that he'd come into the office. He wouldn't mind a little more alone time, but he wouldn't mind seeing some of his favorite staff, either. He did mind the appearance of the man who walked through the door without an invite.

"What the hell do you want, Max?"

Crabtree strolled to the desk like the cocky bastard he was. "Just curious why you're here."

"It's my office. I have every right to be here."

"Only if you're cleared to return to work. Are you?"

"I'm not ready to return to work yet, but I will be soon. And you won't be the first to know."

Max pulled out the chair across from Jack and sat. "That's the problem, Morgan. I have to be the first to know. I run this hospital, and I will do everything in my power to protect it, even if that entails suspending a physician's privileges should I think it's in the best interest of everyone involved."

Meaning him. Jack's fury began to heat up just below the surface of his calm exterior. "I will be back, and you can't stop me."

"Yes, I can." Crabtree rose from the chair, looking way too smug. "And I will."

Jack had the urge to lunge over the desk and coldcock the son of a bitch with a left hook. Instead, he chose another weapon that would wound him worse—the truth. "You know something, Max? It took me a while to figure out why you've always been out to get me. At first I thought it was all about Annie, but then I realized you want everything I have, from my wife to my career. Hell, you want to be me. It ain't gonna happen, so you might as well give up."

"Why would I want to be a man who's all washed up?"

"I'm not washed up at all, Crabtree. Just ask Annie. In the meantime, I'll give her your regards."

He saw it then, Crabtree's transformation from confidence to contempt. "You do that, Morgan. Enjoy her while you have the chance, because sooner or later she's going leave you again, this time for good."

Crabtree rushed out and slammed the door behind him, allowing Jack some measure of satisfaction. Very few people existed whom he could claim he truly hated, but Maxwell Crabtree was at the top of the trash heap. And just thinking about the bastard with Annie made him seethe.

He opened his top drawer, removed a paper clip and twisted it over and over until it was misshapen and useless. Then he hurled it across the room, where it landed on the black leather sofa, sparking one good memory to block out the bad. Annie stopping by the office during her lunch break, although he couldn't recall the exact day or year.

She'd closed the door, tripped the lock, announced she was ovulating and proclaimed she didn't care to wait until they got home. He'd depressed the intercom, told the receptionist to hold all his calls; he was going to be a few minutes late for his next appointment. Then he'd joined Annie on that sofa and made love to her. It had been fast, wild and hot. Some of the best sex they'd ever had. They didn't create a baby that day, or even several years after that, but they'd created one helluva memory.

And he'd be damned if his body didn't remember it, too.

After setting her purse and keys on the table in the hall, Anne hurried into the den to find Shelly packing her bag of tricks, apparently about to leave.

"Jack's SUV is gone," Anne said, her voice winded from her haste and concern. "Do you know where he is?"

Shelly slipped the strap over her shoulder. "He went for a drive."

Anne had seen her daughter off to Florida two days earlier with Delia and not her, she'd gone back to work, and now her former husband had been let loose on the streets of Dallas in a motorized vehicle. "He's alone?"

"It's okay, Anne. I have training in driver rehabilitation, and he can handle it. His residual numbness and stiffness are above the right knee, so he has enough mobility to press the accelerator and brake. For the past few days, he's been driving while you were at work. I went along to make sure he could do it."

Anne couldn't control her continued concern. "Are you absolutely positive he's ready for this?"

"If I hadn't thought it was safe, I wouldn't have let him go. This is only one more step toward his independence. That is what you want for him, isn't it?"

Anne didn't know what she wanted anymore, other than Jack's safety. "I'm worried about him."

Shelly patted Anne on the back. "He'll be fine. And I'll be back on Friday."

"That's three days from now."

"My work's almost done here, Anne. Jack has the tools and he knows what to do. The rest is up to him."

After Anne saw Shelly off, she went into the bedroom to shed her smock and scrub pants. When she opened the closet door, she was struck by the familiar scene of Jack's clothes hanging on the rack opposite hers. Jack's shoes set out on the shelves they'd once occupied. Jack's toiletries in the master bathroom. Little by little, he'd moved back into her life, as if he'd never been gone at all.

"Did you have a good day at work, Annie?"

She nearly tripped over her own feet when she spun around to discover Jack standing immediately behind her. "You just took ten years off my life. Stop sneaking up on me."

"I thought you enjoyed me sneaking up on you."

For the past two weeks, he'd gotten quite good at sensual subterfuge, surprising her with kisses when Katie hadn't been around. Suggestive touches when Anne had been cooking in the kitchen. A pat on the butt when she'd bent over to remove laundry from the dryer. Not once had she protested, but not once had she yielded to the voice that urged her to go to him, when late at night the lone-liness and longing had been almost unbearable.

After she walked to the bureau to retrieve a pair of shorts and a T-shirt, she considered scolding him for driving without a copilot. She chose a more casual approach and faced him, clothes hugged against her breasts. "Where have you been?"

He sat on the upholstered bench at the end of the bed and propped his cane between his parted knees. "I went to the hospital. I wanted to see if they'd moved someone else into my office."

Of course he would go to his office, his favorite place, second only to the surgical suites. "I highly doubt they'd replace you."

"Not yet. By the way, old Crabby paid me a visit. I told him I'd send you his regards, and that really pissed him off."

She imagined it did. Max had never hidden his feelings for her in all the years she'd known him. "He's *only* a friend, Jack."

"He wants to be more than your friend."

She couldn't deny that, nor could she stop her smile. "Are you jealous, Jack?"

"Do I have reason to be?"

He never had and never would where Max Crabtree was concerned. But admitting that might prove to be her downfall, so she opted not to respond. "Did you run into anyone else while you were there?"

"Just a few members of the old guard." He rose from the bench without his cane and walked toward her, slowly, sporting the look she now knew so well. The look that indicated he had something on his mind, and it didn't have a thing to do with Max. With the bureau at her back, Anne had nowhere to go unless she plowed him down.

He tugged the clothes from her clutches and tossed them over his shoulder. "I did see the black sofa."

She hadn't thought about that sofa for years, with good reason. "You actually kept that thing when you redecorated the office?"

"Yeah, I did." He moved closer, leaned into her. "I'm glad it's still there. It brought back some good memories." He pulled off the band that secured her ponytail. "You know what else it brought back?"

"An urge to locate a competent decorator?"

He took away the guesswork when he pressed against her. "An erection to beat all erections. I had to stay behind my desk an extra half hour before I was decent enough to leave. It came back on the drive home."

"Congratulations."

"Is that all you have to say, Annie? Congratulations?"

She'd been lucky to get that much out of her mouth. "What do you want me to say, Jack?"

"I want you to say that you'd be willing to try it out, see if it still fits."

"Now?" Her voice sounded tinny, almost shrill. Held an edge of excitement…borderline acquiescence.

"Why not? It's just you and me and my hard-on, all alone in the house."

"Isn't three a crowd?"

"That doesn't qualify in this case, Annie."

Her hesitation was only minimal, her response complete when he kissed her. She didn't know how it happened exactly. She knew only that their clothes flew off and hit the floor before she and Jack wound up on the bed, limbs entangled, naked in the stark light of day. For the first time in two long years. A homecoming that

Anne probably shouldn't risk. A chance she probably shouldn't take. But she was powerless to stop the madness, even though she knew Jack would stop if she asked. She didn't.

In the past, he would always speak to her in a low voice, soft words of sex, until when he finally did touch her, she was more than ready to welcome his hands and mouth on her. Verbal foreplay, he'd called it. But today he said nothing. He didn't have to. He skimmed his hands over her, touched her with the well-honed knowledge of a former lover, confirmed how well he knew her body, even better than she knew it. Her orgasm arrived fast and furious. She refused to believe that Jack had anything to do with it. Considering how long she'd done without the attention, any man worth his salt could have sent her over the edge in less than five minutes. Or so she kept telling herself.

And then he was there, easing into her body, deeper and deeper. A triumph for him, she realized. Thrilling for her, unfortunately. She welcomed the familiarity, and feared the sense of newness that accompanied it. She didn't want to feel anything beyond the physical renewal. She wanted her heart to stay out of it. She wanted to believe that she was only helping him out, helping to prove he was still very much a man. Prove that his sexuality hadn't been stolen away by an insidious stroke.

Yet when she held him so close, she felt as if she, too, had something to gain. Maybe even a return to her own carnality, which she'd learned to deny. She could lie there and let him finish, detached, but her hands wandered over his back as if she had no control over them. She knew well the breadth of his shoulders, the dip of his spine, the gentle curve of his buttocks. As he moved inside her, she knew that his respiration would accelerate, his frame would grow rigid. Knew he would release a satisfied groan, then shudder and sigh softly in her ear. She waited for the signs, hoped for them even, and rejoiced when they all happened at the right moment.

She wanted this little bit of paradise to go on forever, wanted to suspend time, to forget the trials of the past and the uncertain future. But when Jack whispered, "God, I love you," reality settled in like an uninvited guest. Her body tensed, a knee-jerk reaction to a declaration that she didn't know how to answer.

Jack raised his head and stared at her. "What's wrong, Annie?"

She almost told him she loved him, too. But that would only encourage him to pursue something more permanent—a decision she wasn't ready to make. "This is wrong, Jack."

He rolled onto his back, breaking all contact, physical and emotional. "Then why did you do it?"

"You didn't really give me much choice."

"You could have stopped me. Or maybe you didn't stop me because you decided to hand me a sympathy screw. If that's the case, glad you got to come, and feel free to leave now. I won't bug you anymore."

She grabbed the throw from the end of the bed and draped it across them both. "I didn't do it because I felt sorry for you. I did it because I got caught up in the moment. But it doesn't change anything."

"It changes everything, Annie."

"The problems we had before haven't gone away because we made love."

"You mean, one major problem, don't you? The cheating part, since lack of time together hasn't been an issue for the past few months. I barely remember what happened that night."

"Is that because of the stroke, or is it selective memory?"

He turned to his side to face her. "I don't even remember her name. Does that make you feel any better?"

Anne doubted anything about that sorry episode in their lives would make her feel better. Still, some things she had to know, out of morbid curiosity. "I guess I've always wondered what she had that I didn't."

"Not a damn thing."

"And that's supposed to excuse you?"

"I'm not looking to be excused. But if you want to know what I remember, all I can tell you is that I met a group from the hospital at Flynn's. She was a lab tech, I think. She was trolling, and I happened to be her target. I got drunk, and she wanted to get laid. End of story."

Anne prepared to ask the one question that had always plagued her, even though she might despise the answer. "Where did you do it?"

He released a frustrated sigh. "What difference does that make?"

"I think it's reasonable for me to ask if you made love to another woman in our bed."

"Love didn't have a damn thing to do with it, Annie. It was a fast screw in her car in the parking lot."

Anne fought back the surge of nausea. "Please tell me you practiced safe sex."

"I'm not stupid, Annie. Or maybe I should say she wasn't stupid. She was prepared, like everyone else these days. Just to be sure, I got checked out later. So you don't have to worry about me giving you any diseases."

At least she could be thankful for that. "And you've never seen her again, even at the hospital?"

He scooted up against the headboard. "I'm not sure I'd even recognize her if I did. Is that enough detail for you, or do you want me to make something up—such as, I still fantasize about her?"

She focused on the ceiling, anything to keep from looking at him. "I've heard enough details, thank you. I can't help but wonder, though, how many women you've been with since her. And me."

"None."

That brought her attention back to him. "You're going to tell me that in two years you haven't been with anyone else?"

"I made work my mistress, like you've always accused me of doing. When I felt the urge, I relied on the faithful five. I didn't need a magazine or porn. I only had to imagine you."

"I'm having a hard time believing that."

"Believe it." He studied her a moment. "But you can't say the same thing, can you?"

Anne tried to mask the guilt—which was ridiculous, since she had nothing to feel guilty about. "That's really none of your business."

"When it involves that bastard Crabtree, I'm going to

make it my business, whether you like it or not. Why him of all people, Annie?"

Surely, Max hadn't spouted off during his earlier confrontation with Jack. Then again, she wouldn't be surprised if he had. "What did he tell you?"

"Max didn't tell me anything. He didn't have to. I already knew. I went to our restaurant on our anniversary back in December out of some masochistic need to torture myself. I got the hell out of there when I saw the two of you cozying up in a corner table. I waited outside until you got in the car with him and drove away."

She could lie, but then why should she? "Okay, I slept with him, as a *divorced* woman who happened to be lonely."

"And that night at the bar, I was lonely, too."

"We were still married when you fooled around."

"And you ended our marriage long before we ever signed any divorce papers."

They fell silent, the burden of past mistakes hanging over them. Anne didn't know what to say next. She *had* pushed him away before she'd turned him out. But he'd broken too many promises, and then one important vow.

"Are you ever going to forgive me, Annie?"

If only she could find it in herself to be more forgiving. If only she could get the images of him with another woman out of her head. "I'm trying, Jack. But I'm not sure I can forget."

"Then maybe it's time for me to go." He worked his way to the edge of the bed and grabbed his clothes from the floor.

She watched him while he dressed, and realized that things would be so much easier if she let him go now, before she lost herself to him again. But the thought of him leaving to complete his recovery alone weighted her with an abiding sadness. Truth was, she didn't want him to go. Not yet. Not now.

When he took his cane and started for the door, Anne wrapped up in the throw and quickly climbed out of the bed. "Don't go, Jack."

He kept his back to her. "Only if you give me a good reason to stay."

"Katie—"

"Leave her out of this." Finally he faced her. "What do you want, Annie?"

"I want to believe that we can work things out. But I don't know if we can go back."

He rubbed his palm up and down her spine, the way he always had when he'd comforted her. "We shouldn't go back. We have to move forward. All I'm asking is you give us until the end of the summer to see what happens. No expectations."

"No expectations?"

"Only one. We start sleeping together again. In the same bed, the way we used to. And having you in the same bed with me isn't only about making love. That's the place where we had some of our best conversations."

"And our best meals."

He smiled. "Yeah. And some of our best sex."

"Somehow I knew we'd get back to that," Anne added, returning his smile.

He brushed her hair from her face, kissed her gently. "It's still good between us, Annie. We still have a lot of love left to make. And I don't want to miss another moment of it."

1999

Leave it to him to miss his own birthday party. But at least it wasn't the blowout Annie had thrown last year when he'd turned forty. Just a small gathering with her parents and Hank and Ruthie. From the looks of the deserted driveway, the guests had already gone, which meant he would have to face Annie's wrath without reinforcements.

Jack opened the front door slowly, then headed down the hall to the den, taking care not to run into the damn coat tree. He wasn't surprised to find Annie stretched out on the couch, still wearing his favorite red dress, a piece of his favorite double-fudge cake, topped with a single candle, set out on the sofa table before her, along with several unopened presents.

After slipping off his jacket and toeing out of his loafers, he walked to the sofa as quietly as possible. He planned to carry her off to bed and make love to her until she wasn't angry anymore. But his plan went awry when she opened her eyes and said, "It's about time."

"My flight was delayed in Chicago. Two hours, in fact. Are you mad?" Dumb question. He could tell she was seething by the condemnation in her tone.

She sat up on the edge of the sofa and smoothed a hand over her now-wrinkled dress. "I'm disappointed, Jack. When we came back from the trip, you promised me you'd lighten your schedule."

He collapsed onto the chair across from her. "I had intensive training, Annie. I have to keep up."

"You were gone a whole month, Jack."

"Look, Annie, this is who I am."

"It's what you do, Jack, not who you are. And I'm always going to be second best."

He joined her on the sofa. "I've told you that's not true."

"Those are only hollow words unless you back them up."

Exhaustion brought on a solid dose of anger. He shot off the couch and spun on her. "What do you want me to say, Annie? That I'm going to quit? That I'm going to give up a career that took me years to build?"

She rubbed her forehead and closed her eyes. "I want you to say that I won't continue to play second fiddle to your work." She opened her eyes and stared at him. "But I want you to mean it for a change, or else I'll…" Her words drifted away, along with her gaze.

Panic zipped through Jack. "Or else what? You'll start making noise about us separating again?"

"I don't want that to be an option, especially not now." She leaned forward, picked up a small package from the coffee table and offered it to him. "This is my gift to you."

Jack felt like crap, taking a present from her when he'd given so little other than a lot of grief. But to make her happy, he reclaimed the space beside her and tore into the bright blue paper without bothering to remove the bow. He expected a new watch when he lifted the lid on the white box. What he got was a black-and-white photo. An ultrasound photo. His mind didn't quite register what his eyes were seeing, no matter how long he studied the image. He couldn't quite comprehend the significance, not without inviting hope.

When he looked up at Annie, he noticed tears clouding her eyes. "I hope you like it," she said "because we can't take it back now."

"You're pregnant?"

A broken breath slipped out of her mouth and all she could do was nod. He held her then, hating himself for his shortcomings, loving her for all that she continued to give him.

He rubbed her arm with one hand, still holding the results of the sonogram in the other. "When did you find out about this?"

"The week after you left. I wasn't feeling all that well, so I made an appointment with Bill Freed. After he confirmed the pregnancy, I decided to wait and surprise you. I didn't want to announce it over the phone."

He wasn't only surprised; he was shocked, and disappointed that she hadn't informed him sooner. "When is the baby due?"

"Mid-October."

Jack did a quick mental countdown. "That means—"

"I conceived in Italy."

A host of concerns crowded in on him. "You're already in your second trimester."

"I know, but I've missed periods before, Jack. And after all those false pregnancy tests during the years, I was too afraid to believe that this time it was really going to happen."

He wanted to scold her, but she needed his understanding at the moment, not judgment. "You'll be thirty-eight by the time the baby's born. We probably should consider amnio."

She shook her head. "No. That procedure runs the risk of a miscarriage."

"Only a slight risk."

"Any risk at all is too great, Jack. And even if I did learn something was wrong with the baby, I wouldn't care. I'd still love it no matter what."

He could debate the benefits of preparing for a worst-case scenario, but in her line of work, she knew all the possibilities.

After setting the photo aside on the end table, he pulled her closer. "That's one hell of a souvenir you brought home from Italy."

Finally her anger melted, lightening Jack's emotional load. "Bill says the baby looks great. No signs of problems at all. Do you want to know what we're having?"

"A kid who looks like you, I hope."

Her smile brightened the room as it always had, always would. "I meant, do you want to know the sex?"

"Do you already know?"

"Yes."

"Then I want to know, too. I want to know everything from this point forward, Annie. Every ache and pain you have, every time you feel a kick. I don't want any more secrets between us."

Annie laid his hand on her slightly distended belly, which Jack hadn't noticed at all because he'd been too busy to notice. Yet he'd secretly imagined this moment for years, giving Annie the baby she'd always longed for.

"Happy birthday, Daddy," she said. "Meet your daughter...."

CHAPTER 15

"Happy birthday, Daddy!"

Anne looked out the kitchen window to see Jack hobbling alongside Katie as she rode her bike near the curb, singing the birthday song at the top of her voice. Anne had to admit that her daughter was happier than she'd been in years. Together, father and child fueled each other, igniting a bond that would last a lifetime. At least Anne could be thankful for that, no matter what the future might hold. She couldn't remember a time in the recent past when she and Jack had made love so often, and with such passion, as they had over the past few weeks. Very much like the good years in their marriage, she supposed. But then, sex or the lack thereof hadn't been the crux of their problems until the end.

She often wondered if she was caught up in a counterfeit contentment. If she was making a huge mistake, immersing herself in a world that seemed nearly perfect. Jack continued to make progress, grew stronger every day and more sure of himself. He hadn't spoken of returning to work, but Anne suspected he thought about it often, even though his pat reply when asked was, "Who knows?"

Anne knew. She knew in her heart that if given the chance, he would return to all that he'd once been. And that was why she struggled with wanting him to fully recover and in some ways hoping that didn't happen for some time. Yet when doubts still beleaguered her well into the night, she would watch him sleep, and find peace in knowing he would wake up beside her.

As Anne got together the things for the barbecue that would also serve as a celebration for Jack's birthday, he ventured into the kitchen and came up behind her. "Did you buy oranges today?"

She nodded toward the bowl atop the refrigerator. "Yes, but you've never been that crazy about oranges before."

"I'm not going to eat them. I'm going to suture them."

One more step toward the inevitable. "That should be interesting."

He nuzzled her neck—left fair game, since her hair was piled atop her head. "You smell good."

"And you're sweaty," she said. "You better get into the shower before our guests arrive, since you're the chef."

"Why don't you take a shower with me?"

She wiped her hands on a paper towel and faced him. "How do you expect me to explain that to your daughter?"

"We're rationing water."

"Now, that's a good one."

"She's not here, anyway. She rode down the street to have dinner with Chelsea. I talked to her parents about it earlier. She and Chelsea will be back in time to have some of my birthday cake."

"And she went all by herself?"

"It's only three houses down, Annie. And I waited and made sure she got there in one piece."

Chances were, Katie would grow up to be as independent and pigheaded as her father. "I just worry about her, Jack."

"You worry too much about everything. Now, how about that shower?"

"I swear, you're like a kid with a brand-new toy."

"And you've been more than willing to play with it."

Two more seconds, and she would follow him into the shower, in spite of having already taken a bath. Before she jumped on that bandwagon, she was saved by the doorbell. "Looks like someone's here." She took Jack by the shoulders, turned him around and patted him on the butt. "Be a good boy and run along."

"You're no fun, Annie," he muttered on the way out. "You're going to have to make up for it tonight."

She imagined she would, and gladly at that.

And so it went, the return to the constant affection that had prevailed in the early years, when they hadn't been able to keep their hands off each other. Funny, she'd never considered it could be that way again. She'd never allowed herself to hope it could be that way again.

When the bell buzzed a second time, Anne grabbed a

dish towel and wiped her hands on the way to the door. Hank stood on the porch, clutching a six-pack and Ruthie's hand.

"Let the games begin," Hank said the minute Anne opened the door. "I've got the booze."

"And I've got a good mind to flog you for making me the designated driver after the week I've had." Ruthie's smile lit up her mischievous green eyes. She was a self-proclaimed big-mouth redhead, but Anne thought of her as a natural room illuminator. "I've been baking cookies for the damn medical auxiliary fund-raiser."

Anne stepped to one side. "Come in, you two. Jack's running late, as usual."

"He's still on surgeons' time," Ruthie said, then added, "Not that I would ever tell him that."

"Why not? It's true." Anne gave her a quick hug. "It's so great to see you both again."

"Not as great as it is to be here with you," Hank said. "Now, let's get this party started."

Anne led the couple into the kitchen, handed each of them a beer and then invited them onto the backyard deck. They sat in a semicircle and Anne listened as Ruthie talked about their youngest son, a recent college graduate, and the new baby their daughter was due to have any day. Hank called Ruthie granny; Ruthie called him something totally unflattering. Their banter unearthed a deep longing in Anne, and she wondered what it would have been like had she conceived Katie much earlier. Maybe by now she would have a grandchild on the way, too. Maybe she would already have finished school. Maybe the divorce wouldn't have happened. But she couldn't turn back time, or yearn for the impossible.

Jack soon appeared through the patio doors, cane in hand, and immediately leaned to kiss Anne's cheek before he pulled up the chair beside her. She didn't bother to gauge Ruthie's and Hank's reaction; she already knew what they were thinking. The show of affection served as a good indicator that things had changed between ex-husband and former wife.

"Happy birthday, Jack," Ruthie said. "You're looking good for a fifty-year-old man. Have you been working out?"

"I'm forty-nine, Ruthie, so don't rush me." Jack rested his palm on Anne's thigh. "And yeah, I've been doing a lot of working out lately with Annie."

"He's been using his weights regularly," Anne amended, although the damage had already been done.

Hank frowned. "You need a haircut, Morgan. Unless you've decided to go Einstein on us with all that gray coming out."

Jack ran a hand through his hair, which was still thick and, as far as Anne was concerned, still gorgeous, silver and all. "When you've been without something for a while, you appreciate it even more when you have it back," he said, followed by a meaningful look at Anne.

"I'm ready for a refill." Hank stood, empty bottle in hand. "Can I get you a beer, Morgan?"

"Sure thing."

"Why don't you show me to the steaks, Anne? I can use my special seasoning. Might help when Jack cremates the suckers."

"Watch it, Steinberg, or I'll make sure yours is raw."

Anne trailed behind Hank into the kitchen, sensing that his request for her company had nothing to do with the evening meal and everything to do with Jack.

He set the empty bottle down and leaned a hip against the counter. "So how are things going with you and Jack, Anne?" he asked, confirming her suspicions.

"Things are going well, Hank. He's really working hard." She opened the refrigerator, removed the platter of steaks, then closed the door with a push of her bottom.

When she noticed Hank studying her with concern, Anne recognized he had something important to say. Panic threatened to grab hold of her when she remembered that Jack had been in for his annual checkup the day before. "What's wrong with Jack?"

"Nothing's wrong with him, Anne. At least, not when it involves his physical condition. He's as fit as a thirty-year-old, aside from the leg problems."

Anne slid the platter onto the counter, then faced him. "If you're still worried about his mental state, don't be. He's not showing any signs of depression anymore."

"I'm worried about the state of his personal affairs, Anne. As his friend, not as his doctor. I'm wondering what's going on between the two of you, and where you see this heading."

She gave the only answer she could. "We're taking it one day at a time. That's all we can do. All I can do."

"And what will you do when he goes back to surgery?"

She wouldn't let herself think about that right now. "He's not sure he will."

Hank sighed. "You and I both know he will go back, and he should. He's got more talent than most of the docs in the state combined. Maybe even in the country. Will you be able to handle that decision?"

Anne traced the pattern on the granite surface, realizing her hesitation would cost her. "I'm trying not to get his hopes up, in case it doesn't happen."

"And that would suit you fine, wouldn't it? Having him retire from the field."

Her anger began to build, and she had to draw on all her fortitude not to lash out at their friend. "You're being unfair, Hank. Of course I want him to go back to work. If that means returning to surgery, then I don't have any say in the matter, do I?"

He streaked a hand over his beard. "Look, Anne, I know it's none of my business, but when you left Jack, I was one of the people who had to pick up the pieces. He went into a downward spiral, and for a while, I wasn't sure he'd pull out of it. All I'm saying is that I don't want to watch that happen again."

"Neither do I." And she didn't. He'd already been through enough.

"Then if you can't accept that he could very well go back to work, even sooner than you think, maybe you should cut him loose now."

She resented Hank's intrusion, his advice, no matter how well intended. Despised that she recognized the truth in his words. "You're probably right, Hank. But I can't even imagine not being with him while he's still trying to get well."

"You still love him."

Hank posed the words as a statement of fact, not a question. And to this point Anne had refused to admit it to Jack. Had barely admitted it to herself. But she longed to voice it, to stop denying it, even if Hank was the first recipient of the admission. "Yes, I still love him."

"Love can go a long way toward making things right, Anne."

Delia Cooper had unequivocally fallen in love—and she planned to share that blessed information with her daughter.

The hospital cafeteria crowd was thinning out, which was why Delia had invited Anne for a late lunch. She would have preferred someplace more private to speak with her daughter, but Anne had insisted that she had only a half hour to spare. That half hour would be up if Anne didn't arrive soon.

Just when Delia decided to page her, Anne rushed into the room, holding an apple and a glass of iced tea, weaving through the tables while greeting several employees on her way.

Anne shoved back the chair across from Delia and dropped into it. "Sorry I'm late. We had a set of twins who didn't want to cooperate."

"They're fine, I hope."

Anne shook two packets of sugar and spilled them into the tea. "They're very healthy, and big. Both almost seven pounds."

"Good." Delia sipped at her water, contemplating how she would inform her daughter of the latest news. News she hoped Anne would welcome, although she had serious doubts. First, she needed to get something else out of the way. "I went to your father's grave site today."

"Any particular reason?"

"It's August 10."

Anne rubbed her forehead as if trying to thwart the onset of a headache. "I'm so sorry, Mom. I didn't even think about the date. I've been so busy lately."

Delia patted her hand. "It's okay, honey. No one expects you to remember everything."

"Forgetting the anniversary of my own father's death is unforgivable."

"I'm sure he forgives you. I certainly do. You've had a lot on your mind." Delia's half-eaten chicken salad suddenly seemed unappetizing. "I took him lilies."

Anne smiled. "Because he used to call you his lily of the Shenandoah Valley."

"See? You didn't forget everything."

Anne rolled the apple around with her palm. "I wish you'd called me. I would have gone with you."

"You had to work, and I had a few things I wanted to say to your father in private."

Anne's eyes widened. "You always told me that—"

"I didn't believe the dearly departed could hear the living. I know." But she'd never believed she would meet someone like Gabe, either. Never believed that Jack and Anne might have a second chance. "I also know this could possibly convince you I belong under psychiatric care, but in a way, I felt your father was listening."

"What exactly did you say to him?"

Many, many things, including that she would always love him, no matter what. "I told him I hoped he could see Katherine, but if he couldn't, I assured him that he would be very proud of her."

Anne's eyes held all the sorrow Delia had felt since her morning sojourn. "During the funeral, I kept thinking that if he'd only waited two more months, then he could have seen her."

Just when she'd thought she'd run out of reserves, tears began to threaten Delia again. "Those things are out of our control, dear heart. I'm sure that if he'd had his way, he would have waited, too." She sighed. "Sometimes it seems like only yesterday that he was scolding me about all the shoes I owned. But then sometimes it seems like forever. Much longer than eight years. I've been so lonely without him until recently."

"Until you met Gabe."

"Yes, and that's another reason I had to go alone today. I felt I needed to let your father know that I would always have a special place in my heart for him. I suppose I was looking for his permission to be with Gabe, as crazy as that sounds."

Anne laughed softly, yet the laughter held no real mirth. "I'm sure Dad got a kick out of that, since I don't ever remember you asking him for permission for anything you've ever done."

Delia dabbed at her damp eyes with a napkin, bolstered her courage, prayed that Anne might understand. "But I needed his permission this time, Anne, because Gabe has asked me to marry him."

Anne exchanged the apple for a spoon, which she

turned over and over in her hands. "Have you given Gabe an answer?"

"Not yet, but I plan to tonight. I wanted to talk to you about it first."

"You're an adult, Mother. You don't require my blessing."

"You're right—I don't need it. But I want it. It's important to me."

Delia waited for what seemed an endless amount of time for her daughter to speak. She wasn't all that concerned with Anne's answer; she would do what she pleased anyway. Knowing that her family supported her would just make it so much easier.

Finally Anne's smile returned. "Am I going to have to be your bridesmaid and wear one of those ridiculously frilly dresses that I'll never wear again?"

"We didn't plan to have a formal wedding, but if you insist, I might make an exception."

"Please, not on my account. A nice, simple ceremony would be better. In fact, you could have the wedding at my house."

Delia relaxed from the sheer joy of knowing that her only child approved. "Then you're all right with it?"

Anne dropped the spoon and held Delia's hands. "Of course I am, Mom. As I've said, as long as you're happy, I'm happy."

"I am happy. Regarding the wedding, Gabe and I have decided we're going to do something different and marry in Vegas."

Anne didn't look quite as disappointed as Delia had expected. "A lot of people marry in Vegas, Mother."

"All right, different for me, then."

"Well, if you're going to run off and do this, then please take pictures. I want lots of photos with you and the Elvis impersonator."

"You and Jack could come along and stand up for us."

"When exactly do you plan to do this?"

"We have a chapel reserved for next weekend."

Fortunately, Anne appeared unfazed by that little bombshell. "As much as I'd love to, Katie starts to school shortly, and Jack is still having therapy once a week."

"How is my dear boy doing?"

"He's doing fine, Mother. Much better than I could have hoped for. He's less dependent on his cane, although he still limps. He's made some fairly amazing strides."

Delia couldn't shake her inappropriate curiosity. "Does that also apply to the bedroom?"

"Stop nosing around, Mother."

"I don't have to nose around. The answer is written all over your blushing face."

"All right. If you must know, Jack's back."

The day was definitely heading in a positive direction. "That's wonderful, honey. Does this mean—"

"It doesn't mean what you're thinking, Mother. We're working on our relationship, but we still have far to go before we can commit to anything."

"But look how far you've already come."

Anne sent a fast glance at her watch. "I need to run."

"Of course you do, Anne. You always need to run when your relationship with Jack is involved."

Anne traded her previous discomfort for anger. "Excuse me?"

"You're a smart woman, Elizabeth Anne. You know exactly what I'm saying. You ran from him a year into your relationship. You almost ran the night before your wedding. You ran when things became too tough in the marriage. When are you going to stop running and realize that the two of you belong together?"

Anne stood and pocketed the uneaten apple. "I can't do this right now, Mother. I have to go back to work."

Anne *had* to retreat into her work, Delia decided. Just as Jack had always done. They were so alike in so many ways, yet neither had enough awareness of those commonalities. "Have a nice day, dear. I'll call you before we leave."

Anne leaned and kissed Delia's cheek. "Tell Gabe I said congratulations." And then she was gone, crossing the cafeteria at a fast clip. At an emotional dead run.

Delia had failed to tell Anne the last request she'd made of Bryce—that if he had any influence on God or guardian angels or whoever might be conducting the celestial show, he'd try for a miracle. For it would take no less than that to save Anne and Jack from a repeat of the past.

CHAPTER 16

Anne's forty-seventh birthday had begun with a mad rush of laboring patients, thanks to a September full moon. Many of the young women were half her age, reminding her she was nearing the bottom of the slippery slope to fifty, and the prospect of arriving there alone. Not if Jack had his way. He wasn't exactly pushing her for a commitment, but he was doing his best to persuade her, including planning a birthday gathering for her later that evening. The jury was still out on whether she would be in the mood to celebrate.

She strode out the delivery suite door and nearly stumbled headlong into her new stepfather—a fact she was still not quite used to. "Hi, Gabe. What are you doing up here?"

He shoved his hands into his pockets and averted his

gaze from the young woman who was wailing in pain. "Actually, I promised your mother I'd talk to you today. Can you spare a few minutes?"

Considering her workload, she would normally have said no. But Gabe's serious tone indicated his wasn't a friendly visit. "Sure. Follow me."

Anne passed by the nurses' station and told the clerk she'd be back in a few minutes, then led Gabe into the nearby break room, where she showed him to a small table in the corner. His sober expression, his nervous demeanor, gave her cause to worry. "Is something wrong with Mother?"

He loosened his tie with one finger. "She's fine. She told me to tell you 'happy birthday' and she'll see you this evening. Oh, and she had the wedding pictures developed."

"Complete with the Elvis impersonator?"

"Yeah. She hunted one down right there in the middle of the Strip. Embarrassed the hell out of me."

"I'm sure it did, but that's our Delia." Anne noticed her stepfather still looked troubled. "What's really going on, Gabe?"

He rubbed one hand over his nape. "It's Jack. Specifically, Jack and Max Crabtree."

If she learned that Jack had confronted Max again, maybe even engaged him in a teenage-boy brawl , then she would write them both off. "Those two have never gotten along."

"Your mother mentioned some of the details," Gabe said. "But this has to do with Jack's return to work. Max says having a doctor on staff who's suffered a stroke is too big a liability for the hospital."

Anne couldn't claim she was all that surprised. Max

would attempt anything to make things more difficult for Jack. "Does he have a valid argument?"

"Not as far as I see it, provided Jack is cleared medically. And that's what's bugging me. Max has met with Nan Travers several times. I think he's trying to pressure her not to sign Jack's release."

Anne had always known Max to be a manipulator, but this went beyond normal scheming. "Nan's a respectable doctor. She wouldn't buy into that."

"No, she wouldn't, not unless she honestly felt Jack's abilities were in question. But I don't believe Max will stop there. He's asked me to find some loopholes. He wants me to contact the board and use strong-arm tactics to convince the members to revoke Jack's privileges when the time comes."

If the time came. Yet Anne couldn't keep fooling herself. Jack's return to surgery was only a formality. He'd spent hours on end, working his hand and studying manuals well into the night. "I really hate that you're in the middle of this, Gabe. But I also realize you have a job to do."

"It's not a problem. I told Crabtree that I'd quit before I did anything to compromise Jack's career."

"You'd really do that for him?"

"Yeah, and for your mother. Love's kind of crazy that way. It's about sacrifice if the situation calls for it, and this one does."

"But sacrificing your job?"

He shrugged. "I was planning on retiring early, anyway. Some things are just more important than a job. Your mother's more important, and her family."

In that moment, Anne realized her mother could not have made a better choice with her second-chance love. Men like Gabe were too few and far between. Men who embraced family obligations.

Gabe pushed his chair back and stood. "I better get back to work, while I still have a job."

Anne rounded the table and gave him a long embrace. "Thank you, Gabe. For taking care of my mother and for defending Jack. I'll see what I can do on this end." Even if that meant having a powwow with the administrator. She dreaded the day Jack would return to work, but she'd be damned if Max would stand in his way.

Gabe affectionately patted her cheek, something her own father had rarely done. "You're welcome, Anne. Hang in there. I'll see you all tonight."

In the corridor they went in opposite directions. As Anne moved past the station, the unit clerk gestured to her, impeding her progress. "Karen asked if you could stay until seven. Casey called in sick."

Happy birthday to me. "Can't you find anyone else, Angie?"

"I've tried. No luck so far."

As badly as she hated to stay, Anne felt the need to continue to prove that she was a valued employee after the fiasco in the spring. "Fine. But I'm leaving right at seven."

Now she would have to call to let Jack know she would be late. Call her mother and reschedule the birthday dinner. And after she left the hospital this evening, she would have to make another call—on someone in person. But she'd stay only long enough to set Max Crabtree straight, once and for all.

* * *

When Anne pulled in front of Max's condominium, her bravado began to wane. She didn't have fond memories of the last time she was here—December when she'd made a colossal blunder by sleeping with him.

His Mercedes was in the driveway and all the lights in his condo were on. That meant he probably was home and she ran the risk that he wasn't alone. If that was the case, she'd invite him outside so she could say her piece.

She drew in a fortifying breath, snatched the keys from the ignition, grabbed her purse from the passenger seat and marched up the walkway, but slowed her steps when she reached the front porch. She hesitated momentarily, then pressed the bell.

All day long, she'd meticulously planned what she would say. That preparation escaped her when Max answered the door, looking both surprised and pleased to see her. "Hello, Anne. What brings you here? Did you finally get enough of old Jack?"

Her courage returned immediately. "I'm definitely here to talk about Jack."

Max held the door open while she walked into the living room, and locked it tight after he closed it. "Have a seat," he said, indicating the navy-suede sofa, where they'd sat the last time she was here, before they had made the inadvisable detour into his bedroom.

She shook off her regret. "No, thanks, I'll stand. This won't take long."

"Suit yourself." He collapsed into the lounger and rested his elbows on the arms, resembling an indulgent king about to hold court. "Can I get you something to drink? Maybe some wine?"

Too much wine had been her Waterloo on that fateful night in December, and he knew it. "I'm here for one reason only, and that reason is I'm asking you to lay off Jack."

"I have no idea what you're talking about."

"You know exactly what I'm talking about. You plan to throw up major roadblocks when he goes back to work."

Max released a rough sigh. "I should have known not to trust Gabe Burks now that he's married to your mother."

"And might I remind you that the surgical unit carries the name of my father? I'm not one to pull strings, but I will if you make trouble for Jack."

He stared at her a minute. "He's suckered you again, hasn't he, Anne? You're obsessed with him. When are you going to learn that he doesn't give a crap about you?"

"Jack cares about me, and I care about him."

"Jack only cares about himself. And it's pretty sorry that he sent his ex-wife to do his dirty work instead of handling it himself."

Anne fisted her hands at her side, her nails digging into her palms. "Jack doesn't know what you have planned. And if he does find out, God help you."

Max pushed out of the chair and strolled toward her. "I'm not afraid of him, Anne. From what I've seen, he's not much of a man anymore. He can barely walk. And that makes me wonder how well he functions in bed these days."

"He's more of a man than you'll ever be." Anne realized that at this rate, she would never get anywhere. She remembered her mother's old saying about trapping more flies with honey than vinegar. "Look, Max, let's call a truce. I admit we've had some good times, but we have to leave them in the past."

"Anne, I've always cared about you, no matter what Jack says."

"If that's true, and if you won't let Jack go back to work for Jack's sake, then do it for me."

He mulled that over for a minute before saying, "Now that I think of it, if I let him go back—provided he's able to operate again—you'll be put back on the shelf, the way you've always been when it comes to his job. And unless you're a total masochist, it won't be long before you'll kick his ass out again."

At least Max hadn't said he would be waiting. If he had, Anne would have happily told him to go to hell. "I appreciate your consideration, Max. Now I need to go home to my family."

She barely had the door open before Max added, "Happy birthday, Anne."

She was amazed he had remembered. But then, he'd always had a surplus of consideration, and usually questionable motives to back it. Before she left, she muttered a quick, "Thank you," then practically ran to the car.

Luckily the process had been relatively painless. Unfortunately she had a hard time believing that Max Crabtree would give up that easily.

Jack had glared at the dozen red roses since they'd arrived that afternoon, resisting the urge to build a fire and burn them. But he'd decided to wait until Annie got home—if she ever did—and let her have them first. Then he would request an explanation for why Crabtree was sending her flowers.

He already knew why. The bastard was lying in wait like the snake that he was. Waiting for Jack to mess up with Annie again.

When he heard the door open, then quietly close, he had the strongest urge to meet Annie in the hall and demand answers. He forced himself to stay in the chair and wait. She entered the room and immediately noticed the vase, then smiled.

"This is a nice surprise," she said as she walked to the table and bent to smell the flowers.

"They're not from me."

Following a look of confusion, Anne unpinned the card from the ribbon—the card Jack had already read and memorized.

Thinking of you on your birthday, Anne, and wishing you were here. I miss you. Love, Max.

The sorry son of a bitch.

Annie dropped the card onto the table and frowned. "How good of him to remember. I'll toss them out later."

"Where have you been?" Jack had tried to remain calm, but the words had emerged cold and accusatory.

"I told you—I had to work late."

He'd always been able to tell when she was lying, and tonight was no exception. "I called to ask if you could pick up some milk on your way home. They said you'd left at seven. It's almost eight-thirty."

She sat on the sofa and leaned forward, hands folded on her thighs. "The traffic was bad on the freeway."

"You don't take the freeway home."

"I didn't come home immediately. I had somewhere I had to go."

Jack didn't like the sound of that one bit. "Where?"

"If I tell you where, you have to promise you won't be angry."

"That depends. If this has anything to do with Crabtree, I'm not going to make that promise."

She stood and moved to the back of the sofa, as if she needed to put it between them. "It does have to do with Max."

Jack could no longer control his anger and shot to his feet. "Dammit, Annie, why him? Am I not enough for you that you had to go back to the bastard?"

"It's not what you think, Jack."

"Then you better start explaining, because my imagination is running wild."

"Let's not discuss this here."

When she headed for the hallway, Jack moved faster than he had in a long time and caught her arm. "Did you sleep with him for old times' sake?"

She wrenched her arm away. "I'm not even going to justify that with an answer."

He followed her into the foyer. "I deserve an answer. Did you?"

"You're acting like a jerk, Jack, and I don't like it!"

"Well, I don't like the thought of you climbing into bed with a man I despise. With any man, for that matter."

"Right now, I don't care what you like."

"Stop yelling at each other!" Katie commanded from the top of the stairs, before slamming her bedroom door.

Anne sent him a withering look. "Great. Our daughter now knows the sordid details."

"I'll go talk to her."

She pressed past him and headed up the stairs. "I'll handle it."

Jack stood at the bottom of the staircase and waited for Annie's return. He hated that he'd upset Katie. Hated that he'd lost his temper. But he couldn't take it back now.

Anne returned a few minutes later, clearly sick at heart.

"Is she okay?" Jack asked.

"She told me we were acting like children. I explained to her that sometimes moms and dads got angry with each other, and I apologized. Then she informed me that she was going to sleep, and that she'd 'appreciate it if we would be quiet.' That's a quote."

Jack rubbed his jaw. "Maybe we should continue this somewhere else."

"Maybe we should drop it for now."

"I can't do that, Annie. Not until I have some answers."

"Fine."

Silently they walked through the hallway and into the bedroom. Once there, Anne turned to him, a thoughtful expression on her face. "Katie's never heard us argue before."

"I remember us having some pretty serious verbal knock-down, drag-outs."

"Before she was born. After that, we stopped fighting."

He considered the conjecture for a moment, and realized Annie was right. "We stopped talking altogether."

"We treated each other with indifference, even when we were angry."

"We did it to protect her, Annie."

She held her arms tightly to her middle. "We can't blame Katie for our mistakes."

"I'm not blaming her. I'm blaming us. At least at one time we had enough passion to fight. And we had one helluva time making up."

He could tell she tried not to remember, tried not to smile, but she didn't succeed with either. "Yes, we did."

He circled his hand around her neck and reeled her closer. "So do you want to go duke it out in bed?"

"Not until I tell you why I went to see Max tonight."

"Okay. I'm listening."

"Gabe stopped by the unit this morning and told me that Max is trying everything, ethical and not, to keep you from going back to work. He also tried to recruit Gabe in his dirty dealings, but Gabe refused. I went to see Max to ask him to stop the underhanded tactics."

Damn Crabtree to hell. "You don't have to fight my battles for me, Annie. I can handle Crabtree."

"I know, but it was something I had to do." An air of determination came over her. "Fight him, Jack. Prove to him that you're capable of being the surgeon again."

Jack had never expected Annie to say that. "I'm sure going to make the effort, babe." Taking a chance, he kissed her. Risked that she would reject him. Amazingly she didn't, although the kiss didn't last long enough.

"Happy birthday," he said.

"It's been interesting, to say the least."

"By the way, your mother stopped by and left some pot roast and your gift."

She backed out of his arms. "I guess I should see what she came up with. Anything has to be better than what she gave me last year."

"What was that?"

"A calendar featuring studs of the Southwest."

Jack laughed. "Delia's a character."

"That she is. Do you want something to eat?"

"No. I want you to open my gift before you do anything else." He moved to her side and nodded toward the nightstand. "It's over there."

Anne seated herself on the edge of the bed, while Jack kept his distance for the moment. She picked up the package and shook it. "Something tells me it's red and skimpy and probably looks great on a twenty-year-old."

Jack sat beside her and hung his arm over her shoulder. "It's definitely going to look great on you." But only if she agreed to wear it. "Hurry up and open it."

As always, she unwrapped the gift at a leisurely pace. For once he wished she would just rip into it without worrying about keeping the bow intact. After removing the lid, she lifted the tissue paper to find the surprise he'd planned for weeks.

She stared at the blue-velvet box for a few moments before finally opening it. And then she stared some more.

"I had the diamond from your old set remounted," he said. "I found the ring in the jewelry box. It took me a while, and for a few minutes I thought maybe you'd either hocked it or flushed it."

"I wouldn't do that." She lifted the box and studied it more closely. "It's beautiful, but—"

"Don't say I shouldn't have done it, Annie. I should have done it years ago."

She slipped the ring from its holder, but she didn't put it on. "What exactly does this mean?"

Jack felt as though he'd been thrust back to that day at the lake, nerves and all. "It means I want to marry you all over again."

She smiled tentatively. "You've been watching too many commercials."

This wasn't going at all where he'd planned for it to go. "This is reality, Annie. We've been living like husband and wife for the past few months, so I think it's time we make it official."

She put the ring back in the box and set it aside. "I'm not ready for this yet."

He'd been a total fool to believe she would accept the ring without any argument. He might be fooling himself if he believed she would ever accept it. "Okay, Annie. There's no rush. I just needed you to know how I feel and where I want us to go from here."

"It's not that I don't appreciate the gesture, because I do. I have to have more time."

"How much more time, Annie?"

She folded and unfolded the hem of her smock, keeping her eyes centered on the floor. "I don't know yet. Most days I don't even know how I feel."

He framed her face with his palms, encouraging her to look at him. "Do you still love me, Annie? And if not, then what the hell are we doing?"

"I don't know."

"You don't know if you love me, or you don't know what we're doing?"

"Yes. No. Okay." She sighed with resignation. "Yes, I love you, Jack. I've never stopped loving you for a minute, even after you left. But we have to have more than that."

At least she'd given him that much, even if she hadn't given him the answer to his proposal. "It's enough, Annie. We'll work on the rest."

She stood and began backing toward the door. "I'm going to say good-night to Katie, grab a bite to eat, then get ready for bed. Can I get you anything?"

Yeah, more of her attention. But if she was determined to avoid him, then he'd make do for now. He'd bury himself in the one thing that had always provided comfort when she hadn't been willing to do so. "I've already eaten. I have some reading to do. I'll be in the den so I won't bother you."

"Okay. I'll see you later, then."

He wanted her to issue a protest, tell him she'd be waiting for him in bed. He wanted her to come back in the room and say she'd reconsidered. But after watching the door for a good ten minutes, Jack realized that wasn't going to happen. And he began to wonder if they would ever find any common ground.

Later that evening, Anne ate her leftover dinner alone, opened her gift from her mother—an Elvis snow globe—alone. Went to bed alone.

She waited up for over an hour, hoping that Jack would finally join her. A little past midnight, she drifted off to sleep in the desolate bed, only to be awakened sometime later when she felt the mattress shift beside her. She checked the bedside clock to discover dawn would arrive in less than two hours. She questioned why Jack hadn't bother to wake her when he'd come to bed, yet she knew the answer. He was disappointed. He'd wanted her to make a decision she wasn't quite ready to make. To commit to him again without hesitation. To give him everything, when she wasn't certain if he'd do the same.

By attempting to convince Max to let Jack go back to work in the near future, she'd all but given her former husband permission to return to his former self—the revered surgeon, obsessed with his calling, determined to be the best, disregarding her needs.

Only time would tell how far Jack would go to reclaim his status, and that would be the test of his commitment to his family. That would either convince Anne he had changed for the better, or that his conversion into a man who'd been attentive and caring for the past five months was just a front for the doctor who preferred surgery to family dinners. Medicine to making good memories.

Regardless, she would stand by him until he was the best he could be, for to do anything less would be selfish on her part. Yet she had the strongest feeling that during the process, she would be spending many more nights alone. Again.

At least she still had Katie.

1999

"Please don't let this baby come until tomorrow." After almost ten hours of grueling labor, Anne never believed she would say such a thing. But then, with all the futile years of trying, with all the disappointment, she'd never believed she would have a baby, either. Being eight centimeters dilated at last check, she doubted she'd get her wish that the baby would arrive later rather than sooner.

Jack feathered her hair from her damp forehead and smiled. "That's a switch, Annie. A few minutes ago you threatened to deliver it yourself. Not to mention you're two weeks overdue."

"It's half past midnight."

"Yeah, it is."

"It's Halloween, Jack. No one wants to have a baby on Halloween."

Anne gritted her teeth as the next contraction hit, whereas she should have been breathing through it.

Jack rubbed his hand down her arm and loosened her grip on the side rails. "Try to relax, babe. It'll be over in a minute or two."

She rode the painful wave holding his hand, drawing from his strength, until at last the contraction subsided. "This is a lot tougher than I'd realized."

"That's why they invented epidurals, Annie."

"It's too late for one now." Anne hadn't wanted anything to dull the pain, as insane as that now seemed. She'd wanted to feel every contraction, every sensation, take everything to memory, since this would probably be her one and only child. "I don't care whether it takes another day if it means having a baby on the first of November instead of Halloween." And to think she'd scoffed at other pregnant women for making such inane statements. But then, she'd never been on this side of the bed before.

Jack picked up a cloth and wiped it over her brow. "Think of it this way. If we have a Halloween baby, then you won't have to worry about choosing a new theme every year for the birthday party."

"That's brilliant, Jack. We have to have the baby before I start planning birthdays." She studied his face a long moment. "Are you sorry we learned the sex?"

"No, Annie. I'm not sorry at all. Let's just hope they're right and we don't have any surprises. Otherwise our son's going to hate his pink room."

Speaking of surprises... Hank stuck his head in the door and waved, only one of many of Jack's colleagues who'd stopped by for progress reports. At this rate, anyone who didn't know Anne might believe she was suffering from several serious diseases. "No baby yet?" he asked.

Now she understood why women were so irritable during labor. Men and their stupid questions. "Does it look like we have a baby, Hank?"

Hank held up his hands in surrender. "Uh-oh. You better get the doctor, Jack. She's getting bitchy, and that means she's getting real close."

As soon as Hank said it, Anne felt the first urge to push. "He's right, Jack. Get the doctor."

"I'll do it," Hank offered, then disappeared out the door.

"Where's Mother?" Anne asked.

"I sent her home. I told her I'd call the minute we had something to report."

She wanted to insist he call her now; she needed her mother with her. But Anne also realized Delia hadn't been sleeping well since August. Since her husband's death.

Sarah, the night charge nurse, breezed into the room, fortunately without Hank in tow. Anne didn't relish the prospect of Hank getting an up-close-and-personal look at her cervix. "Time to get to work, Anne," Sarah said.

"I've been working." And blowing and panting, along with a little groaning.

Sarah moved the stool to the end of the bed and instructed Anne to bend her knees. "I'm going to check you and see what's what."

As if Anne didn't know the routine. She'd followed it a million times herself.

"You're fully effaced and fully dilated, Anne. The baby's head is right there. You can go ahead and push."

When the next contraction arrived, Anne bore down with what little strength she had left, tuning in to Jack's encouragement, to the traditional ten-second countdown, delivered by Sarah.

After two more attempts, Sarah told her to relax a minute and Jack tried to touch her forehead, but she shoved his hand away. He took her mood swing in stride, as he had all evening. When she hadn't wanted him to leave for even a minute, he'd stayed by the bed. When she'd told him to get the hell out of the room and her life, he'd continued to stay, consoling her, comforting her.

After an hour of futile attempts to deliver, and

overcome with exhaustion, she wanted to just lie back and sleep. Wanted to will her uterus into a state of suspended animation. But her body wouldn't let her. Neither would Jack. He'd become the cheerleader. Her champion. And hopefully she would reward him with a beautiful baby soon, because she wasn't sure how much more of the futility she could take.

"You need to stop for a bit, Anne, and breathe through the contractions." Sarah stood, stripped off her gloves and tossed them into the refuse bin. "I'm going to go page Dr. Freed."

Anne caught the look Sarah exchanged with Jack, and sensed something was wrong. She knew exactly what was wrong when Jack asked, "Do you want her on her left side?"

"Good idea," Sarah said as she headed out the door.

"Roll toward me. Annie."

In a haze, Anne complied, until reality seeped back in. "The baby's in distress."

"The heart rate dipped below a hundred, but only slightly. It's probably nothing."

Rationally, Anne realized chances were the baby would be fine as soon as she entered the world. But love, not logic, ruled at the moment. "We can't let anything happen to this baby, Jack."

He leaned over the rail and kissed her cheek. "Nothing's going to happen, Annie. I'm not going to let anything happen to our baby, or to you."

And somehow Anne knew he wouldn't.

"Hey, folks." Bill Freed strolled into the room, with

Sarah at his side. He slipped on a pair of gloves and claimed the stool at the end of the bed. "I hear you're giving us trouble, Anne. You should know better."

Anne closed her eyes and endured more poking and prodding while she prayed that everything would be okay.

"This baby's got a big head," Bill said. "Must take after her father."

Jack looked at Anne and grinned. "Is it as big as a pumpkin?"

"Can we stop with the Halloween humor?" Anne huffed through the sudden onset of burning pain, her body's demand to bear down.

"I'll do what I can, Anne," Bill said. "But you might have to have a section."

She warred with what was best for the baby and her own desire for a vaginal delivery. "Only if we have to."

"Can we get a pediatric doc down here, Bill?" Jack asked. "I think it would make Annie feel better."

Anne loved him so much at the moment. Loved him for knowing exactly what she needed. Loved him for erring on the side of caution.

Bill nodded at Sarah, who picked up the bedside phone and made the request before returning to the O.B.'s side.

The next few minutes passed in a blur as Anne struggled to deliver the baby. She pushed with all she had left, Sarah applied pressure to the fundus of her uterus, Jack coaxed her with soothing words—and Bill Freed announced, "It's a girl."

Then came the sound Anne had heard thousands of

times. That precious wail of protest. Only tonight, it was her baby's cry. Her and Jack's baby.

Through a veil of tears, she watched Jack cut the cord. Watched as the pediatric resident carried the perfect baby with the cap of golden hair to the nearby warmer, then proclaimed they had been blessed with an eight-pound-two-ounce healthy little girl.

Katherine Anne Morgan.

Sarah lifted the swaddled baby from the warmer and handed her to Jack—and Anne acknowledged she would never forget that moment. Never forget the undeniable love in her husband's face as he held their daughter. Never forget the tears filling his eyes, this stoic doctor whose world revolved around the science of saving lives. Never forget the reverence in Jack's voice that broke slightly when he whispered, "Welcome to the world, Katie."

CHAPTER 17

"Is that why you call me 'pumpkin,' Daddy?"

Katie waited for Jack's response, but Anne realized he had mentally escaped to somewhere else, to where he'd been during the entire telling of the birth story. Probably to the O.R. zone. "Jack, Katie asked you a question."

He finally stopped stretching the rubber band wound around his right index finger and thumb—stretching he'd begun to do over and over the past few weeks until Anne wanted to tear the band away and pop him with it. "Sorry, kiddo. What did you say?"

"She asked if that's why you call her pumpkin. Because her head was big."

He brought out the smile reserved for his daughter, the one that never failed to charm her. "You're still my little pumpkinhead."

Katie left the couch and planted herself in Jack's lap. "That's baby stuff, Daddy."

"I know, and you're eight years old now. A seasoned second-grader." He raked off her witch's hat and put it on his head, bringing about Katie's giggle.

When the doorbell rang, Katie snatched the hat from Jack and stuck it back on her head. "I'll get it this time."

"Make sure it's tricker-or-treaters before you answer the door, sweetie," Anne called as Katie rushed away, the black cape her grandmother had hand sewn flying behind her.

"How was the school party?" Jack asked.

"The usual. Lots of junk food. It was nice of Katie's teacher to combine Katie's birthday with the regular festivities." Anne paused a moment, then asked the question she'd been meaning to pose all evening. "How was your appointment with Nan?"

"Okay from a neurological standpoint. CAT scan looks fine. I still have the leg weakness, but at least I can read again, and the fine motor skills are back to normal. Nan cleared me to return to work as soon as I think I'm ready."

Anne didn't quite understand why he sounded so dejected. "You should be jumping for joy."

"Kind of hard to jump with one bum leg. If it's not any better by now, then it's probably not going to get any better."

"If you had to trade your ability to run with operating again, would you?"

He flipped the rubber band onto the table. "No. I'll manage during surgery."

"When do you plan to go back?" A query she'd purposefully avoided until now.

"I'm not sure yet. Maybe after the holidays."

She attempted to gather some enthusiasm, but her efforts, along with her voice, fell flat when she said, "That's great, Jack."

"Don't sound so excited, Annie."

Although this was the answer to his prayers, Annie also recognized that with each milestone, each successful surgery, she risked losing him all over. Some days, she felt he was already gone.

"That kid was creepy," Katie said as she bounded back in the room. "He had a fake knife sticking out of his head."

"I hope you don't have nightmares tonight. Speaking of which…" Anne climbed off the couch. "Time to get ready for bed."

"It's my birthday, Mom. Can't I stay up later?"

"It's also a school night," Jack added. He braced himself with his cane and stood. "Come give your old decrepit dad a kiss."

"What does *decrepit* mean, Daddy?"

"It means he's tired," Anne said. "Now, let's go."

"Don't wait up," Jack said. "I'll be in the den."

As if Anne wasn't well of aware of that. He'd transformed the room that he'd once claimed was his prison into his own private classroom, where he spent many a night studying, sometimes with her help. But not tonight. He'd have to make do without her.

She waited while her daughter readied for bed, distracted by thoughts of her fragile future with Jack. Katie only made things worse when she asked, "Is Daddy going to live here always?" as she climbed under the covers.

If only Anne knew the answer to that, she'd be glad to confirm it—or deny it. "Katie, when we talked about Daddy staying here, it was only until he was well. And he's almost well."

Katie spiraled her hair around one finger, looking as though she might cry. "But he wants to stay here. I know he does. Don't you love him anymore?"

Yes, and that in itself was a problem. "Let's just take it one step at a time."

That was the only thing Anne could promise her daughter. The only thing she could promise herself. Yet somehow she knew that her blissful days with the Jack she'd grown to love all over again were numbered.

"Jack, it's Thanksgiving. Can't you give it a rest?"

Seated with his back to the den sofa, Jack glanced up from the orange he'd been suturing for over an hour, searching for perfection and almost finding it. Almost. "I've got to make sure I can do this is right before I turn myself loose on live patients."

She didn't look at all pleased at his response. "But it's almost midnight. You've been at it since Mom and Gabe left. You didn't even tell your daughter good-night."

He reclined against the sofa and shook out his aching hand. "I'm sorry. The time got away from me."

She perched on the end of the chair across from him. "You haven't even scheduled any patients yet. You still have time to practice."

This was the part she wasn't going to like—something he'd been avoiding telling her for over a week. "I've got patients scheduled on Monday. And for the past few days, while you've been at work, I've assisted Chen on a few cases."

Her expression turned to stone. "Actually, I heard that rumor at the hospital, but thanks so much for confirming it. Is there anything else you've been keeping from me?"

He hoisted himself up onto the sofa and prepared to let her have her say. "I'm sorry, Annie, but I knew you'd be upset. You pretend you're okay with me going back to work, but you're not happy about it. In fact, my guess is you'd wish I'd just throw in the towel."

She stood and paced the room. "That's not true. For two hours the other night, we went over all the instruments. You outlined the procedures to me in detail so many times *I* could perform a bypass or transplant. What else do you expect from me?"

"I expect you to understand why I have to do this."

She stopped midstride and faced him. "I understand it all too well, Jack. You're determined to go back to being the way you were before the stroke. And I'm beginning to realize that's not all good."

He knew exactly where this was heading. Knew that if he made one wrong step, he'd widen the emotional gap between them. "If you're worried I'm not going to be around enough, you're wrong. This is only part-time."

"For now, until you're back in the groove. Then come the long hours, the trips around the country to learn new procedures. The influx of residents you have to teach. You won't have time for me or for Katie."

"Why are you so damn determined to believe the worst, Annie?"

"Because I've been there before. I've already started to see it happen. You've been up until all hours of the night, sometimes even in the morning, and I go to bed alone. We haven't made love in over a week. You haven't even kissed me for days. What am I supposed to believe?"

Unfortunately she was right. He'd become so obsessed with fighting for his career he'd disregarded her needs. "Come sit down with me, Annie. Let's talk this out."

"I'm not sure I have anything else to say except I can't do this again."

He shot off the sofa and shuffled over to her. "As soon as I get back into a routine, I promise I'll make sure we spend a lot of time together. Maybe we can go away some weekend after the first of year. Delia can watch Katie."

"You've been promising me that since Katie was born, Jack. All of it. A return trip to Italy. Private practice. You've never made good on those promises before. I have no reason to believe you will now."

"I'll prove it to you, Annie." He couldn't seem to control the anxiety in his voice, the feeling that everything was about to fall apart. "For God's sake, don't write us off again because of my past mistakes."

She bit her bottom lip, showed the first signs of tears. "You can't give me what I want, Jack."

He circled his arms around her and held her close. "Just tell me what you want, Annie, and I'll do my best to give it to you."

She tipped her head against his chest, her tears dampening his T-shirt. "I want you to move back to your apartment."

He lifted his face with his palms. "Don't do this to us, Annie."

"I don't have a choice, Jack. This is about my emotional health and Katie's. The longer you stay, the closer we become and the harder it will be for you to leave. Because you *will* leave. You'll go back to your real love, surgery, and you'll forget about us and what we need from you."

He wanted to shout at her. He wanted to curse. He needed to plead. To beg if he had to. "You're asking me to choose between you and my life's work. There's not a damn thing fair about that."

"I'm not asking you to choose. I'm asking you to let me go, Jack. Let us go."

He probably should let her go, but instead he held on tighter. He struggled to find the right words to change her mind. Amazing that he could save lives, but he didn't know how to save a relationship with a woman he couldn't stand the thought of losing again.

But he *was* losing her.

He'd already lost her.

He realized that the moment she stepped back, reached into the pocket of her robe, withdrew the ring she'd never worn since he'd given it to her on her birthday and enfolded it in his hand. "Someday you'll find someone who'll appreciate you for the remarkable man you are, Jack. Someone who's stronger than I am."

"I don't want anyone else, dammit." He never had, never would.

"It's too late, Jack."

Then she turned away from him and left the room. Left him completely alone, paralyzed with sorrow and in some ways fear. That fear quickly dissolved into fury. He hurled the ring across the room, following with his cane. Then, using one forearm, he cleared the table where he'd been working so diligently to become the surgeon again, unaware that with every stitch he made, he was sealing the end to their relationship.

But not without one last stand. A strong sense of purpose sent him through the house as fast as his bum leg would allow. His steps faltered and he nearly fell in the hallway, but that didn't stop him. He was going to show Annie how much he loved her, convince her that she had to give them another chance, even if it took all night.

When he arrived in the bedroom, he found the light on, but no Annie. He also discovered she'd put his suitcase on the empty bed. He felt as though he'd been thrown back in time to where they'd been two years ago, when she'd said she didn't want him in their house any longer, the one they had built together. That she didn't want *him*.

If that was the way it had to be, fine. He'd give her what she wanted, because he loved her that much. Enough to let her go a second time. He'd return to his apartment, to work, and carry on without her—and wish every day of the rest of his sorry life that he could be the man she needed.

She knew it would be difficult to watch Jack tell his daughter goodbye, but she hadn't realized how difficult. Hadn't realized how painful it would be to see her daughter cry in her father's arms, begging him not to leave, before Katie looked at her with undeniable hatred, as if she had been the one to completely destroy her little girl's world.

Anne also hadn't realized that her own mother, whom she'd called to take Katie for the day, would appear so disappointed, on the verge of tears herself, when she led her granddaughter out the front door, leaving Anne and Jack alone in the bedroom. And Anne hadn't expected the depth of the ache that would settle over her when she entered the room she'd once shared with Jack, several years ago and not so long ago, the closet now absent of his clothes, as if he'd never been there at all. But he was still there, standing before her, the final bag resting at his feet. The final goodbye still waiting to be said.

She couldn't find it in her shattered heart to say anything other than, "I'll be at work on Monday. The usual shift. If you get a chance, stop by the unit and let me know how it went with your surgery."

He looked so grief-stricken Anne wanted to leave now. Leave him before she could no longer contain her own grief. "I can't do that, Annie. I have to have some time to sort this out. I have to have some distance."

Anne understood, yet that didn't make the thought of not seeing him at all hurt any less. "Okay. Take care of yourself, Jack. Katie needs you."

"And you don't."

If she said she didn't, she'd be handing him a lie. "I want you to be happy."

"I'm not sure what being happy means anymore, Annie.

I only know that over the past few months, as hard as it was, I was happier than I'd been since we were last together."

She tried to smile, tried even harder not to cry, but she failed at both. She recognized why this goodbye was so much tougher than the last. Two years ago they'd parted in anger, with harsh words and angry accusations. Today they would part quietly, acknowledging the love that still existed between them wasn't enough to make things right. But even if she'd known for sure how this would end, she still wouldn't have taken a moment of the past few months back. All the heartache, the sorrow, the successes. The inevitable goodbye.

Jack retrieved the last bag and hung the strap over his shoulder, the cast of unshed tears in his dark eyes. "If you don't care to remember anything else, Annie, remember this. I have never stopped loving you. I never will."

Anne watched him head to the bedroom door, but called him back when she noticed the box sitting on the bureau. The same box full of mementoes that she'd discovered in his apartment all those months ago. She hadn't even realized he'd brought it home.

When he turned, she saw the trace of hope in his expression. Saw it fade when she said, "You left your pictures on the dresser."

"You keep them, Annie. I don't need any reminders. I remember everything now."

Moments later the front door slammed, physically jolting her. Now she was completely alone, with no one to witness her mourning.

She picked up the box and carried it to the chair near the window, determined to immerse herself in the past to forget the present, and the future that seemed so desolate. She opened the lid, and more tears clouded her eyes when she found the framed photo of her that had once resided by his bed—a sure sign he was removing all the reminders, moving on with his life. She shifted it aside, withdrew the packet of pictures from the trip to Italy and came upon the photo the waiter had taken of them at a small outdoor café. She and Jack looked so content. So in love.

They had been in love, always in love, and willing to work through their differences. Anne had never believed they wouldn't get through the rough patch two years ago, until the day Jack had announced his infidelity. Since then, she'd worn his mistake like an emotional shackle, unwilling to forgive him, when in fact in many ways she'd been guilty of cheating, too. Not in a physical sense, at least not while they were married, but she had confided in Max through the years when she'd had troubles with Jack. A mental affair in some ways, although Max had never measured up to her husband. He still didn't, and he never would.

If only she could take back her own stubborn pride. If only she could take back that morning and the wounding words she'd said to him. But it was simply too late.

2005

"Where have you been?"

Jack looked startled over finding Anne in the kitchen—*their* kitchen—at this hour of the morning. He also looked disheveled, his hair mussed, his face unshaven, his shirt and slacks wrinkled.

He took a cup from the cabinet and said, "I had an all-night case."

"You're lying. When I tried to reach you earlier to ask if you could pick up Katie from T-ball practice, I called the Surgery desk and they said they hadn't seen you since yesterday."

Coffee in hand, he turned and reclined against the cabinet. "Why do you even care where I've been? You're the one who left and ran home to your mother."

Maybe she shouldn't care, but she did. And though it pained her to ask, she had to find out. "Who is she?"

"You don't know her."

Anne felt as though she'd been gut-punched. She'd honestly expected him to say he'd spent all night at Hank's, maybe even slept in his car after tying one on at the neighborhood bar. And though she'd worried, suspected even, that he'd been with another woman, she'd stupidly wanted him to lie about it, not confirm her worst fears.

She let the truth sink in, willed away the tears. She would cry later, when he couldn't see how deeply he'd wounded her. "How long has this been going on?"

"It was one-night stand. It didn't mean a thing."

"You're a smart man, Jack. You should be able to come up with something better than a cliché."

He tossed the remnants of his coffee into the sink and set the cup down hard on the counter. "Do you want to know why I did it, Annie? I did it because I wanted to hurt you as badly as you've hurt me. You took my daughter away from me. You won't even give us a chance to work out our problems."

Problems that now seemed too insurmountable to work out. "Maybe we could have tried again, Jack, but not now. Not after this."

He strode to the kitchen island and shoved back the stool across from Anne's, knocking it over. "Don't seventeen years of marriage count for anything, Annie?"

"Obviously not to you. Otherwise you wouldn't have cheated on me."

"I'm not proud of it. I wish the hell I could take it back, but I can't."

Anne could no longer trust him. Couldn't trust that he hadn't done this before on all those nights he was supposedly operating. She slid from the stool to stand her ground, even though she felt that her trembling legs would betray her, just as Jack had betrayed her. "It's over, Jack. I want you out of the house."

She caught the hint of desperation in his eyes. "I promise it won't happen again."

"It's too late for promises."

She whirled and headed for the bedroom they'd once shared, marched straight to the walk-in closet and began yanking his clothes from the rack, hangers and all, and throwing them onto the floor. Then she caught sight of the aged blue sweater hanging on her side of the closet, the one he'd given her their first Christmas, along with the promise of sharing many Christmases to come.

"I love you, Annie. That should mean something."

She wrapped her emotions in a steel cocoon and, through a rush of angry tears, ripped the sweater from its hanger, spun around and threw it at him. "Right now I hate what you've done to us, Jack. I hate you."

"That makes two of us, Annie. Because right now I hate myself."

CHAPTER 18

Jack hated where he found himself now, seated on a bench in the surgical dressing room, reflecting on the past few weeks without Annie, as he'd done nonstop since she'd told him goodbye for good. His leg still hurt like hell, but not as badly as waking up alone. Going to bed alone. Knowing he would face another long day without her. He'd mistakenly thought immersing himself in work might save him from the isolation, and he'd been a damn fool to believe it.

"I figured I'd find you here."

He looked up to see Hank leaning back against the locker. "What are you doing here this time of night?"

"A patient of mine came to the E.R. with a hot appendix. Jones has her in the O.R., so I decided to stop by and talk some sense into you."

Jack raked his cap off his head and dropped it to the

floor, which he'd been contemplating for a good half hour. "I don't need a lecture on how I should slow down and take care of myself."

"That's not what I was going to say, Morgan. I was going to tell you to get your head out of your ass."

"If my head was up my ass, I couldn't operate."

"This isn't about your surgery prowess, Jack. This is about you and Anne."

He shouldn't be surprised Hank would broach that subject, even if the point was moot. "In case you haven't heard, there isn't a 'you and Anne' anymore. She threw me out again."

"I know. Ruthie told me. And I feel partially responsible."

That definitely got Jack's attention. "What the hell do you mean?"

"When we were over at the house back in the summer, I told her to cut you loose if she couldn't accept you going back to surgery."

He resented his best friend's interference, even though in the grand scheme of things, it hadn't mattered. "She would have done it anyway, Hank. It was only a matter of time."

Hank rubbed his beard, something he always did while engaging in deep thinking. "You know, Jack, for the past eleven months I watched you overcome some pretty hefty odds to get back to where you are now. A lot of men wouldn't even have attempted it. That's why it's so hard for me to understand why you won't fight for Anne."

Yeah, he'd accomplished a lot. He'd recovered most of his memory, his knowledge and skill, but look at what he'd lost. "I can't win, Hank."

Hank joined Jack on the bench. "Let me ask you something, Doc. When you went back into the O.R., did it give you as much satisfaction as being with Anne?"

He'd experienced a sense of achievement, maybe even triumph, but it hadn't compared with what he'd had with Annie. "Not really."

"Does the hero worship measure up to having Anne's love?"

"Not even close."

"Then fight to get her back, dammit."

If only he knew how. "The only way I might even stand a chance is to give up medicine altogether, and it's still a slim chance. This way, if I can't have her, at least I still have my job."

"I'm not saying you should give medicine up completely, Jack. Maybe you should consider just giving up the surgical aspects."

At one time that seemed incomprehensible. "How do you propose I make a living?"

"You'll come up with something." Hank slapped Jack hard on the back and stood. "You still love her, my man, and that's really all that counts."

After Hank left, Jack tried to imagine what it would be like not to operate again. Not to know the adrenaline rush when he held life in his hands. Yet holding Annie again meant more than performing surgery.

He didn't know what his next move would be, but he did know Hank was right. He had to fight for Annie, or face living without her. And he wasn't willing to do that, not without giving it one more shot.

* * *

The twelve-foot evergreen in the corner didn't appear quite as majestic to Delia this Christmas morning as it had in years past. Though she'd taken great care to decorate the tree with sparkling white lights, ornate angels and ribbons of gold, the holiday had lost its luster. The one person who would have brought the joy back was missing. Jack.

Surrounded by mountains of discarded wrapping paper and myriad boxes, Katherine and Gabe sat on the floor, playing with the mixed-breed puppy Jack had saved from the pound and presented to his daughter the night before at his apartment. But that precious little ball of fur could never replace a precious father. Still, if all went as planned, the holiday could be salvaged—as well as Jack and Anne's future.

The sounds of Anne playing the piano filtered in from the hallway—Pachelbel's "Canon in D"—the same piece Anne had performed during her recital at the age of twelve. The same song that had played as she'd walked down the wedding aisle on her father's arm. Obviously, Anne hadn't forgotten the music, or the memories.

Now seemed as good a time as any to have a little chat with her daughter, before returning to the ordeal of making the holiday dinner. Delia walked to the hearth, slid the tan envelope from the mantel and tucked it beneath her arm. "I'll be back in a bit," she told Gabe before heading into the nearby parlor. She found Anne still seated at the piano, her hands resting lightly on the keys, her eyes closed. Although her daughter would qualify as middle-aged, Delia couldn't help but think Anne looked like a teenager. One who'd lost her best friend. But then again, she had.

Delia slipped onto the bench and laid the envelope on her lap. "You miss him, don't you?"

Anne slowly opened her eyes, not bothering to wipe away the tears. "If I say yes, will you promise not to lecture me?"

Delia held in her hands something that should be much more effective than a sermon. She unfastened the packet, withdrew a white envelope and offered it to Anne. "It's Jack's Christmas gift to you. The first of three."

Anne turned the envelope over, removed the document and simply stared at it for a few moments. "What is this?"

"Exactly what it says it is. Full tuition for your return to school in the spring, bought and paid for by Jack."

"I can't believe he did this."

As far as Delia was concerned, the best was yet to come. "And should you have any concerns about who will help with Katherine, then you need to take a look at this." She removed the second document, a set of pages bound by a clip, and rested it in Anne's lap. "This is a contract. Jack told Gabe to give you a copy. Basically, it says that Jack is going to head the cardiology research program at the hospital."

Awareness dawned in Anne's expression. "He's not going to operate anymore?"

"Only on a very limited basis. He'll be assisting on certain cases, and he'll still be doing some teaching, but for the most part, he'll be working normal hours. He made sure that clause was included before he accepted the offer."

"And Max—"

"Will be leaving at the first of the year. I believe he's accepted a job in Seattle." After Delia had used her clout with the board, convincing the members that Max Crabtree was a detriment, not an asset, to the hospital.

Anne shook her head as if trying to clear away the confusion. "I don't understand, Mom. Jack loves surgery."

"He loves you more, dear heart."

Delia allowed a moment for that to sink into Anne's stubborn brain before she said, "The last of three gifts, Jack plans to give you himself. A trip. You need to be at the airport by 6:00 p.m., bags in hand. I've agreed to take care of Katherine while you're gone."

Anne's eyes widened with surprise. "Where am I supposedly going?"

"You'll find out as soon as you arrive at the airport."

"That doesn't give me much time," Anne said.

Anne, always the planner. A trait Delia acknowledged she'd passed on to her daughter. "You have plenty of time to pack a bag if you go home now."

"I meant, time to think about whether I should go on a trip with Jack."

Delia was beginning to believe she'd raised a daft daughter. "Oh, for heaven's sake, Elizabeth Anne, there's nothing to think about. If you don't go, you'll be wasting two tickets, because Jack refuses to go without you. Worse, you'll be wasting another chance to be with the only man you've ever loved."

When her daughter failed to comment or to move, Delia placed the documents on the bench between them and framed Anne's shoulders with her palms. "First of all, what I'm about to say doesn't mean I don't love Gabe, because I do. He's been a godsend. But your father will always be my first love, just as Jack will always be yours, and nothing will ever change that. You might find someone else later, but you will never find someone who loves you as much as he does. It's high time you forgive him. You both need to forgive each other, because you can't have true love until you've learned to grant grace."

Anne tipped her head against Delia's shoulder. "I'm so scared, Mom."

"I know you are, honey. But all you have to do is take that leap of faith. Jack will be there to catch you. He always has been."

Jack Morgan hated airports. Hated the chaos, the confusion and the crowds. But the woman striding toward him across the terminal made the hassle worthwhile.

Unlike the day he'd met her, she wore traveling clothes, not a little black dress and heels. She had her luggage, not her mother, in tow as she elbowed her way through the masses waiting to be cleared through security. Yet in so many ways, she still looked the same as she had twenty-four years ago. Time hadn't erased her beauty, or all the things he still loved about her.

He left the chair and raised his hand to garner Anne's attention, his pulse accelerating as she came closer. He couldn't believe she'd actually decided to meet him, even though Delia had called earlier to assure him she would.

It seemed to take Annie forever to arrive, and when she did, she seemed unsure. Jack couldn't claim too much confidence, either, when she skipped the usual greeting and said, "Can we go somewhere a little more private so we can talk?"

He should have known better than to get his hopes up. She could still walk back out through the sliding doors. She could still say they were making a mistake. He didn't have a choice. He had to listen to her, even if she planned to say things he didn't want to hear.

Jack picked up his cane and nodded toward his right. "There's a place over by the elevators."

They rolled their suitcases to the alcove and set them aside, then faced each other. A moment of uncomfortable silence passed before Annie spoke again. "I have to say this, so if you'll bear with me."

"I'm listening." And praying she didn't say she'd changed her mind.

"My mother's always told me I'm too unforgiving, and she's right."

When he started to protest, Annie held up her hands. "Wait and let me get this out before you comment."

She hesitated a moment before continuing. "Today I realized how many important things you've given me. I'd been so angry I'd forgotten what an extraordinary man you are. I'd forgotten all the times you were there for me, and instead focused on the times you weren't. After you left, I began to understand how much I've relied on your support over the years. But today you proved how much you're willing to sacrifice to make this work."

"You're that important to me, Annie."

"I realize that, Jack. But I would never ask you to quit surgery. It's who you are."

"It's what I do, not who I am," he said, tossing her words back at her. "Who I am has a lot to do with loving you. And you're worth the price, Annie."

She reached out and took his hand in hers. "I'm so sorry for everything. For my stubbornness. For being so unbending and bitter that I forgot what's really important. We should forgive each other for the mistakes. That's all I know to say."

"Just say that you still love me, Annie. That's all I need to hear."

"I love you, Jack. I always will."

She moved quickly into his arms and held on tightly. They stayed like that for a while, clinging to each other, before Annie pulled away first and smiled. "This place we're going to—does it have good weather and good food?"

"Yeah, but not many miniature golf courses."

She laughed. "I can't believe you remembered that."

"Some things you never forget, Annie, even when you're too sick to remember." He dropped his arm from around her and withdrew the ring from his jacket pocket, the one he'd tried to give her not long ago. "I brought this, just in case. But you don't have to wear it if you're not ready."

"I'm ready, as long as you do the honors."

She held out her hand and let him slip the diamond on her finger, as he had the first time he'd proposed all those years ago. "It's nice to have it back where it belongs." To have them back where they belonged.

But she still looked hesitant. "Where do we go from here, Jack?"

With the hand that had given him the gift of healing he touched her face—a face he wanted to see every morning for the rest of his life. The last face he wanted to see before he died. "One thing I've learned over the past few months, Annie, it's better to take things one step at a time."

And the next step would be to return to the place in which they'd found some common ground. A good place to begin again.

Sorrento, Italy
Twenty years later

On a quaint terrace overlooking the bay, together they watched the sunset, content to sit in silent communion, side by side, hands joined. She wore the aged blue cable-knit sweater that helped keep the memories alive. He wore his favorite pair of cross-trainers, though he only dreamed of running these days. In the past, they might have viewed the panorama from the rocky shoreline, yet the passage of time had taken somewhat of a toll on their mobility. But not on their spirits. And not on their love for each other.

For many years, Jack and Anne had made an annual sojourn to this healing place, seeking a respite from the world, renewing their strength and commitment to each other. Tonight they spoke of their good fortune in having witnessed Katie grow into a remarkable woman, on her way to becoming a skilled surgeon. Jack talked about his joy when he'd walked his daughter down the aisle, and Anne reflected on the miracle of attending the birth of their grandson. They continued to celebrate their original anniversary, viewing the two years they'd spent apart as only a bump in the road.

Yet the path they had traveled to arrive at this peaceful juncture hadn't been without a few difficult twists and turns. Two years earlier, they had lost their beloved Delia, who, as she'd always said she would, simply went to sleep one night and drifted out of their lives. Jack's unerring support had seen Anne through the crushing grief, and she had found comfort in knowing that her mother had spent her final days with a man who had loved her well.

Four years ago, the realization that life was truly short had begun to sink in, and they'd both decided to retire, leaving behind their careers—Anne as the hospital's director of nursing, Jack as a renowned teacher and surgeon—to spend more time together. And since that day twenty years before, when they'd returned to this haven to renew their vows, they had known great passion, though several times they had again almost given up. But memories—both the good, and the not so good—had shown them that anything worth having was definitely worth the fight. And fight they did, only to find that making up was still the best part of the battle.

As the stars began to appear in the darkening sky, Jack stood and held his hand out to his Annie. With arms around each other's waists, they continued their journey, holding steadfastly to each other. Through trial and error, they had discovered that to successfully navigate obstacles, to keep from falling, it was best to walk the way together.

And to take life one small memory, one small step, at a time.

* * * * *

Happily ever after is just the beginning…

Turn the page for a sneak preview of
A HEARTBEAT AWAY
by
Eleanor Jones

Harlequin Everlasting—Every great love has
a story to tell.™
A brand-new series from Harlequin Books

Special? A prickle ran down my neck and my heart started to beat in my ears. Was today really special?

"Tuck in," he ordered.

I turned my attention to the feast that he had spread out on the ground. Thick, home-cooked-ham sandwiches, sausage rolls fresh from the oven and a huge variety of mouthwatering scones and pastries. Hunger pangs took over, and I closed my eyes and bit into soft homemade bread.

When we were finally finished, I lay back against the bluebells with a groan, clutching my stomach.

Daniel laughed. "Your eyes are bigger than your stomach," he told me.

I leaned across to deliver a punch to his arm, but he rolled away, and when my fist met fresh air I collapsed in a fit of giggles before relaxing on my back and staring up into the flawless blue sky. We lay like that for quite a while, Daniel and I, side by side in companionable silence, until he stretched out his hand in an arc that encompassed the whole area.

"Don't you think that this is the most beautiful place in the entire world?"

His voice held a passion that echoed my own feelings, and I rose onto my elbow and picked a buttercup to hide the emotion that clogged my throat.

"Roll over onto your back," I urged, prodding him with my forefinger. He obliged with a broad grin, and I reached across to place the yellow flower beneath his chin.

"Now, let us see if you like butter."

When a yellow light shone on the tanned skin below his jaw, I laughed.

"There…you do."

For an instant our eyes met, and I had the strangest sense that I was drowning in those honey-brown depths. The scent of bluebells engulfed me. A roaring filled my ears, and then, unexpectedly, in one smooth movement Daniel rolled me onto my back and plucked a buttercup of his own.

"And do *you* like butter, Lucy McTavish?" he asked. When he placed the flower against my skin, time stood still.

His long lean body was suspended over mine, pinning me against the grass. Daniel…dear, comfortable, familiar Daniel was suddenly bringing out in me the strangest sensations.

"Do you, Lucy McTavish?" he asked again, his voice low and vibrant.

My eyes flickered toward his, the whisper of a sigh

escaped my lips and although a strange lethargy had crept into my limbs, I somehow felt as if all my nerve endings were on fire. He felt it, too—I could see it in his warm brown eyes. And when he lowered his face to mine, it seemed to me the most natural thing in the world.

None of the kisses I had ever experienced could have even begun to prepare me for the feel of Daniel's lips on mine. My entire body floated on a tide of ecstasy that shut out everything but his soft, warm mouth, and I knew that this was what I had been waiting for the whole of my life.

"Oh, Lucy." He pulled away to look into my eyes. "Why haven't we done this before?"

Holding his gaze, I gently touched his cheek, then I curled my fingers through the short thick hair at the base of his skull, overwhelmed by the longing to drown again in the sensations that flooded our bodies. And when his long tanned fingers crept across my tingling skin, I knew I could deny him nothing.

* * * * *

Be sure to look for A HEARTBEAT AWAY,
available February 27, 2007.
And look, too, for
THE DEPTH OF LOVE
by Margot Early,
the story of a couple who must learn
that love comes in many guises—
and in the end it's the only thing that counts.

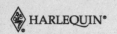

Every great love has a story to tell™

These deeply emotional novels
show how love can last, how it
shapes and transforms lives, how
it's truly the adventure of a lifetime.
Harlequin® Everlasting Love™
novels tell the whole story.
Because "happily ever after"
is just the beginning....

Two new titles are available
EVERY MONTH!

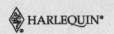

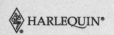

HARLEQUIN®

EVERLASTING LOVE™

Every great love has a story to tell™

"I'm yours. And you're mine."

Eve Swango and Tommy Baca belong to each other. Always have. Always will. For decades now, they've shared a passion for exploring the wild, subterranean depths of a New Mexico cave. Their cave. In this fascinating and original romance, two lovers learn that the deepest feelings last the longest....

The Depth of Love
by **Margot Early**

> Buy
> *your copy*
> *this March!*

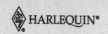

EVERLASTING LOVE™

Every great love has a story to tell™

COMING NEXT MONTH

#3. *The Depth of Love* **by Margot Early**
"I'm yours. And you're mine." Eve Swango and
Tommy Baca belong to each other. Always have. Always will.
For decades now, they've shared a passion for exploring the
wild, subterranean depths of a New Mexico cave. *Their* cave.
In this fascinating, moving and original romance, two lovers
learn that the deepest feelings last the longest....

#4. *A Heartbeat Away* **by Eleanor Jones**
One morning Lucy McTavish meets a stranger named
Ben in a London park. The connection between them is
immediate and powerful, but it's also perplexing. As their
lives intersect in the weeks that follow, Lucy begins to ask
herself, has Daniel Brown, her soul mate, her greatest love—
her husband now gone—kept his promise after all?

www.eHarlequin.com